farewells
and
FOREVER

Farewells and Forever
Untouchable #12
Copyright © 2022 by Heather Long
Cover: Crimson Phoenix Creations
Editing: Leavens Editing
Proofreading by Lunar Rose Editing Services

Farewells and Forever/Heather Long – 1st ed.
ISBN: 978-1-956264-48-7

For Blake, who wouldn't shut up about me writing Frankie.

For Steph and Elisabeth who became some of my biggest cheerleaders.

For Sara, Alyssa, and Jane, who demanded more (lovingly) even when Alyssa coined the phrase "Team Mad at Heather."

For Jeni, who proofs every single audio.

For Lauren, who helped build the soundtracks.

*For Tate, who cheered me on and said turn the screw a little harder. *winks**

For every single one of my readers.

Thank you.

Series so Far

Rules and Roses

Changes and Chocolate

Keys and Kisses

Whispers and Wishes

Hangovers and Holidays

Brazen and Breathless

Trials and Tiaras

Graduation and Gifts

Defiance and Dedication

Songs and Sweethearts

Legacy and Lovers

Farewells and Forevers

Foreword

Dear Reader,

We're here. Book 12. The final book of the Untouchable series. I bet you thought we'd never get here. I said in the last book that finishing the final "cliffhanger" in the series was a heady experience, but finishing this one? This was amazing.

I won't lie, there were tears. Not at the end, no, but at some key moments within the story itself. Some of them weren't even the most "important" ones.

As I wrote this, one of the thoughts in my head all the way through was "this is my love letter" to Frankie and the guys. It's also my love letter to all of you, the readers, who have been with them through their ups, their downs, their rules, their changes, their struggles with communication, their arguments, and even that horrible moment when two of them broke up for a time.

From the day she learned about her mother's affair to that whopper of a Daddy lie to the moment she earned her emancipation to the final confrontation with Maddy just outside a public bathroom, Frankie and the guys have been there for each other. Car accidents. Illness. Mean girls. Long-distance relationships. New family. Grief. Love. Friends. More.

They've earned their happily ever after. It has always been my belief that a happily ever after is a work in progress. It's not a final moment where you cross a t or dot an i. It's all the little moments, the hurried meals, the quick text messages to say I love you, the times when you pick up the burden because they need you to those lazy days when you can just sit and breathe.

Happily ever after is never the end of the story. It's the continuation, it's the big moments and the small ones. It's life. A life you live together. A life where you fight, you make-up, you cheer each other up, sometimes you just cry. You fail. You succeed. You get overwhelmed. Sometimes, you just need a hug.

I thought saying goodbye would be hard, but it's hard to say goodbye to a life you know they are going to keep sharing, living, celebrating, and quite probably laughing their way through.

This series has been such a gift for me in so many ways. I am ready to move on to new characters, new challenges, and new moments—but never doubt for an instant that Frankie and the guys won't always be right there in the back of my mind.

In honor of this being the final installment, I added four bonus scenes to the very end. These bonus scenes are flashbacks. In my reader group, when books hit review goals, I write bonus scenes. Sometimes they are alternate points of view. Sometimes they are scenes that take us back to the time before Rules and Roses. These four scenes are the details of when Frankie met each of the guys in her life.

Never hurts to throw a little nostalgia at the happily ever after, you know?

Just thank you. Don't forget to check out the afterword, join my group, leave a review, and in general, just keep being awesome.

Normally, this is where I'd do the housekeeping notes, but this is the last book. If you haven't read the first eleven, you should probably start there.

xoxo

Heather

Chapter One
I'M WALKING ON AIR

FRANKIE

"Hey, Frankie," Jake called with a grin, his phone pointed right at me as we walked toward the plane. "What are we doing?"

As tempted as I was to flip him off, I just laughed. "About to jump out of a plane."

"How are you feeling about that?" His eyes danced as he glanced at me over the top of his phone. I swore he was like a kid at Christmas. Had been since I said yes. I managed to shoot Jake a thumbs up and a laugh while I shook my head.

"Hi, everyone," the man walking next to me said. Older than all of us by at least two decades, he'd also been our "jump" instructor. His grin was almost as engaging as Jake's. "I'm Jake too," he said almost tongue in cheek while holding up his own phone. It appeared that filming was going to be a thing. "Our girl here likes Jakes, apparently."

"Hey now," Jake called from ahead as he kept filming me. The guys were all in with sky diving, and apparently this was a big deal cause it was my first time. But I wasn't the only *virgin* on this flight. "Watch the flirting."

"Ignore him," Jake, the instructor, said with a hand on my shoulder. He'd already gone over my rigging—twice—as had the guys. Then he'd shown me how to go over theirs with the same kind of thoroughness. "We're going to get on this plane here." He turned his own phone toward the plane where Coop, Archie, and Ian waited.

"Okay," I said, trying to keep the nerves out of my voice. It was one thing to talk about this, to practice—when we were on the *ground* and something else entirely to get on a plane with the intention of jumping out of it.

"We're going to go up two miles," he said, aiming the phone back at us.

"Yay." I summoned a smile and Jake cracked up. Coop whistled, then did a *whoop whoop* and I laughed. "We're going to go up two miles," I repeated Jake the Elder, Jake's name for him, not mine.

"Then we're gonna jump," Jake the Elder continued.

"We're going to jump out of a perfectly good plane," I ad-libbed.

"We're gonna fall for…" Jake the Elder trailed off, holding up one finger to me.

"One minute?"

"One mile," he corrected. That was a long way to fall. I swore my stomach plummeted for me. "One mile," he repeated. "If we fall for one minute, we've gone too far. That's gonna be bad."

I would not throw up.

I would not.

"We'll fall for one mile," he said, raising his hand. "Then we're going to hang out." I high-fived him, but I was pretty sure it lacked any real enthusiasm. "Sound good?"

"I can't wait," I told him, laughing, even as I blinked back tears. I wasn't going to throw up. Excitement vibrated through my system.

"You're going to be great," he told me, lowering his phone. "We can still do it in tandem if you change your mind."

"We talked about that," I said, pushing a loose tendril of hair back. I'd braided all of it, but there were wisps still escaping. "AFF works for me."

"Okay." This time he offered his fist and we bumped them together. "Then let's get everyone on and airborne."

My Jake caught me in a loose hug and a quick kiss as Jake the Elder continued on. "You good?" The caution and worry in his eyes couldn't hide his excitement.

"I'm awesome," I informed him. "Or so you all keep telling me." Still, my hands were trembling.

"You are awesome," he murmured, gripping my hands between his. "The absolute fucking best, Baby Girl. You don't have to do this."

I wrinkled my nose. "Don't even start. I know I'm freaking out—a little—but I'm also excited. The more you guys keep telling me I don't have to, the more nervous I get. So, if you want to stay here on the ground, Benton, I'll be the blonde—up there, free-falling."

He laughed, dragging me in for a hard, firm kiss. "As if I'd let you go up there without me."

"Let's go," Archie called. "Some of us would like good luck kisses too."

I grinned as Jake threaded his fingers with mine and we crossed the last few yards to join them. The plane was going to be crowded. In addition to the pilot, there were two professionals for each of us to jump with. They would be babysitting us. They said we would all fit, but it was still a tight squeeze.

We had to sit on the plane in the order that we were jumping. Jake was going first, so he would be the last on. I was going right after him—I won the rock, papers, scissors match with the boys—then Archie, followed by Ian, with Coop last.

I gave each a kiss before they climbed on. Jake the Elder was one of my pros, and his son, Benjamin, was the other. Benjamin was only a couple of years older than us. He offered a fist bump as we waited to climb on.

All too soon, we were all loaded into our seats. The butterflies in my stomach turned into full-fledged dragons as they waged war in my stomach. In addition to our group, there was one more guy jumping with us and he had a camera.

"Memories," Archie declared when he hired him. "And you guys can use it for your next video if it comes out great."

Business and pleasure. They were silly. My stomach dropped again, but I kept my smile in place cause our happy cameraman kept pointing it at me.

The guys wanted to track every minute. I got it. I might throttle them later, but I got it. I blew out a breath as the wheels left the ground and we were climbing. I actually liked flying now, but this was not first-class on some huge jet or on Archie's luxurious private plane.

This was more like a prop plane and I swore I could feel every bump, dip, and lift we hit.

"How are you doing, Frankie?" Jake the Elder yelled, and he had to yell because it was so loud. If anyone else was talking, I couldn't hear them over the engine.

"Nervous," I muttered.

"What?"

"Excited," I yelled back, and his grin promised me he'd heard the earlier comment.

"You're gonna be fine," Benjamin yelled from next to me. "We'll be with you every step of the way. Just relax and enjoy it."

Right. Relax.

I'd do that once we were on the ground and I had that bottle of champagne Archie promised—provided I didn't puke. The higher we went, the more the anticipation coiled in my belly.

"Anyone you want to say hi to?" Jake the Elder asked, holding up his phone, and my Jake glanced back at me, laughter in his eyes. I made a face at him and he grinned wider.

Waving a hand, I said, "Hi, Dad, see you soon—hopefully."

Jake cracked up and Archie tugged my braid. I glanced back at him and he stole a kiss. "I'll be right behind you," he yelled.

"You just want to stare at my ass," I called back. The guys around us laughed. Fortunately, there were a couple of women among our jump instructors, so I wasn't going to choke on testosterone overload.

"Hell yes, it's a gorgeous ass." Archie winked. Behind him, Ian lifted his chin. The sheer confidence in his eyes shored up some of my own. Behind him, Coop crossed his eyes and stuck out his tongue.

God, I loved them.

"Eyes front," Jake the Elder said. "We're almost to our jump point."

Really?

I tried not to grimace. There were a pair of lights on the side. One said don't jump and it was currently illuminated. The one below it said jump.

As if summoned by my thoughts alone, it lit up.

"Goggles on," the instructors with Jake called back, and I tugged mine on and made sure they were secured tight. We weren't wearing helmets. But we had to have the goggles on before they opened the doors because the wind would be too much.

All too soon, the door ahead of Jake slid open. I shuddered at the rush of wind that just got louder.

Thumbs raised ahead of me as they got ready. On impulse, I leaned forward and gripped Jake's shoulder. "I love you," I yelled toward his ear and he twisted to look at me and mouthed the words back.

One squeeze of his shoulder, and I let go. This was insane. We were all absolutely crazy. Jake and his partners were at the door and he blew me a kiss before he jumped, with both of them going right after him.

No hesitation.

"Here we go," Jake the Elder said, even though the wind tore his words away. The cameraman had already jumped and I half-stood to make my way to the door.

Holy shit—gazing out at the land below—my heart fisted. Was I really going to do this? Had I lost my mind? This plane was perfectly safe. The land looked like something out of a cartoon, a fanciful patchwork quilt of green.

"Ready?" Benjamin yelled, and I glanced toward the guys. It had only been seconds, even if it felt like an eternity. They all wore grins of anticipation and Coop managed to look nervous. I wasn't sure how much of that was real and how much of it was for me. I blew them a kiss and then jump-fell.

The wind seemed louder out here, but not. I was falling, but I spread out my arms and legs like they'd taught us. Below me, I could see Jake's dark blue shirt.

I wanted to turn around and look at the guys, but I didn't dare. A wild scream tore from my throat. This was *amazing*. Terrifying? Yes. Insane? Absolutely. But it was like flying too.

What did they call it in the movie? Not flying but falling with style.

I cracked up again. The wind pushed at my cheeks and I could feel my skin rippling even as my braid snapped out behind me.

A vibration on my wrist pulled my gaze to the watch that said thirty seconds.

Holy shit, I'd already been falling for thirty seconds. Fresh laughter exploded out of me. This was the absolute best thing ever. I moved my right hand to the cord as my wrist vibrated again.

"Now," Jake the Elder called and I tugged. Even prepared for the way the chute would snap open and pull me upward, it was still a jerk. Little huffs of laughter escaped that sounded a lot like squeaking to me.

I glanced back up, but I couldn't see the guys past my chute. The bright yellow-green of it seemed to almost glow. It matched Jake's below.

Pulse racing, I kept glancing around us as we half-floated, half-glided back to the earth. I adjusted my pulls when Jake the Elder or Benjamin yelled. It allowed us to alter directions, though not like driving, but definitely like targeting.

For one minute, I'd been free-falling, and it took another three or four to travel the last mile as the wind filled my ears and a smile stretched my lips so hard, I was worried my cheeks would cramp.

The pure fountain of elation bubbling up within me was almost indescribable. All too soon, we were approaching the ground. Jake was already there, climbing to his feet.

"Relax," Jake the Elder called. "Relax your legs, you've got momentum."

The lessons replayed in my head, and even as I told myself to relax, I still found myself trying to jog as I touched the ground. But it was hard to run forward a little, when my muscles were almost pure noodles. I was falling, landing on my ass and laughing.

One of the other instructors was there to help, and I all but fell on my ass the second time I tried to stand.

"Don't stand up yet," Benjamin said as he pulled free of his own parachute. "Just breathe…relax. It's the adrenaline rush…"

Oh, that was why I was shaking like a leaf and my muscles all seemed to have turned to rubber. He popped the catch on my harness to help me out of it. Jake the Elder gave me a hand up and I staggered a little. My braid was half-gone and I swore part of my hair looked blown up.

"How was that?"

"That was fucking awesome," I swore, still laughing.

"Baby Girl," Jake called, and I high-fived Jake the Elder and his son for real, before I staggered over to meet Jake. He let out a *whoop* and picked me up into a twirling hug. I laughed as I held onto him.

When he paused, we turned to watch Archie land. He did not land on his ass at all; he actually made the glide-in landing look easy and jogged to a stop.

I threw my arms up and let out a girly scream for him as I cheered.

His grin was as wide as mine felt. With swift movements, he unlocked himself and then he was striding toward us. I gave Jake a swift kiss before he set me down, and I stumbled right into Archie's arms for a fierce hug and kiss.

"You were fucking awesome," he declared. He high-fived Jake and then we turned to watch Ian, followed by Coop. Ian landed damn near as gracefully as Archie had. He added a slide in at the end, more like he was stealing a base or something.

Coop didn't even try, he just lifted his legs and slid across the grass like he meant to do it. The rubbery muscles in my legs began to cooperate and I was skipping toward them. Well, not really, more like a halting run, but Archie and Jake were with me.

Giddy. I was giddy like I was still falling, and Ian caught me up in a kiss that threatened to send me flying all over again. He lifted his head and gave me a searching look. "You're shaking."

"Adrenaline rush," I promised him, then nuzzled another kiss to his jaw before Coop got there.

"Gimme," he demanded. "I risked my life and need a kiss like the action hero I am."

The guys half-snorted and half-laughed as I wrapped my arms around Coop's neck. "You're always my hero," I whispered and his grin gave me real wings. From fierce to heated to protective to playful, they were my everything. I cupped Coop's nape as he teased my lips apart with a kiss that was a lot slower and a lot more demanding than the others.

But I wasn't the only one shaking, so I wrapped him up tighter. Nothing said thrilling like willingly jumping out of a plane for the guys you loved or them doing it to be there for my first jump.

"Ah," I sighed as I leaned back and Archie eyed me.

"That sounded pretty lusty and profound."

I grinned as Coop finally put me back on my feet. I still had something of a drunken stagger, though I loved it. "It was—it is."

Honestly, I wanted to rub my thighs together and drag one or all of them off somewhere to get naked and get them to fuck me sideways. All of them together, one at a time, or all of the above. I was not picky at the moment.

As it was, my nipples tightened as I clenched my inner muscles to try and suppress the reaction or some of it, at least while we had an audience. Light flared in Jake's eyes and I caught Ian's speculative look.

Yeah, I was not covering my responses well at all.

"Gonna share?" Archie asked, glancing toward our cameraman and making a cutting motion with his hand. "Thanks! Go ahead and send the whole thing over and the invoice, yeah?"

"You got it, Mr. Standish."

Mr. Standish. It really suited him when he got that in-charge look.

"You guys did good," Jake the Elder said as he clapped me on the shoulder. "Your girl did great. Come on up to the road when you're ready and we'll drive back."

"Thanks," Jake said to him, shaking his hand. All the guys did. They shook all of their hands, but I could feel their attention and how tightly it focused on me.

Soon as they had all moved ahead and were out of earshot, Ian gave me a look. "Angel?"

"I'm just—thrilled, honestly. I mean, that was a hell of a turn-on, and yes, I'm very fucking horny right now, so the sooner we find some privacy, the better—but…" I paused cause Archie's jaw fell open briefly before a wicked grin spread across his lips, and Coop threw his head back and laughed.

"But?" Jake prompted, giving Coop a shove.

"But—I love that we popped our cherries on this together." Because we had. We'd done the jump classes together and the guys could have done their first jumps earlier, especially Jake, because I'd been in Paris for a week getting Rachel moved in—but they waited for me.

"Hell yes, we waited," Archie muttered. "You are *always* worth waiting for."

Ian was closer, and he cupped my chin, tilting my head back as he chuckled. "He's right, Angel—and you need your rings back on." Then he opened his palm. The four rings that interlocked were waiting for me. I'd worried about losing them mid-jump, so I'd tucked them into his pocket.

I held out my hand and he slid them on in the correct order while the guys watched.

"Better," Jake said.

"Agreed," Coop sighed.

I lifted my hand to look at them. They were right. The lack of them had left my finger naked.

"You sure we can't elope?" Archie asked abruptly, and we all looked at him. "I mean, I get waiting until next summer. We want graduation done and Jake's parents are getting married at Christmas—but who says we can't just elope and not tell anyone else. Then they can all come to that wedding and we get to have our own."

Fuck. That was tempting.

"My mother will kill me," Ian said. "So will Jake's and Coop's."

True. I reached over to link my fingers with Archie's. Hank and Eddie would roll with it… "The Dad Bros wouldn't be thrilled either, and Chloe might cry."

The last was a secret weapon. Archie growled, tugging me to him. "Fine, we can't make her cry. But June first, Miss Curtis, and you're gonna be Mrs.—"

I put my fingers against his lips and he made a face. "We haven't decided on that yet," I reminded him. "But we will. We'll decide on everything. I promise." Moving my fingers, I kissed him lightly. "I said 'yes,' remember?"

His whole expression softened and he nipped my lower lip. "Yes, you did."

"Right. She absolutely did. Now, hand her over," Jake said, stretching out a hand. "She said something about being horny, and we need to get on that right now."

"On that?" I challenged and Jake grinned.

"Baby Girl, don't even pretend you can't wait for every single one of us to get on *that* meaning you. Sooner, rather than later, yeah?"

I mean—he had a point.

"Thank you," he said when I didn't argue and then scooped me up. "Last one to the car has to wait for three orgasms," he said and then bolted. I whooped as he took off running.

Archie raced past him, and to my shock—so did Coop. When Ian passed us, I gave Jake a look because he slowed from running to walking. "What did you…"

I wasn't the only one suspicious because Archie fixed him with a look. "What was the small print?"

But Jake didn't answer until we were tucked in the privacy of the limo Archie had waiting for us. "I said; the last one to the car had to wait for three orgasms to share her. I didn't say whose orgasms."

Smug.

So smug.

But I collapsed into him laughing as Archie pursed his lips and Coop cracked up. Ian just shook his head.

"Dude, revenge is gonna be sweet," Archie informed him,

"Bring it, Standish. Our girl likes it when we compete for orgasms."

Yes, I really, really did. I liked it even more when they went to work on my first while we headed back to the house. Winner- winner, Jake, Ian, Archie, and Coop for my dinner.

Chapter Two
LIFE IS A HIGHWAY

COOP

"Family meeting starts in five," Archie called as he came in the door. Considering the rest of us were already sitting around the table, dinner in warmers, ready to be served, I wasn't sure who he was reminding—himself or us. Jeremy had set everything up before he and Miss Abigail had gone to meet Ms. Bradshaw in the park.

I liked Ann, she was becoming something of a fixture in Jeremy's life. It meant she was at the brownstone more often, and she was good for Frankie. I glanced over at the love of our life, where she currently had one physical textbook open, a second one open on her e-reader, and a third one on her phone.

Our beautiful overachiever was twelve credits away from her bachelor's degree. Despite cutting back on classes, she'd continued to add one each summer to make up for the ones she didn't take in the fall and spring semesters.

A bright green-eyed gaze snared mine. Busted for staring, I grinned. Her lips curved, then she blew me a kiss and I winked. Moments like this were just—perfect.

There really was no other word for it. Jake had graph paper in front of him with a design he'd been sketching for the last half-hour. It was a light plane from the looks of it, and Bubba was in a text conversation with their manager.

They'd finished a half-dozen songs in the last two months. Four were being offered to the manager for the recording company's other artists. The last two, they were going to record on our mid-autumn break when we headed out to the Hamptons.

The house there, had been gradually becoming more and more our own. Archie and Frankie had actually redesigned an entire set of rooms and the work had been done while we traveled. When we came back, we had a huge suite just for the five of us, with the biggest fucking bed I'd ever seen.

To get to our bedroom, you had to go through a game and movie room that Archie kitted out like our teenage geek dreams - from the wet bar to the one-hundred-inch screen that descended from the ceiling to the array of video consoles tucked into the convertible coffee table.

The oversized sofa also boasted two lounges on either end. Extremely comfortable and perfect for when we randomly would get in the mood. Frankie loved the fabric on her nipples. The height and the angle were perfect for getting the right thrust.

Blowing out a breath, I stood and shoved that particular train of thought to a different track. I'd already been thinking about peeling her out of that tank top and shorts since I'd first realized her braless state and the very deliberate swing to her hips when she came down from her shower.

Note to self, shower time needed to be taken advantage of more. "Getting another glass of wine," I said. "Anyone else?"

"Beer would be good," Jake said at the end of a yawn as he stretched. "I'll get it." He cracked his neck and then his shoulders before he leaned over to drop a kiss on the top of Frankie's head. "Ten more minutes, Baby Girl, and you need a break. You've been working on that all afternoon."

"I know," she said without looking up, but she did catch his hand with her left and gave it a squeeze. The light danced over her rings, and the possessiveness ripped through me like a Texas thunderstorm. "Ten minutes should be enough to finish this section. I need to draft a full proposal and I wanted notes to take with me when I meet with Eddie."

Bubba glanced up from his phone, his gaze assessing as he swept it over the books, the devices, and the way her pen moved at speed as she took notes. "If you're only doing another ten minutes, then wine to go with dinner?"

Lifting her head, she glanced at me, then Jake, and finally Bubba. "Yes, please. Now, stop interrupting me, or it's going to take longer."

I chuckled as Bubba tugged her hair gently and went to get the wine. Archie took slightly longer than five minutes. He came down just as I got a second bottle opened that Ian had brought out and then gave Frankie the rest of the first bottle. It filled a four-ounce glass and we had the second for the food.

Jake had brought out three beers. Archie glanced at the wine, then the beer, and ran a hand over his face before picking up the beer.

"Babe," he said as he leaned over and smoothed his hand over her hair. She tilted her head up and gave him a lazy kiss.

"Three minutes left," she murmured and he chuckled. Yeah, we were all nuts for her. I loved how they loved her. Loved how we all loved her, really.

I started dishing out the food. Bubba shoved his phone away and we built Frankie's plate first. When she lifted her head, snapping her book shut, Jake helped put it all away and even stowed his own graph pad.

"Family meeting over food or after food?" Archie asked as he took his seat. In no time, we all had massive plates of roast beef, roasted potatoes that were still crispy—how the fuck did Jeremy do that—roasted Brussels sprouts, and fresh bread.

"Depends," Frankie said as she cut into the meat. "Are we going to argue in the meeting? Cause if so, I need chocolate and more wine before that."

"You feeling okay, Beautiful?"

"Cramps. New IUD the doctor recommended is better, but it's making me a little crampy this month." She made a face. "Too much information?"

"About you?" Bubba said with a snort. "Never. But if you're cramping, we can move the meal to somewhere more comfortable for you."

"I'm good," she promised, and there was nothing evasive or dismissive in her posture or her words. The only thing she did was shift to sit on her leg. "I am. I've had much worse, but I just don't want to argue while we're eating."

"Fair enough," I said. "But I don't think this is an argument so much as a debate. It's October. We're seven months from graduation. Time to decide where we want to live after—if we're staying here, going back to Texas or moving to California."

Her eyes rounded and Archie frowned at his food.

"Truth is," I continued, because the family meeting had been my idea after all. "You guys," I motioned to Jake and Archie. "You can pretty much work anywhere. There's some freedom in building your own company. Bubba can write his music anywhere, as long as Frankie is around." Then there was Frankie. We all glanced at her. "But you've been looking at taking on more at Standish…"

She bit her lip as she studied me. "I have been," she admitted. "I actually like working with Eddie."

"He definitely likes working with you," Archie told her with a grin. "You've got a lot of sharp insights. You're a natural, but that said—if taking over Standish is the goal, we're better off in New York—at least, for another four to five years."

I nodded thoughtfully.

"Wait—take over Standish?" Frankie gawked at him. "I don't want to run the whole company."

Archie gave her an indulgent look as he lifted his beer. "Babe, trust me, that company has been my legacy my whole life. If you do decide to run it, you won't be alone. Promise."

Her laughter wreathed the room. "I like working with Eddie. I like working with you and Jake. I adore working with Ian." She shot me a smile. "I'd love to work with you, but I'm not qualified, so I'm going to be your personal cheerleader."

"Does that come with one of those cute little cheerleader outfits? Cause, I'm definitely feeling that."

I wasn't the only one who focused on her. "You know," Bubba said slowly. "Halloween is coming."

She would be too if she dressed in that outfit.

Rolling her eyes, Frankie raised her wine glass. "Noted. Skimpy cheerleader outfit. Lots of skin?"

"Uh-huh," Jake said, wiping his mouth. "The only place you're trick or treating is with us."

We all laughed.

"And on that note, let's circle back to the meeting portion of our meal." I broke the end off of one bread loaf to butter. "I've been looking into a Master's program."

I had all of their attention.

"If I want to get licensed, most states require you get your master's degree in their state, then I can test out and do my clinical hours, and I can license as a clinical therapist. That's still my goal. I like working with kids." I'd actually upped my volunteer hours this year. They'd offered to add me to the payroll once I was in clinical hours, but that wouldn't be for another year to a year and a half.

I was good with that.

"So, you need us to make the call now so you can apply to the program you want?" Frankie cut into her meat and then studied me. "I like New York. I always kind of thought we'd just be here for school, but… I like the city and I love the house in the Hamptons."

Archie smiled at her. "Well, they are ours. The brownstone and the Hamptons house. We could add a third up north in Westchester if you like—or Boston."

I had to bite back a smile at the faintly sour look on Archie's face. He loved her siblings, but the only child in him struggled when my sister or Jake's were there. Frankie's were a lot younger and so full of zest. He loved her little brothers and sister, yet that zest often made them too much.

Little Chloe genuinely was a miniature her in some ways, and that threw me back to elementary school. Her brothers, on the other hand, were hellions and I loved it. Bubba and Archie might complain, but they loved the little shits too.

"I don't actually want to have a house there," Frankie admitted. "It's weird that we have two places already."

"Three," Archie said. "Well, technically four. There's the house in

Texas, and your grandparents are probably going to leave that house in Connecticut to you."

Silence draped the table as Frankie stilled. Jake shot Archie a glare, but he didn't take his gaze off Frankie.

"I get it, you're still pissed at them," he continued. "You have every right to be angry with them, Babe. But it's been almost two years—and you've talked to them twice."

Frankie sighed and lifted her head. "I don't know if I can ever forgive Patience. I know Maddy was her daughter, and she wanted to protect her—I get that." Her mouth twisted. "Or maybe I don't. I know you guys would do anything to help me, including lie to everyone we know. But it's hard to even think about the way she risked you."

That was it in a nutshell, and I wasn't the only one who glanced at Archie. The threat Maddy had been to *him* had been incredible, and more than once, Frankie had been caught right in the middle.

"But I'm here," Archie said softly. "Maddy isn't. Patience was a fool, but I don't think she ever meant you, or me for that matter, any harm. Eugene… he definitely didn't. They're weak people, but they're your grandparents and they want to know you."

I got where he was going with this. We'd all discussed it on and off for the last few weeks. The conversation sparked when she'd been in Paris with Rachel and Eugene sent a card to her. That card had sat unopened for three weeks after she came back.

When she opened and read it, I had no idea, and she hadn't told us what it said. "Beautiful," I said, stepping in. "What Archie is saying, what I'm saying, is we don't want you to look back someday with regret. Forgiving her might be hard, but you'll never get there if you keep them cut out of your life."

"To be perfectly clear," Jake added. "We don't give two shits about her feelings. You're the one we care about and your huge fucking heart."

Bubba nodded slowly when she glanced at him. "They aren't wrong, Angel. No one will judge you if you choose not to, it's always your choice."

"But Grandpa Ted liked them," Archie said, bringing it full circle. "Fuck if I know why, though he was a good judge of character most of the time. So, there has to be something there to value."

She looked back at her food and began eating again. The silence was telling, so we all backed off, resumed eating, and waited her out. I would kick Archie for bringing it up *now*, except there never was going to be a "right" time to discuss her grandparents and her feelings on that subject.

We finished eating and then moved upstairs to our living room. Frankie curled up on one corner of the sofa, fresh wine glass in hand.

"New York," she said finally, then glanced at us. "We stay here? Whether we live in the city or the Hamptons or Archie gets to build us a house in Westchester."

Jake laughed and I grinned. Archie didn't even look remotely humbled by the declaration. "I like it. And I love the idea of building us a house. We don't need to move yet. We're good here. But eventually, we'll want a place to expand."

"Agreed," Bubba said. "Which means Coop can work on his master's here, and we can discuss where we want to have the wedding."

"I still say we elope," Archie kicked back on one of the chairs and put his feet up. Jake was scrolling through movies, more to just do something than looking for real. However, we would end up watching one. "Tell no one, go get married, then come back and plan a huge party and make it a commitment ceremony or a reveal party, you know?"

"As much as I kind of like that idea," Frankie said. "We still have three problems with that."

"Give them to us, Babe. We can't fix the problems without the parameters."

A smile flashed across her face, alleviating some of the earlier melancholy. "There's the legal issue of five people getting married."

"We're working on that," Archie said. "Legal we can handle. The ceremony itself is for us, and it's our emotional commitment."

"Goddamn," Jake said, then gave a low whistle of appreciation. "You've really grown."

"Yeah, fuck you too," Archie said with a smirk. Everyone laughed, even Frankie. Bubba slid over and picked her right up before settling her in his lap. When the tension drained out of her, I nodded. That was what she needed and Bubba must have felt it as she curled into him.

"Back to the wedding," Bubba said. "We need to pick a date, a place, and who we want to officiate. Then we need to decide how formal we want to be. Do we want to say our own vows?" Bubba focused on her. "Do you want to walk down an aisle, or should you be the one at the front while the four of us walk to you?"

Oh…hey. "That's not a bad idea," I said. "When it comes down to it, we are the ones who pursued you."

Frankie chuckled. "You also made me untouchable."

"Hell yeah, we did," Jake said with more than a little pride. "I'm still sorry that hurt your feelings, but I'm not sorry we kept the schmucks away."

"While I'm certain she has long since forgiven us," I jumped in. "Let's not pick at old wounds, shall we? What were the other problems, Beautiful? You said the legal issue is one."

"The name issue," Frankie said. "Do we want to change any names? I mean—Frankie Curtis Brennen Benton Rhys Standish is a bit of a mouthful."

"You can handle it," I teased. "You handle all of us just fine, and I speak from experience."

She flushed, but she also laughed.

"Lose the Curtis," Archie suggested. "Then you're Frankie Brennen Benton Rhys Standish—Mrs. Standish for short."

There it was, the wild smile on his face and the gleam in his eyes. I got it. The idea of her being Mrs. Brennen was definitely appealing, but Archie wasn't wrong. If we went with all the names…

"Okay, legal issues, name issues," Jake said, ticking them off. "What's our third problem?"

Lifting her head, Frankie studied all of us. I braced for it, because whatever it was, we'd fix it or tackle it together.

"Kids," she said slowly. "We've really not talked about it since… the new year. Do we want them?"

"Hell yes," Archie said. "Eventually. When you're ready."

"Agreed," Bubba and Jake said almost in the same breath. But I caught the look she sent me. The one that said help.

"Beautiful, we're not in a rush. Bubba's twenty-two, we're twenty-one, almost twenty-two. We're not graduating for another few months, and then I'm going after my master's degree while you take over the world, and Bubba writes the soundtrack for two evil geniuses who will be creating all the neat new tech. We have *time*. We want kids—when the time is right for it. What do *you* want?"

She sighed as Bubba rubbed her back. "Being a mom scares the hell out of me."

"Frankie," Jake leaned in to catch her free hand, "you are not your mother. You have *never* been your mother. You have that big ass heart, and you have all four of us. We're going to love every single child we make, no matter whose sperm wins the race…"

I rolled my eyes. Really? Making sperm into a competition.

"…you're going to be an amazing mother. Your kids are gonna be so fucking lucky to have you. That said, nothing happens until you're ready. If that day doesn't come, well, there's nothing wrong with having the freedom to be naked any time of day and fuck like rabbits on the sofa if we want to."

It was Frankie who rolled her eyes. "You guys will do that anyway."

"Yes," Bubba agreed. "We will. The point is that we make the decision together. No one is doing this alone. Whether it's you taking on a more pivotal role at Standish or Coop getting licensed—those two trying to build the next best thing without blowing anything up."

"Hey," Archie said. "We haven't blown anything up in months."

"We're also not done with the test engine," Jake said drily. "Yet."

Laughter spilled out of Frankie, and she tucked her head against Bubba's shoulder. He kept rubbing her back while Jake rubbed his thumb over her palm.

"I love our family," she said softly. "I don't want to lose this—"

"Then we don't," I promised. "We keep talking, we keep working together, we build the future we want. We do it *together*. That doesn't mean we won't have hiccups or stumbles. But we pick each other up, we steady each other, we pick up the slack when someone else needs it."

"What he said," Jake agreed. "I love our family too. Fuck it, if names are an issue, I say we all change our names to something so we match and the only mouthful you have to deal with is us."

That set her off laughing even as Archie groaned. I caught Bubba's eye and gave him a questioning look. He wore a tiny worried frown, tensing into a line between his brows. With a gentle shake of his head, I got it.

Later.

Probably have to go running, but I'd do it.

"Sorry, Coop," Frankie murmured, which yanked my attention right back to her.

"For what, Beautiful?"

"You called the family meeting and I sort of wandered all over the place with it."

"Angel," Bubba said in a soft, almost scolding voice that held way more affection than irritation. "That's the point of a family meeting. We're all agreed on New York. Coop's going after his master's to get licensed. We'll back him up and ensure he doesn't burn out." He kept rubbing her back as he ticked the items off. "We'll figure out the names and the legalities. We want kids when we're ready, and if it happens before, we roll with it. Oh, and Jake and Archie will continue with their endeavors while hopefully not blowing anything up. That about it covers it, right?"

We nodded.

"Great," I said. "Movie time and give her to me, Bubba, time to share."

He chuckled as I rose and slid her out of his lap and shifted her over onto mine. Not that I took her far, we just sat on the sofa as well.

Frankie wrapped her arms around my neck and pressed a kiss to my jaw. "I'm proud of you."

I grinned. "Right back atcha, Beautiful. We got this. Now, without looking at the screen, pick a genre…"

Archie cracked up. One of our favorite movie games. Pick a genre. Pick a number. Hit play and watch whatever crazy thing we got.

A genuine smile curved her lips. "Action."

"Number?" I asked.

"Four," she teased. "The perfect number."

She was way too damn tempting. I kissed her and she arched into me as I teased her lips apart. The guys laughed and Jake groaned but it wasn't until I dragged my head up that I got why.

The fourth movie was *Demolition Man.*

Eh, it worked. Besides, Frankie loved the three shells jokes and the jingles. But I had that stupid bologna one stuck in my head all night.

There were worse things. I also had a cuddly Frankie in my lap, even if I had to share her.

Chapter Three

I FEEL YOU

FRANKIE

The slow stroke of a hand over my hip lulled me out of sleep. Gentle, teasing traces of fingers gliding down my thigh and then back up again. The sheet whispered over my skin as the warm body pressed against my back shifted to press a very thick, very hot dick right against my bare ass.

"Hmmm," I murmured. "Happy birthday."

Coop chuckled as he kissed along my shoulder to my throat. I didn't even have to look to know the sun was not up, even if he certainly was. "Definitely a happy birthday to me," he whispered the words as he nudged my thighs apart.

Biting little kisses sprinkled with teasing licks and gentle sucks sent tiny shivers through my system. When I would have rolled over, he tightened his grip and teased fingers all along my pussy.

"So fucking wet for me already," he said with a little hum of appreciation. I bucked against his hand, but he nudged his cock right against my entrance as he gripped my thigh and lifted it.

It took only one firm push and he filled me right up to that point of pain. A gasp spilled from my lips as he bumped his hips to mine.

"Hmmm," he echoed his earlier hum before biting down on my earlobe. "Ma belle fille. Donc parfait pour moi. Mon meilleur ami. Mon amour."

His accent was terrible, but the words were so heartfelt. My beautiful girl. So perfect for me. My best friend. My love.

"Je t'aime tellement," I confessed. His rumble of appreciation as he began to rock into me just lit me up. From the piercing on his thick tip to the fatness of his cock that was always so damn much to take, I craved him, and he let me know how much he adored me.

I barely noticed the faint buzzing noise before something locked over my clit, and the stimulation jerked my eyes open as I went from teasingly full and content to utter desperation. My pussy clenched around him, but he kept me in place with one well-locked arm around my shoulders.

Pressed against his chest, I couldn't do much more than rock wildly against what had to be a clit vibe or sucker—or fuck—my thoughts shredded as he kept thrusting. The tighter I clamped down on him as the pleasure spasmed through me, the more he grunted as he had to force his way in and out.

It was too much and not enough. My nipples ached and I dug my fingers into his arm as the first orgasm crashed down on me. I tried to move away from the pulsations teasing my clit, but I had nowhere to go.

"Come on, Beautiful," Coop huffed against my ear. "Just come. Don't fight it. This is what I want right here. My once and future wife screaming my name."

Well, he got what he wanted because the next orgasm seemed even more powerful as he deepened his thrusts. Between the suction on my clit sending my eyes rolling and the force of his strokes hitting me so deep inside, that even the gentle tease of those metal balls framing his tip struck lightning, everything whited out as I was nothing but pleasure and motion.

Wetness escaped me as I floated back into my body. But that wasn't Coop. If anything, he seemed even thicker inside me as he kissed and soothed. The stimulator had vanished, and he massaged my breasts as I tried to catch my breath.

"There she is," he whispered, and I tilted my head back to look up at him. He was just another shadow among shadows. "Can you turn around, Beautiful?"

I wasn't even sure I could move. The liquid heat inside of me had dissolved all of my limbs, but what the birthday boy wanted…

"If you need help," Jake said from the darkness. "Just say the word, Baby Girl."

Startled, I flexed around Coop and he groaned. "Fuck yes."

"Her, not you." Laughter threaded Jake's voice and I grinned.

"I can move," I managed to say. Oh, look, I found my words. Course, moving meant sliding off Coop's dick, and that had us both hissing as I tried to shift. Warm hands caught mine and the callouses were a dead giveaway, as was the shape of them.

Jake swooped in for a kiss that stole my breath as he all but peeled me off of Coop. I wrapped my arms around his neck, thrusting my fingers into the lengthening mass of his hair. He'd stopped keeping it short so the length was nearing his shoulders, and I fucking loved to play with it.

"Stop hogging my birthday present," Coop "complained," though there was far more laughter in his voice than any actual irritation.

"Hmm," Jake hummed, sucking my tongue against his. The minty taste of his mouth reminded me that I hadn't even brushed my teeth, but he didn't let me up for a second until he was ready to turn me around.

Heat blew through me like a hot summer day as he took his time turning me and then pressing right up to my back. His cock was right there, heavy and thick, where it pressed against my spine. "Can't blame a guy for wanting to taste how sweet she is fresh off an orgasm."

"No," Coop agreed, and the fact it was still so dark in the room just seemed to amp up the sensuality in their voices. "But I can be selfish cause…"

"…the birthday boy gets what the birthday boy wants," Jake finished for him as he cupped my breasts and massaged them. "Pretty sure what he wants is you, Baby Girl." He teased the shell of my ear with a kiss. "He's the best kind of best friend, because he invited me to the party."

Fuck, that was hot. A moan escaped me as Jake pinched my nipples, amping up the liquid heat in my system until it turned to lava.

He glided his hand up and down my torso, then dipped his fingers between my legs and let out a distinct growl against my ear.

"Yeah, our girl is very hot for you, Birthday Boy. You ready for her?"

"Fuck yes," Coop answered, and his hand found mine almost unerringly. Like they'd choreographed the motion, Jake massaged my clit in three swift brushes that had me trembling before he lifted me while Coop tugged.

Straddling Coop, I gripped the base of his cock and lined him up. Between them, they thrust me down until he filled me again and I let out a soft cry as Coop latched his mouth on one nipple.

The warring sensations cascaded through me. Fire skated over my skin, hot and cold, that only magnified where they touched me. I'd been in a lazy waking state when Coop started, but I was edging toward desperation all over again as I sank down on him.

Jake fisted my hair and tilted my head back before fusing his mouth with mine. Coop thrust upward as he sucked against my nipple and I sank one hand into his hair as I reached up for Jake.

Writhing between them was one of my favorite places to be. "Forward," Jake said against my lips before turning me to Coop again. It wasn't hard to obey that command because Coop lifted his face to mine and then tangled our tongues as I began to roll my hips.

The pressure was so perfect as Coop pushed up to meet my every downward shift. It kept edging right along too much as my inner muscles just spasmed away, particularly if he shifted and my clit bumped against him.

Warmth drizzled against my ass, and then Jake speared two fingers into me. The pressure went from exquisite to intense and I gasped against Coop's mouth.

"Fuck," he groaned into my lips. "Hurry up, man, this is heaven and hell."

He wasn't wrong. My nerves kept lighting up, then Jake scissored his fingers and I bucked between them. Too much. Not enough. Coop dragged me back to him, rubbing between my shoulder blades.

"Right here, Beautiful, focus on me." The roughness in his voice was a direct contrast to the sweetness in his words. I could drown in the care they wrapped me up in. "Jake…" The last came out an actual growl.

"I'm there, aren't I, Baby Girl?" He punctuated the question by pulling his fingers free and replacing them with his dick. Slicked up with lube or not, it was a tight fit. I tried to relax my muscles, but I was shaking almost too much. Coop's abdominals tightened as he pulled back a fraction and then Jake thrust in.

Crying out, I dug my fingers into Coop's shoulders. The trembling racked me from head to toes. For a moment, we just hung there, suspended. It was so much like that first time in Colorado.

Sweat dripped down my forehead, my heart thundered in my ear, or maybe it was theirs. Jake pressed against my back as Coop slid his hands away and then he braced Jake. The perfect frame around me as we all seemed to acclimate to the pressure.

They were going to tear me apart, and I was so ready for it. This was…"Happy birthday," I whispered to Coop. "To me, too—apparently."

Laughter exploded from behind me, and Jake eased back as Coop pushed up and it took them no time to find their rhythm. It was perfection. I caught the motion and rolled my hips, chasing them both as they see-sawed in and out of me.

Head back, I kissed Jake as he nipped at my lips and Coop kissed up the column of my throat, only to capture my lips as I turned back to him.

"Wanna try something," he informed us in between gasps of air, and Jake let out a groan.

"Fucking birthday boy," he muttered and I giggled.

"I'm trying," I promised.

"Succeeding," Coop teased, then nipped at my pulse. "Roll."

The command in his tone was hot, but I wasn't sure who he directed it at. Jake seemed to have no such doubts because we rolled, all three of us until Jake's back hit the bed and I was flat against him, pushing him even deeper.

All three of us groaned and then Coop laughed. "Oh yeah, this is better."

And by better, he meant he had more control because he thrust so deep, electricity sparked through my system and Jake cursed against my ear in between kisses.

"That fucking piercing," he muttered and I laughed. It was too damn early to be this drunk.

"Don't hate," Coop said, and I could taste the wild grin in his smile. "Could have been you."

"Could still be me," he gritted back out between his teeth and I arched up to chase Coop's dick as he pulled back and then Jake dragged my hips down, impaling me firmly on his dick.

"And it could be me," I teased though I already had a piercing in my belly button and another one currently railing me.

"My piercing is yours," Coop reminded me as he slammed home, and the orgasm they'd been edging me on spilled over. I hooked one leg around Coop to hang on as I began to shake in earnest, clenching down on both of them until they hissed.

They tried to rock into me, chasing their own release, but I barely let either go, and when they came, it was a whole new rush. Coop kissed me as he gave three short, jerky thrusts before his own orgasm stole over him.

Sticky, hot, and fused almost into one, it felt like we clung together as the storm of emotion and sensation began to pass.

Eventually, petting hands and light kisses roused me from the sensual haze and then Coop eased back. The loss had me almost weeping. A moment later, Jake rolled me onto my side and then he eased away too.

Fuck. From too full to too empty. But they didn't abandon me. If anything, the petting strokes began getting firmer and then they were trading me back and forth for kisses.

Light had just begun to edge at the windows, promising a new day, when Ian and Archie arrived wreathed in the scent of coffee and sweet treats.

"Someone got the party started early," Archie said dryly and I grinned at Coop. He winked at me.

"Birthday boy gets what the birthday boy wants," I said in a totally wrecked voice. "Though, I'm hoping he wants to spend the day in bed because I'm not sure I can move after that."

His grin grew positively devilish. "A day in bed sounds perfect. Want to skip class with me, Beautiful?"

"Yes." I didn't even care what was on the agenda today. I had no meals or meetings booked cause it was Coop's birthday.

"Yes!" He fist-pumped and then laughed when Archie waved coffee over me.

Did I track that cup lovingly? Yes, yes, I did. That would get me to sit up. As it was, I didn't care that we were all nude. None of us did. It was a little messy, but I didn't care about that either.

"Dude, that's cheating," Jake said even as he rolled off the bed and to his feet. There was the barest moment of stagger that Ian steadied before he handed him his coffee. "Not that I'm complaining."

Laughter bubbled up through me as it rippled through the guys. Coop scooted up to sit against the headboard, then he tugged me back toward the pillows with care before Archie handed me my coffee.

Ambrosia.

"Yours," Archie continued as he passed a second cup to Coop, along with a card.

I hid a smile at the sight of it and sipped my coffee. As boneless as I was, that sent a fresh surge of energy through me.

"Hold that thought," Jake said after taking a swallow of coffee and setting it down. He staggered into the bathroom. I almost choked on the coffee in an attempt to not laugh at him. The guys weren't so kind.

"You look like you've been skipping workouts," Ian said, almost idly. "Should get you back into training if stepping up with Frankie is leaving you so wrecked."

"Yo, Bubba?" Jake called. "Bite me."

I smothered another round of giggles as Ian sat on the foot of the bed and winked at me.

"Dude, shut up and take a leak already. We're waiting on you out here." Archie let out a huff of disgust before he sank down in a chair and then eyed me briefly. "Babe?"

"For real? I don't even know what my hair looks like."

His grin grew far more wicked. "It looks very fucked, like the rest of you. Please?"

Rolling my eyes, I propped up my knee and spread my arms wide.

"Fuck yes." Archie pulled out his phone and snapped a photo. Then another. Coop photo-bombed—well, kiss-bombed, I suppose— when he dragged me into one and Archie laughed. "Like you think that's gonna discourage me."

"You were the last thing on my mind," Coop promised as he nuzzled another kiss. I grinned against his lips and then turned to take a drink of my coffee. He tasted like fresh coffee too. Was there anything sexier?

Jake wandered out of the bathroom, reclaimed his cup, and grinned at me. Between his glorious tattoo and sex rumpled hair, I had to admit there was definitely something sexier in the room—all four of them.

My pussy clenched and ached at the same time. Not that I was remotely complaining.

"I'm back," Jake said. "You can open that now."

"Gracious," Coop retorted. "Since it's *my* birthday."

"It is your birthday, and you are the bestest boyfriend and fiancé."

"Hey," came three equally snarky voices in varying degrees of outrage, but I just waved them off.

"Birthday boy."

"Yeah, yeah." Archie smirked. "I get that title in just a few days."

"Yes, you do, and you're the bestest fiancé too."

"You're just catering to my ego." He appeared considering for a moment. "I'll allow it."

Fortunately, he put his coffee cup down cause a pillow smacked him in the face a second later.

"Wait your turn," Coop informed him with an unrepentant grin and the guys laughed when Archie just flipped him off.

I loved them so damn much.

Coop handed me his cup to hold and I watched as he opened the card. It was thin, one hundred percent camouflaging the contents as just an ordinary birthday card.

The front had a giant horn on it and a piece of cheese, declaring him the great cheese on the cheesiest of birthdays. He snorted, then flipped it open and the business card fell out.

Frowning, he picked it up, and for a moment, his whole expression froze. It wasn't the only thing inside the card, but I could almost see the thoughts racing behind his gray-green eyes.

The business card read:

Cooper Brennen, Ph.D. Licensed Clinical Therapist

Practice Coming Soon

"Guys…"

"You," I told him, "are going to be the best damn therapist ever. You are great with those kids, and they love you. We love you more. You want to get licensed in New York, and we want you to know that we're with you every step of the way."

There was no mistaking the misty look in his eyes as he stared at me. "I mean—this is great—but what I really wanted was a pony."

"How about I ride you like a pony later?"

He tossed the birthday card. "Sold." Then he kissed me again as the guys laughed. The card didn't go far as it fluttered down onto the bed, along with the list of the best degree programs in the state for clinical child psychologists. A list we'd put together with help from his advisor and his boss at the community center.

"I love you," I whispered.

"Hmm, me too," he agreed, then laughed almost hard enough to make our teeth clack when my stomach gurgled. "Guys? Please tell me there's food for Frankie somewhere so that she can ride me like a pony later?"

"Yeah, but we gotta get dressed for it," Jake said, stretching a hand out to me. "Jeremy's fixing breakfast and there are a few gifts waiting downstairs. We also promised your mom you'd video call her before Frankie steals you away for—well, I won't tell you what for. Some surprises are just better experienced."

I let Jake help me up, grimacing only a little at the mess running down my legs. The boys all looked very pleased with themselves. "Be nice, gentlemen, and if Coop's in a good mood, I bet I can ride you all like ponies today. I'm feeling adventurous."

With that, I carried my coffee into the bathroom as Coop muttered, "Best birthday ever," behind me.

Twenty-five minutes and one blowjob later, Coop and I were the last two down the stairs to breakfast. Jeremy just gave us an indulgent look as he set out the food, including the sparkling cinnamon rolls with a candle stuck in them.

It was the most ridiculous thing, but Coop grinned at it. I knew the moment he noticed the new picture we'd hung on the wall in the dining room. It was a mural with three panels made by all his kids at the community center—their impression of Mr. Coop.

"Later," Coop said against my ear as the guys talked about the pickup game that weekend and Jake's upcoming hockey season. "I'm gonna cry like a baby about that."

I turned into his kiss and whispered, "Your secret is always safe with me."

It always would be.

Chapter Four
LETTER TO ME

ARCHIE

Leaning back against the Bugatti, I checked the messages on my phone. Frankie sent a rather delightful rant on her contracts and acquisitions management professor. Apparently, he was a snore, a bore, *and* a misogynist. Lips pursed, I scrolled through the series until I got to the last message.

> Frankie
> I have no idea who thought he was worth hiring, but I'm tempted to ask if we can get him fired.

Followed swiftly by…

> Frankie
> Tempted, not actually asking.

.

Then another:

I didn't laugh, mainly because there were three dots indicating that she was typing. Then the message came in and I laughed.

The adorable little winky face at the end, coupled with the smirk, was just so her.

I sent back.

Two kisses were her only response. I flicked a look at the building and then flipped over to the browser on my phone to look up the name of her instructor. Never hurt to be prepared if she asked me about him. I was reading his bio when Eddie came striding out of the building, loosening his tie.

"Sorry," he called. "Hong Kong ran long."

Checking the time on the phone, I raised my brows. "It's almost midnight there."

"Exactly," he said, making a face with a sharp shake of his head, pulling the tie all the way off. "I got here at five. They were punctual, and the meeting started at six. But London was late."

"Have you introduced Frankie to international meetings yet?"

But Eddie didn't answer, he was staring at my car. "This is new."

I laughed. "Yes, and it's a gift. I don't get to take her out often, so be honored."

He shot me an indecipherable look. "I already was."

Right. That was enough emotions for that.

"As for Frankie and international meetings, no, I did have her sit in on the meeting with some of our French partners over the summer, but I wanted to test her language skills and our translator's."

I had zero doubt in my mind that she had passed, but I waited to continue the conversation until we were in the car. "How did it go?"

"Excellent. Even our translator was impressed, and theirs was delighted. It's been the first time in four years I got a concession out of them. We'll be able to work out of that airfield we wanted."

"She mentioned the airfield was still in negotiations because the company from Norway had made a significant offer." She'd also been very proud of herself because of the wording they'd used.

"She also said the wording suggested it was already in the past, and they might be trying to leverage us for a higher fee, so I hard balled at five percent less than our first offer…"

"And they came back five percent higher?" I got this game and heard him and Grandpa Ted discuss it way too many times. "But you stood fast, and they finally dropped it to one percent below your original offer and you caved.'"

"One point five," he said with more than a little pride. "One point five and the right to renegotiate in five years."

"That's a good deal. Not bad for an old man."

His snort made me laugh as I pressed the button to get the engine rumbling to life. The latest text from Frankie popped up on the dash screen.

Frankie

> You looked up his name,
> didn't you?

I chuckled.

"Whose name?"

He waited while I checked traffic before I accelerated. We were heading out to Long Island for the afternoon to inspect the last of the changes the contractors were to have finished once we were back in the city.

"Frankie's contracts and asset management professor is making her crazy."

"Runkle," Eddie said as he stretched his legs. "Kind of a quirky guy and definitely an acquired taste."

It didn't surprise me that he knew who the man was. The Bugatti handled like a dream as I flowed through traffic. It was nice that it wasn't too damn busy in Midtown today. It would be even better once we got on 495.

"Misogynist?"

Eddie frowned sharply. "Not that I know of. What kind of shit is he pulling that she's asking that?"

The immediate defensiveness pulled another grin from me. "She was on a rant. He's a snore, a bore, and a misogynist. But she doesn't rant about many people, not even teachers she's disliked in the past. So, either he critiqued her harshly, or he's a special kind of stupid."

Scratching his jaw, Eddie looked thoughtful. "I've met with all of her professors. Since I'm still acting as her official mentor, I leveraged it to get a look at them, and I talked to the dean of the college to pull some strings on the classes she got into."

Nope. Didn't surprise me in the least.

"No, I didn't tell her, and no, I didn't overstep. Much."

"I'm not saying a word," I told him. I didn't have to say a word.

"That's a very mature stance."

"You're protecting her interests and making sure we know who is influencing her and keeping the sleaze bags who like to seduce their students away from her."

"Could be a healthy donation that saw a rearranging of certain schedules to avoid any legal entanglements the college did not want coming their way." The smugness in his voice was well-earned.

I offered him my fist and he gave me a side-eye.

"Just fist bump, Dad, and accept the compliment."

He grinned, touching his knuckles to mine. "The dad is more than enough of a compliment."

"You did good. Just take it and run."

"Premise accepted." He shifted in the seat. "She runs like a damn dream."

"I know." It was my turn to be smug. The Bugatti had spent a lot of time in the garage. I didn't get to take her out anywhere near as much as she deserved. With winter coming, she'd be locked up tight and warm soon enough. Still… Frankie got me this car for Christmas a couple of years earlier.

It meant far more than she probably realized. Or maybe she did. It wasn't the cost, though, but the fact she'd spent so much when I knew how frugal she tended to be. How frugal she probably always would be, despite the volume of wealth she had without me.

With me?

Yeah, we were sitting pretty, and extravagant gifts were undeniably my love language. She'd become so fluent that she not only got me a car, but she also got me a car I could love and appreciate without being transported back to the Ferrari.

Any wonder on why I loved her?

"So," I said once I finally got us out of the city. He glanced up from his phone. "Let's talk about the future a little…"

While I didn't look at him directly, I caught how he braced

himself.

"It's not bad news," I said with a hint of exasperation. "Seriously, I know we've had a long history of me only talking to you when I was on the attack and you only speaking to me when you had to—but I think we're both past that."

"I'm sorry," he said abruptly, then held up a hand. "Before you tell me this is a settled matter between us, I don't think it can ever be truly settled. I fucked up. Plain and simple. So, I'm sorry that you ever thought the only reason I spoke to you was because I *had* to. What I *had* to do was grow up and get over my resentments. Took me too damn long to do that."

"You were in love with her, Dad," I said, and I could afford to be understanding on this front. "Before Frankie, I would never have understood the depths that I could go to. I saw what I was doing when I thought she was never going to look at me the way I looked at her."

The stunts I'd pulled. The girls I'd just used to scratch an itch and move on.

"No one was ever going to be her. Muriel wasn't. And I was the reason you were stuck with Muriel."

Eddie sighed. "No, Archie, you were *not* why I was stuck with her. You were and *are* the best thing I've ever done. To be honest, that was a happy accident, because Jeremy and Dad made you the man you are. You might take after me in some ways, and I damn well appreciate them, but the simple truth is I can't go back and be the father I should have been."

"Well, we will go forward now," I said. "We've been doing pretty good. I mean, you see that little smile Frankie gets when we talk without arguing?"

He laughed. "There isn't anything you won't do for her."

"Nope. Not a damn thing, which brings us back to the future. So, if you're ready to let go of apologizing for the past—which I get and I appreciate, but I don't need. Not anymore. We have the future. I have a future with her and we want you to be a part of it. So if you can meet me on that bridge, I think we're going to be okay."

"Okay, well, I'm walking out on the bridge. What are we talking about with regard to the future?"

"Prenuptial agreement, and since it will be directly related to my stock shares in Standish, I wanted to be the one to tell you."

His expression sobered. "I'm listening."

"However, the legalities are worked out, and the marriage is not just Frankie and me. It will be me, the guys, *and* Frankie." I'd actually given this a lot of thought while the guys and I had discussed it over the last few months. "Naming conventions are still TBD—"

"You're changing your name?" Shock rippled through his words.

"Maybe," I admitted. "It's part of the discussion. Four last names for Frankie is huge, but then again, we're all in this together, so maybe one last name for all of us is the way to go. It's again—still TBD."

His lips compressed, but he said nothing.

"You don't have to like it, Dad, and yes, you can weigh in on it— but let's stick with the prenup for now. Fair?"

Blowing out a breath, he flexed his hands. "Thank you. I was biting my tongue and that shit hurts."

I laughed. Cause he wasn't wrong. Biting your tongue sucked. "Good. Look, this is what I'm thinking. Collectively, Frankie and I have the bulk of the wealth in the family. Bubba's not to be sneezed at because while he plays humble, he's starting to rake in the royalties— both of them are—for their work as Bound Hearts. Jake's designs are the foundation of our engineering division, and Coop's going to make the world a better fucking place. "

Flicking a look to my right, I checked his expression, which was intent but not negative—an excellent sign.

"But right now, Frankie and I have the bulk of the wealth. If and when Patience and Eugene pass away, Frankie stands to inherit a lot more than she realizes. At least, as far as I know, she does—but that's only relevant to the possible future. She might just flat-out donate that money."

"That reminds me," Eddie murmured. "For later, we need to discuss expanding the foundation. I think that's a good place for her to get her feet wet after school."

It used to worry me when we would be on the same wavelength like this. Not so much right now. "Got it."

"Okay, continue. You two control the bulk of the financial assets, but Jake and Bubba both bring significant future investments into the relationship, and Coop's assets aren't tangible but infinitely valuable."

"Perfectly stated." I liked that summation.

"Comes with the territory. Proceed."

"What I want to do is set up a prenuptial that covers all five of us, balances the assets in an equitable split, designating Frankie and any children she produces as the ultimate beneficiaries, but balanced so that if *anyone* in the group, myself included, decides on a split—everyone is taken care of."

"That's—that's a tall order, Archie," he said slowly. "You're basically looking to pool the assets collectively, creating equal portions for each person, then if—one or two leave, no matter the circumstances, they are entitled to financial remuneration including stock shares and future profits?"

"I trust them, Dad. I trust their love for Frankie. I trust their love for me." Sometimes, it floored me to say it aloud. "But I want us to all be equals. It's important to me that no one feels like the power— financial or otherwise—is tilted against them. What I have, they get in equal partnership."

"We'd have to get board approval if this involves your shares in the company, that's—that's a significant chunk that would then be split. Especially if you and Frankie pool those shares."

"Can you sell it to them? I mean, you're currently the majority stockholder."

"Because you signed a power of attorney over the shares Dad left you to me." The comment made me grin.

"He was always trying to get us to communicate and work together. We are, so his legacy is in good hands. Besides, you and I both know that 'office life' is not for me. That shit bores me to tears, even if I can play all those corporate games. You want to bring me in to scare the crap out of people with my wild, reckless ways—do it. But you love the wheeling and dealing. I don't."

"You'd be good at it," he said, but there was acceptance in his voice.

"Just because I'm good at something doesn't mean I want to do it. I like building things. You need me, and I'm there. Frankie needs me, and I'm there. Otherwise, I'm content to ignore the board and the shareholders and go build a better car or a better plane…"

"How is that going?"

"Not gonna jinx it," I said, rolling my head from side to side. "But Jake's definitely on to something, and if I can make the converter do what we want it to do, I think we're going to revolutionize travel."

"See, I hear that note of pure glee in your voice, and I want to head out to Brooklyn and poke around your shop." He raised his hands. "Don't get touchy cause I won't. Dad was right, you want to build your legacy and you're damn smart. So, we'll just keep backing the winner."

"Thanks."

"You're welcome." Then he sighed. "Okay, have we talked to any attorneys about this prenuptial agreement?"

"Not yet. I've been working on the wording in my head. I haven't even brought it up to Frankie yet. I thought about talking to her first, but I like bringing her a plan. We have many group decisions to make, and we're all discussing those—this one—this one I want to have mapped out before I put it in front of her."

"You want all the exits buttoned up, so she doesn't worry about taking advantage."

Exactly. "Dad, she's never cared about the wealth. What she saw in me was never the money. Fuck, she used to give me hell for spending any on her. I've worn her down over the years, and this car is proof that she gets it. What is the good of money if you can't spend it on the people you love?"

"True," he said in a quiet voice. "I went to Connecticut a couple of weeks ago."

Woah. "What?"

"It was my anniversary with Maddy," he admitted. "I know it shouldn't matter—"

"Dad, of course it matters. I didn't like the woman, but it doesn't mean I don't get what she meant to you. I'm sorry you went up there alone."

"Thank you, but it was something I needed to do." He sighed. "My point is—Maddy cared about the money. She cared when she thought it was leverage and set out to prove everyone wrong on that she didn't need it. Then she cared because she wanted the power back. The money—it was always there. I'm glad it's not like that for you and Frankie. If she doesn't like the prenup—if any of them don't really, don't make it about the money."

That was food for thought. "I won't do it and make it a done deal without discussing it with them. I just wanted to have a plan in place beforehand, a road map so they—and I for that matter—know it can be done and how."

He nodded but didn't say anything more. I mean, what was there to say. About fifteen minutes from the house, he scratched at his jaw.

"So—Frankie and *any* children she produces…"

"She's not pregnant, Dad."

"I wasn't asking that."

"We're not planning on a pregnancy anytime soon."

"Wasn't going to ask that, either, smartass."

I grinned. "Then what were you going to ask?"

"Hank has the inside track. He's going to be a grandpa to any child of hers."

"Yeah," I said slowly.

"I want in on that deal too. How do we negotiate to make that happen?"

I opened my mouth then snapped it shut with a little click of my teeth. That was really not even on my radar for questions. "You know— pretty sure all you have to do is ask…"

"Good. Then consider this me asking. I'll get a meeting on the books with Frankie…"

"Dad?"

"Let us finalize the marriage and graduation first. I'll ensure you have a pre-contract lock on the grandpa status—unless you want granddad?"

He looked thoughtful. "I'll concede the first call to Hank. Then I get my pick. The other dads can get in line."

I did not laugh.

I didn't.

"Seems reasonable."

"Good." He grinned. "I'll make sure you have the pre-contracted agreement in your email on Monday."

"You know what?" I laughed. "I'm good with that."

"Excellent." He rubbed his hands together. "Do we need to talk to the contractors about a future nursery or kids' rooms? We should also look into the various pre-kindergarten programs. Some of them fill up—"

"Dad?"

"Too much?"

"A little, but thank you."

"You want us to focus on the future, well, I'm going for best grandfather. Jeremy already has the edge, so I'm gonna have to work extra hard."

I don't think I *stopped* laughing before we got to the house.

Chapter Five

BROTHERS AND SISTERS

FRANKIE

"I swear, if you don't leave my shit alone," Alec said with just enough menace to sound believable. "I am going to pound you."

Leaving the kitchen, I glanced into the living room where Alec and Craig were in a full-on glare-off. Someone had turned the console games on and there was a game frozen on the screen.

"I'm not hurting you," Craig hurled back. "And you're grounded from the Xbox until you catch up on your projects."

"That doesn't count this weekend, jerk." As furious as he sounded and the threats he'd issued, Alec kept his hands at his sides, even if he flexed and curled his fingers like he wanted to punch something. "That's *my* game. You didn't even ask."

"Cause you would have said 'no,'" Craig retorted. My brothers were so different from each other, except when they weren't. At thirteen going on fourteen, Alec had hit a growth spurt over the summer. He was easily as tall as me now. I had a feeling he'd catch up to the guys rather spontaneously at some point.

"You're such a pain in the ass. Ugh."

"Well, you're an asshole!"

"Boys," I said quietly, and they both jerked around to look at me. The age difference was just two years, but Alec really towered over Craig and Chloe at the moment. Puberty sucked. I wasn't so far removed from it that I didn't remember that. "Alec, come give me a hand, and, Craig, you can play a game that isn't one that belongs to Alec."

"Awww," they both protested in almost the exact same tone. But Alec's scowl deepened, and for the first time since I met him, he actively glared at me. I hated to break this to him, and I probably would refrain unless he was too much of a little shit, but he was kind of adorable still. And Jake had a much meaner scowl.

Come to think of it, so did Coop. He didn't get mad often, but when he did—hello.

"Or you can go up to your room while I talk to Alec," I informed Craig. "But what you aren't going to do is get away with being rude. He's your brother. He's not asking you to do much, except to ask before you touch his things. It's just common courtesy. I know for a fact what Kelly would do. So keep pushing me."

For a second, Alec's fierce frown vanished as amusement flashed in his eyes. No sooner did that happen than he screwed his face back up into something terse. "Mom said we were to behave for Frankie."

"You know what, Alec," Craig said as he clenched his fists as if he were ready to launch at him. "You're a jerk. I'm going upstairs." He bumped his shoulder against Alec hard as he passed him, though it didn't do much to move his much larger brother. Craig stomped all the way up the stairs and then a door slammed.

"He's such a baby sometimes," Alec muttered.

"And you were an ass, but we don't all grow up at the same time or at the same rate." The oven beeped behind me and I jerked my head toward the kitchen. "Let's go. We should talk before lunch."

I walked back into the kitchen and waited for him to join me. I'd put potato skins in the oven cause the kids all liked them and so did I. It was a chilly weekend that kept threatening snow, but so far, none had fallen. Kelly and Hank were away for the weekend, going to some school thing, or maybe it was a work thing for Kelly.

Honestly, I didn't remember. It was a weekend with the kids and I'd looked forward to it. Archie was supposed to come up with me, but he'd gotten tied up with some component that kept failing, and when he and Jake vanished down that rabbit hole, I told him it would be fine if I went on my own. As much as I liked having the guys here, it was good for me to just get to know the kids.

Normally, we didn't have these issues. They argued, but I'd never seen them so angry with each other. Maybe I needed to be around more for that. The door to the kitchen opened, and Alec walked in. He frowned at me as I pulled out the tray of potato skins and then slid a second one in.

"Did you really just call me an ass?"

"Yep."

"You know, Mom doesn't like that kind of language."

"Really?" I pursed my lips. "Huh. Learn something new every day."

"She doesn't like when we use it or when it's directed at us. In fact," Alec continued, folding his arms and raising his chin like he was about to give me a lecture, "she disapproves of that type of language entirely. I don't think she'd care for your attitude."

"Entirely possible," I agreed with him as I picked off a piece of the bacon from one of the potato skins and munched on it. "What do you think she'd say about *your* behavior?"

"I think she'd be disappointed in me, then wonder what kind of example you were setting. You realize that Craig and Chloe are a little young for this kind of language."

Oh boy. "How old were you when you learned to cuss?"

"We're not talking about me," Alec said. While he didn't stomp his foot, he looked pretty pissed. "You're supposed to be the big sister here, setting the example. I told you this, remember? What kind of an example is calling me an ass?"

"Calling a spade a spade." I picked up one of the potato skins and leaned back against the counter. "Alec, you're thirteen, not thirty. You were pissed because Craig was playing your game when you're not allowed to. It had nothing to do with him touching your stuff. It had to do with him touching something you're not allowed to touch. So, you were bullying him cause you're bigger and you're older. You use your size and your attitude—"

When he opened his mouth to protest, I held up a hand.

"Zip it. You asked a question, I'm answering."

He glared at me, but I didn't blink as I met him stare for stare. I could go toe to toe with Jake in this mood. He did not worry me in the slightest.

"Fine," Alec declared, flopping his arms around then folding them as he dug his heels in stubbornly. He'd listen, but he didn't want to, so I better make it good.

That explained some of my own temper. Maybe Hank's laid-back attitude masked a temper too. Food for thought.

"That fight with Craig wasn't about Craig. So, tell me what it was about," I said, switching tactics. "And come eat, cause while I can eat all of these, I am supposed to make sure you guys eat too. The second tray can be for Chloe and Craig when they come down."

"Why do you think something is wrong?" Bewilderment cracked

through his stony expression. "You were just saying I was bullying my brother." The last definitely insulted him.

"You were, but according to you—and to Jake's sisters—picking on your younger siblings is a sign of love. However, sometimes, especially when you're already irritated, they're just easier targets." Blake and Becca got into it like that a lot. Not with Louisa so much.

"Are you filming me?" He twisted to look around the kitchen, and I blinked.

"Why would I be filming you?"

"To put it on TikTok or something about pranking your younger brother." He looked moderately outraged.

"Well, while that might be funny, I'm not. I had too many people post pictures of me and rip on me on social media when I was in high school. I'd never do that to someone else."

The speed at which he yanked his head around to stare at me when I said that answered my question. Someone was giving him a hard time…

"Probably never told you about that, huh?"

He shook his head slowly.

"Okay, grab us some sodas, and I'll get food on the table. I want to show you something."

Whether it was my change in tone or what I'd already told him, he didn't argue. He even grabbed the sour cream. With twenty minutes left on the oven for the rest of the potato skins, I waited for him to sit down before I pulled out my phone.

"It'll take me a minute to find them, but I know some of them never came down—I just got older and didn't care. Go ahead and eat."

It took me a full ten minutes to scroll back far enough to find the posts in my messages. They were way down. I suppose I should have deleted them a long time ago. But I just hadn't thought about them in years.

"Here we go." I slid the phone over to him and then picked up a potato skin to eat while he studied the screen. After wiping his hands, he scrolled upward.

"What a bitch," he finally said, and I bit back a smile.

"She definitely was. It hurt back then. Not that she thought that about me—I mean, I did get to the point where I didn't care because nothing I said or did would ever change her mind. She hated me because she was jealous. I'd like to offer you a platitude, but the simple fact is—some people just suck."

"You tried to make her stop?" His expression was so tense.

"Well, the guys did. Pretty sure they would have done the same thing to her if she didn't, but I didn't want them to do that. Rachel, on the other hand, roasted her pretty hard and clapped back regularly. It didn't make Sharon stop. She just kept digging in her little comments and posts. I did break her nose. That shut her down some—I don't recommend that last part. Largely cause I do like your mom and I don't want her to actually get mad at my advice."

He laughed. "I don't think my stuff is this bad."

"So show me yours—tell me what's eating at you. I might not be able to do anything or offer you a platitude, but I have some experience in these areas. I also have a social media guru we can consult if we have to."

That pulled a real laugh out of him, but then his ears went red. "It's—it's not about me. It's—there's—there's a girl I like. I mean, I don't like her like a girlfriend. I just like her like a friend. But she's pretty, you know. Only, she doesn't think she's pretty. Then some of the guys made some jokes about her in class, and one of the girls posted it. It kind of went from there."

"That sucks. What did you do?"

He wasn't looking anywhere but at the table and his shoulders drooped. "I didn't do anything—I mean, I wanted to slug the guy who made the joke, but Dad says the minute I hit someone, I've already lost the argument."

Depends on the argument. But I didn't say that aloud.

"I can't tell the girl what I think of her cause she'll just run and tell the teacher or anyone else and say I was bullying her—kind of like you said I was with Craig." He made a face. "It bugs me, I should do something, but I don't know what."

"Want an idea?"

He studied me for a moment. "You said what you did, didn't work. How would that help?"

"Well, I'm not talking about what to do about them—directly. I'm talking about what you can do for—" I raised my brows.

His ears went a little deeper red. "Her name is Emma. Don't— don't tell Dad? I mean, I think Mom knows, but Dad always wants to give me good advice, and he's great and stuff but—"

"Your secret is safe with me." I held up my pinky. "I swear."

He hooked his pinky with mine. "Okay—what's your idea?"

"Send her a message and reach out to her. Being picked on sucks, especially if you think everyone else thinks the same things. It hurts. Maybe you can't *fix* it. But you can be her friend."

For a moment, he just stared at me. "Like—you want me to call her?" You'd have thought I was suggesting he go and egg her house; he was that appalled by the idea. "Girls are weird, Frankie, no offense."

"Well, none taken, but I thought you liked her."

"I do," he said, then took a bite of one of his potato skins. "I just— when you're nice to a girl, they think you're into them."

"And that's bad?" I pulled one of the potato skins in half so I could dip it into the sour cream.

"I mean—kind of. Maybe." He made a face. "I don't know. Girls get weird."

"Sure, but boys are pretty weird too. You don't see me judging you for that." That got a smile out of him, even if it was a little reluctant.

"What would your guys have done?"

"What would they have done, or what would they do?" Because what Archie had wanted to do was destroy them. Course, so had Rachel…

It took him a minute to decide what his answer would be, and three more potato skins disappeared in the meanwhile. Some of the sour left his disposition too. Bad enough to be hungry, but hungry and frustrated? Yeah, that was a recipe for disaster.

I got up and retrieved the next round of potato skins before the timer went off. They'd need a couple of minutes to cool.

"What did they do?" he asked finally.

"They were my friends," I told him. "They walked me between classes. They stared down the people who stared at me. They shut down the gossip. Jake got into more than one fight—not advising that but Jake's got a wicked left and right cross, so—he took real exception when people called me names."

"They were your friends?"

I nodded slowly. "They didn't care who saw them with me. They didn't worry about what other people said about them. In fact, I'm pretty sure Archie loved it when they tried to talk about him." He could really eviscerate people with that talented tongue of his. "Be her friend," I told him. "As I said, you can worry what other people will think about you, but that's kind of a shitty way to be about someone you like. Even if you don't like-like her—you like her enough to care that she's hurting. So, what are you going to do about it?"

"I should probably send her a message, huh?"

"Might be a good start. Is she in the class you're behind on?"

He blinked. "I'm not behind cause I don't know how to do it. I just thought the assignment was stupid."

"Ask her for help."

"I don't need—"

"Maybe not, but it's an excuse to talk to her, right? It's a way to pick up the phone and start a conversation. You could start with a text, then work it up from there."

"Oh," he said slowly, then blinked at me. "That wouldn't be so bad…but what if she thinks I'm dumb?"

I had to bite back a smile. "Do you think Ian is dumb?"

"No, he's brilliant. Great musician."

"Do you know he asked me to tutor him in math for four years?"

"But—" Alec's jaw dropped. "They're brilliant. That's a great idea." He bounced up and then started to rush out but turned around to clean up his plate, then grabbed his soda and kissed me on the cheek. "You're not so bad for a sister."

"Hey, Alec," I called. "You're not so bad yourself. Just remember—be her friend so she knows you are. Okay?"

"I can do that. And I'll tell Craig and Chloe to come eat—and I'll apologize to Craig and tell him he can play my game."

He rushed out and up the stairs before I could comment. The fact that he then yelled his apologies and that they needed to get down here and eat before the door to his room slammed, just made me laugh.

"Frankie," Chloe said as she and Craig came in. "Can we watch movies this afternoon?"

"Yep, but first, I have to beat Craig at that game he was playing."

She grimaced as Craig got all smug-faced.

"Don't worry, I'll show you how to play it too."

"Wait, what?"

"Go ahead and eat. I just need to text the guys really quick."

"I'm never getting a boyfriend," Chloe announced. "They are way too much work, and guys suck."

"As if anyone wants you for a girlfriend," Craig snarked. Then she pinched him.

Hard.

"Ow," he complained. "See, this is why they won't."

"Good," she told him, and I had to bite the inside of my lip to keep from laughing.

"Just eat your food and stop picking on each other for five minutes."

Opening up our group text message I sent,

TOGETHER
WITH THEIR FAMILIES

William, Klara
&
Alicia

REQUEST THE HONOR OF YOUR PRESENCE AT
THEIR MARRIAGE AND RECOMMITMENT
CEREMONY

Sat | 10 | Dec

AT HALF PAST FOUR IN THE AFTERNOON AS
THE SUN SETS ON THE PAST, THEY WILL JOIN
TOGETHER FOR THE FUTURE.

CALISTOGA HOUSE
ELMWOOD

Reception to follow

70

Chapter Six
HERE COME THE BRIDES

JAKE

It seemed almost surreal to be back in Texas, where the Christmas decorations filled the yards and the stores while the air conditioning was blasting. A cold front was coming in by the weekend, though, and there were ice storm warnings coming with it.

As often as this had been our holiday season, I was already missing New York. There was a foot of snow on the ground. A stark contrast to when we'd made a foray to Rockefeller to see the tree after they lit it this year. The live performances had been fun and it had been just a great night all the way around. A nice break from the finals grind.

"Hey," Frankie said, pulling me back to the present. She was fixing my tie—something she'd perfected over the last two weeks of fittings. My parents' wedding was a kind of bohemian marriage between tradition with their unique flavor of love. "You good?"

I grinned at her as I gave her a once over. Klara had asked Frankie to be her best woman, which—I couldn't blame Klara for that, Frankie was definitely my best woman. My only one. Blake, Becca, and Louisa were bridesmaids. Bubba and Joe were groomsmen, and I got to be Dad's best man.

"I'm good," I promised her, tempted as hell to kiss the pink slick of gloss and color right off her lips. But considering she'd endured a whole litany of color testing with the girls to make sure she complemented without dominating, I was pretty sure she'd pop me.

Worth it.

"You look edible," I teased, taking advantage of the closeness to adjust her tie. Frankie wasn't in a full suit like me, instead, she wore a waistcoat that matched mine over a billowy long-sleeved shirt. Similarly, her tie had been designed to match. But whereas mine was just blue with a silver pattern on it, hers seemed to practically sparkle under the light.

Or maybe it was just Frankie.

"Well, you need to curb your appetites for now. If I mess up this hair, Klara and Alicia might genuinely have a nervous breakdown."

I frowned. "They're that bad?" That made no sense.

"It's their wedding day, and before you say they were married before," she continued, smoothing down my jacket. "I think that makes it even more nerve-wracking."

"Because it didn't work out the first time." I sighed, tension fisting my gut as she linked her fingers with mine. Eyes closed, I rested my forehead on Frankie's. "Should I say something to them?"

"I think you being here, being a part of their day and supporting them, says a lot."

"How'd you get so smart?"

"Born this way."

I chuckled.

"Okay, it's my wedding day, you two," Dad said as he came out of the backroom and smoothed down his suit. "It feels weird not to be in my uniform."

"I think you look great, Bill," Frankie told him and I shifted to face him.

"You do look kind of weird," I admitted. It wasn't like he was in uniform all the time, but… "Mom is going to appreciate the gesture, though."

"Yeah?" Dad, who did not fumble, fucked his tie up.

After squeezing Frankie's hands, I turned to him. "Let me help."

"I'm going to check on Klara," Frankie murmured, pressing a kiss to Dad's cheek. "You really do look great. Almost as good as Jake."

He laughed, some of the tension cracking. When she turned to me, she winked before all but sauntering to the door.

"You got lucky with that one," Dad said to me after the door closed behind her.

"Yes, I did." You'd never get an argument out of me on that subject. I loosened his tie and went back to work retying it—just another layer to the weird of the day, I supposed.

"Is this when you threaten me?" Dad asked and I quirked a brow.

"Do I need to threaten you?" Cause we'd had a few conversations after he and Klara had begun to actively pursue Mom again. Then why now? Why not sooner? What were they planning on changing? Could they change? Most of it was none of my business except…

"I love your mother," Dad told me as I finished the Windsor knot with one last adjustment. "I always have."

"I know."

"We're determined to make this work."

"I know that too."

Dad halted my backing up with a hand on my shoulder. "Do you?"

"Pretty sure you were clear on that last year when I asked you if you were serious because I didn't want Mom hurt again. I had a front-row seat to that for years."

"You were pretty pissed off at me."

Sighing, I met his gaze evenly. "Yeah, I was. Pissed at you. Pissed at Klara. I think some part of me was angry with Mom but…"

"It's tough being mad at Alicia," Dad admitted. "She always seems so much more delicate, but she's tougher than me and Klara put together."

"She had to deal with my hell-raising," I pointed out.

"She did a damn good job with all of you." He tightened his grip then let me go to back up himself. This closeness between us still had a way to go. Dad was a tough guy. He wasn't the kind of dad who'd been in touch with his feelings like Joe and could express them easily.

But at the same time, I hadn't doubted that he cared—until things went sideways for them. "I chose her," I told him, and while this wasn't unfamiliar ground for us, I'd grown up a lot in the last ten-plus years. "I don't know exactly why things didn't work out back then. I know Mom was lonely in Germany. She—she warned me when she realized we were all dating Frankie that a multi-person relationship wasn't easy. That— you have to think of everyone's needs, and sometimes, you're not all on the same page. I'm not asking you to explain anything to me."

"Good, because I wasn't going to," Dad said with a hint of a smile. "There are some things we can talk about, Jake—"

"Dad," I cut him off. "Seriously. Totally fine if we *never* have that talk. But, and I say this as someone who loves and respects all of you, hurt Mom again, and I'm gonna pin you down so Klara can kick your ass."

For the first time in our lives, I was pretty sure I'd stunned him, because his mouth opened and then snapped closed twice without him saying anything at all. Then a real laugh escaped and some of the tension tightening the lines around his eyes eased.

"You know what, I don't think Klara would need you to pin me."

"Honestly, pretty sure she doesn't, but respectfully—I'd do it anyway."

We were still chuckling when a knock announced Joe and Bubba's arrival a split-second before they opened the door. Like us, they were in suits, and, yeah, Frankie still looked a lot better than any of us.

"We good in here? No blood to clean up? No tempers to defuse?" The easy smile on Joe's face softened the inquiry, but he wasn't wrong to make it. If you'd asked me back in high school whether I'd even speak to Dad again, I'd have said the chances were low to almost nonexistent.

"All good," Dad said as he held out a hand to greet Joe with a quick handshake and a second for Bubba. "Civilian life is still taking some getting used to."

"You'll get there. Alicia will whip you both into shape in no time."

"Looking forward to it."

"Did you see Frankie?" I asked Bubba in a quiet voice and his grin grew.

"She looks good in a tie."

Yeah, she did. Gave me all kinds of ideas for later, when she was just in a tie—and nothing else. Bubba's grin promised I wasn't all that mysterious with where I was going with my thoughts.

"We doing good on time?" I asked instead, after checking my watch. The ceremony was scheduled to begin at four-thirty, so they were taking their vows at sunset. Winter in Texas also meant we could have part of the ceremony outside if they'd wanted.

Elmwood was a classic-style mansion and resort; it even had an outdoor gazebo in addition to the indoor chapel and wedding room for larger parties.

"Yeah, we're good. The officiant has arrived." Bubba pulled his phone out. "Coop says that most of the guests are here and seated. Oh—his mom brought a date."

We both shared a look. Coop was not a fan of his mother dating, though he'd been trying to get on board.

"Klara and Alicia are both ready, and hey, look—" Bubba turned the phone so I could see the pictures of each of them sent by Frankie. Cause she'd even included a message of *ooh-la-la, Jake's mom is hawt.*

It was so damn wrong, it was right.

"Is that the girls…?" Dad started to ask, but Bubba withdrew the phone and snapped the screen off to make it dark.

"Sorry, sir. My orders were clear. You don't get to see either bride until the ceremony."

Joe laughed and clapped my dad on the shoulder. "Guys, go on out for us? I want a word with Bill."

"Yes, sir," I said with a nod, more than a little relieved. Dad freaking out was not on my bingo card. "We'll see you down front, Dad."

"Jake—" He caught me before I left and then gave me a hug. It wasn't near as awkward as it used to be. The hug was fierce but brief. "Thank you for being here for us."

"My pleasure," I said, and I meant it. "I mean, call this practice for us in a few months, you know?"

He groaned. "Well, that makes me feel old."

"Glad I could help." I grinned and then followed Bubba out the door. Bubba, who kept chuckling. "Laugh it up," I told him. "You know we're going to be doubly freaked."

"Yeah, but we'll have each other and Frankie. We'll be fine."

He had a point.

Twenty minutes later, I could admit that my palms were sweating. Dad seemed calmer, which was good. The "ceremony" room had been laid out like a triangle with three different approaches to the center. The guests would circle around them, as would the wedding "party."

As Best Man, I would follow Bubba and Joe, then Dad after me. Louisa and Frankie were standing for Klara. Blake and Becca were with Mom. Dad was the only one with three attendants, but then Joe would just move to Sara afterward.

Coop and Archie were with the guests. I caught sight of the guy sitting with Carly. He seemed in one piece. Coop must have decided he was all right. Trina was on the other side of Carly.

There were quite a few familiar faces out there—both military and non-military.

When Frankie joined Bubba and me at the center, she winked. Then the wedding march started. The mix of traditional with eclectic was what made this ceremony something special.

Sara, who was officiating, was the last to join us before Mom, Dad, and Klara began their walk down the aisle. Mom looked radiant. They'd skipped "wedding" dresses of any kind. Instead, she was in a dark blue, off-the-shoulder evening gown, while Klara wore one that matched it in a lighter shade of blue.

Dad's tie matched both of them. They were both wearing silver jewelry, and they looked—*happy.* Mom's grin when she saw me and then the girls just widened. One at a time, she paused to give each of us a kiss. Dad followed her, though he just shook my hand, and then Klara.

Pretty sure that wasn't in the script, but we all rolled with it. Including Frankie and Bubba, who also got affection from each of them. The ceremony itself was pretty simple, though I liked how direct the wording was. It wasn't just Mom and Dad getting married this time, they were marrying each other, but they were also marrying Klara.

Mom and Klara both wore little smiles of disbelief when they slipped their rings on each other. They would all sport two rings each now, and hey, I kind of liked it.

Did my gaze dip to Frankie's hand where all four of our rings rested? Hell yes it did. I didn't even mind when she caught me and my eyes blurred a little. Must be something in the air. Allergies were pretty common this time of year, cold front or no cold front. It had been in the seventies and sunny when we flew in.

Bubba bumped my shoulder as his mom said, "Normally, we would ask if there is anyone here who knows why these three should not be joined together as they desire, speak now or forever hold your peace."

A ripple of nervous laughter spread through the room.

"But in light of how hard these three have worked to repair their relationships, to rebuild their communication, and to find a way to balance their lives with each other so they can be together again, and the simple fact that they have never stopped loving each other, you can all just keep your peace and hush."

Real laughter filled the room and I even had a stupid grin on my face. So, I glanced over my shoulder and said, "You heard her. Hush."

Coop shot me a subtle middle finger, but we were all grinning too hard to care.

"With that in mind, and with the vows you've taken, and by the power you've vested in me," Sara continued. "I now pronounce you wife-husband-and-wife. What you three have put together, let no one else tear apart."

Dad swept Mom right off her feet and into a kiss. I put my fingers up to my lips and gave off a shrill whistle as they straightened and she went to Klara, and it was Klara who dipped Mom this time. Dad gave them a whistle before it was his turn to kiss Klara.

"You know," Sara said dryly. "I was getting to that part."

At another round of laughter, I applauded, as did everyone. The timing was perfect because outside the glass-paned wall, the sunset was visible over the lake. It really was a new beginning for them.

After a few more rounds of hugs, kisses, and congratulations, we did wedding photos. Thankfully, Archie and Coop stuck around for those, and we were all heading to the reception.

Dinner and a live band turned into free-flowing drinks and dancing.

"You know," Becca said, as she dropped into the chair next to me. Her shoes were long gone. "I thought it would be all kinds of gross, but it wasn't."

"What? The three of them dancing together when Dad lacks serious rhythm? Or the ceremony?"

"Eh, Dad's cute, and the wedding was really lovely. No, I'm talking about how loved-up they all are. Mom and Klara went to the 'bathroom' earlier," she said, making air quotes. "And they were gone way longer than a normal trip, and Mom was all—"

"Nope." I put a hand over her mouth and her eyes turned wicked as she fucking laughed at me. "We do not need to discuss this ever. Let them have their privacy and go find yourself a wedding date hookup or something."

"Jake," Blake said as she smacked my shoulder and took over the chair on the other side of me. Frankie was currently dancing with Archie or—no, she wasn't. I frowned as I scanned the dance floor. "Frankie had to go to the 'bathroom,' too," Blake told me with a smirk. "Don't worry, Archie went with her."

I'll just bet he did. Bubba was near one of the doors to the hall and he caught me looking and just gave me a thumbs up. Okay. Bubba knew they'd gone, and either he was covering or making sure no one bugged them.

Good call. Still made me paranoid if I couldn't track her in a room like this.

"You can butt out of our sex lives, too, Blake," I informed my sister and she wrinkled her nose.

"I never want to discuss your sex life. That's disgusting."

"Thank you. Same."

"So why are you telling Becca to go hook up with someone?" She eyed me, and she wasn't alone. Becca had a wine glass she'd stolen from me, but since it had barely more than two swallows in it, I didn't care.

"Cause I'm right here and it'll be fun to embarrass her," I said with a grin, and they both groaned. Louisa, on the other hand, ignored all of us and was out on the dance floor with some kid who was not quite as tall as she was, but he kept his hands in the right places.

He could live.

It was a half-hour later when a slightly disheveled Frankie returned and I helped fix her tie before tugging her out onto the dance floor with me.

"Having fun?" I asked as she looped her arms around my neck.

"I am," she admitted. "I thought it was a lovely ceremony. Give you any ideas?"

"Yep, I'm joining Archie's camp and say we elope and throw a party later. That way, we can get to the consummating part super quick."

"Yeah, I'm pretty sure they already took care of that." She nodded to where Mom and Dad were dancing alone.

"Don't want to know," I told her, even if I was grinning. If they'd managed to sneak off, then good for them. "I'm talking about us, Baby Girl."

"I know you are," she said as I swung her around and then pulled her right up to me. Her arms tightened. "I loved how they did this—it was simple but elegant. It reminded me of a lot of them. But it's not—"

"It's not legal," I whispered. "The three of them are going to go and flip a coin on who gets to marry Mom this time. It was her and Dad before and I think he wants that again, except Klara also wants to do it and since *that* is legal, they might do that. Either way, they want Mom protected by their benefits."

Which made sense to me. I also loved that they loved her enough to make that concession. It also kind of explained why they didn't marry each other all those years of the separation. They were missing Mom.

"I don't ever want to do that," I said, locking eyes with Frankie. "No matter what happens with all of us, even if we fight—especially if we fight, cause let's face it, I'm me—I don't want to spend years apart. Those months between junior and senior year *sucked*."

"Agreed. Now stop worrying and kiss me. Ian and I are going to sing for you guys tonight, then as soon as the wedding trio leave, we can go back to our hotel."

I grinned. "I love the way you think." I loved everything about her. When her lips parted under mine, I sighed. Yeah, elopement was looking better and better.

Chapter Seven
TEENAGE DREAM

FRANKIE

Christmas was quiet and relaxed. In some ways, it was like the calm before the storm. It seemed unreal that we were already in the last semester of college. Well, undergrad anyway. Coop had already begun to fill out his applications for graduate school and gather his recommendations. The excitement in his eyes when he told us about the program at Long Island University via their Brooklyn campus was magical. NYU also had a master's program, but it didn't lead to licensure.

I loved it for him. Though he kept saying *if I get in* and it threw me back to all those months of college prep and sweating over applications and essays. "You'll get in," I told him. "You have two other schools already lined up, you know what you need to do and you want it. You'll get in."

"They prefer candidates to be bilingual."

"Well, you have a wonderful tongue," I promised. "I can help you with that. Does French count?"

His groan just made me laugh. "You start tutoring me in French, then I'll never get anything done."

"I can teach you the dirty words," I said with a wink. Then I spent an afternoon doing that. Granted, it didn't get his applications done, but he seemed to feel better afterward. If he decided to work on his bilingual skills, then I'd just take a Spanish class with him.

I'd taken a lighter course load this semester. I only needed one class for graduation, so I'd added a couple of history courses for the hell of it. Jake had a hole in his schedule, too, so now we were doing film History of New York. It was going to be so much fun.

We had time to add basic Spanish if he wanted to get started.

"Hey, Angel," Ian said as he gripped the chair back behind me and leaned down to give me a kiss. His lips were chilled and cold rolled off him even as he tugged off his coat. It had been frosty outside when I'd ducked into our favorite coffee place to warm up while I waited for him to get out of class. We hadn't had as much snow this year as in the last three, but the cold had been pretty brittle.

"Hey," I greeted him. "I ordered your coffee." I didn't have any classes today, so I'd timed it to get here only a few minutes before him.

"This," he said as he wrapped his hands around the cup, "is one of the reasons you're the best."

"I'd ask for a list, but I'm pretty confident in how much you love me," I teased him and his deep blue eyes filled with laughter. "You've even written songs about me."

"Oh, just a few." He stretched his legs out, hooking one ankle around the leg of my chair. It pressed his calf against mine. "How are you doing, Angel?"

"Pretty damn good," I told him without any hesitation. "I mean—I thought the new year would be hard. But it wasn't. I know Archie was worried, but he did okay too. He and Eddie both." We'd had Eddie over to spend New Year's with us. The guys introduced him to a series of video games. It was a lot of fun.

"I'm glad," Ian said. "Really glad. Rachel was worried too. I think between us, we had a dozen messages from her checking on you."

I groaned. "I talked to her yesterday, and she wants me to come out for spring break."

"You should do it," he said, and I blinked. "Seriously, go to Paris. Spend a week with your bestie. You can wedding dress shop while you're there if you feel like you need a reason. But you'll be happier knowing you get to see her and check on her for real. Then come back to us."

"What are you guys going to do while I'm gone?"

"Survive," Ian said with more than a bit of drama. "It'll be tough, especially if Jeremy takes a cruise or something with Ann. Or they go for a long week in the Adirondacks. But I think we can manage. I'll even make sure Jake and Archie shower in between work binges on the new engine."

I giggled but sobered. "Coop is gonna be applying to his master's programs, and I don't know how long they take to get back."

"You can call him and flirt with him in French. That instantly takes his mind off of everything." His indulgent smile suggested he had an answer for everything.

"You trying to get rid of me?"

"That's three right there, Angel," he said with just enough seductive promise that I tightened up all over. "And no, I'm not. Although, you're worried about Rachel. You mentioned her three times last week, and you couldn't get her on the phone. Then when she texted you back, you said—"

"Cryptic," I grunted. Rachel had been playing it very close to the vest the last couple of months, since just before Thanksgiving.

I'd been distracted with wedding plans, school, and Jake's parents' ceremony. Not so distracted that I didn't notice how her texts had grown fewer and further between. She said she was busy with school and her apprenticeship with a photographer. She might be. "Maybe I'm just butting in where she doesn't want me. They say friendships sometimes grow apart."

"One, Rachel adores you way too much. She could be busy, that's not unreasonable. But someone who is growing apart doesn't text your boyfriends repeatedly just to make sure you aren't too sad or upset over a holiday linked to what could be a bad memory."

It wasn't enough to make me sad. Not really. I mean, it had sucked, and it was a long few days, but I was all right.

"Two, best friends are precious. They aren't based on the number of messages you exchange or how often you see each other. You two think about each other all the time, and you even take notes on things so you remember to message her about them."

I did that. He was right.

"Three, Rachel's cagey, but she knows you love her. Go see her. You'll feel better. She'll feel better. We'll be right here when you get back with all the reunion sex you could want."

Laughter bubbled through me. "Reunion sex sounds amazing."

"Now, if you don't want to go, that's different. If you want one of us or all of us to go with—"

"I do want to go, and I always want you guys to come with me. But I don't know how forthcoming she'll be with all of you there."

"Then make your plans, Angel. We'll run it past the guys, and you can go spend spring break in Paris with Rachel. She can brag and take a lot of beautiful pictures of you."

"Thank you," I said. Sometimes I forgot how well he saw what I needed even before I did. "You know, we haven't talked about recording that new album yet. You finished the last of the songs, right?"

"Most of them. We have one more that we were working on, but I haven't been able to get the bridge where I want it. If you have some time on the weekend, we can drive out to Long Island and work in the studio there."

"Oh, that sounds like a good excuse to have some rest for all of us." I propped my chin on my hand as I studied him. "Unless you just want to steal me away for the weekend, in which case, I'm all in."

"Now who is reading whose mind?" He held out a hand and I gripped it. "I like it when we make time for each other. You're always shifting your schedule to come to meet me for coffee in the middle of the day—even when you don't have classes. You go to Jake's games and his practices. I know you've been out to the shop in Brooklyn at least twice in the last two weeks to check on them. Coop's leaning on you pretty hard right now too."

"I don't mind," I said, and I really didn't. "It's not an effort, at all. I used to worry about not having enough hours in the day or getting too caught up in my own stuff. But I don't anymore."

"No?"

"Nope. You guys tell me what you need more often than not. You hear me when I say what I need. Sometimes, what you need is me, and sometimes it's each other."

"Sometimes it's all of the above."

"Exactly. So, if you want a weekend away with me, Mr. Rhys, I will clear my calendar and we can go out to Long Island, make music, get naked, and just hang out."

He traced his thumb over my knuckles and then down to my rings. "Promise me if anything ever gets to be too much…"

"I'll tell you," I said, crossing my heart with my free hand. "I will. I'm ready to do a new album, though. I'm still not keen on a long tour away from home. But I think we can make it work, we just have to balance around Coop's degree and then work and stuff."

"You're going to take Eddie's offer?" He studied me.

"I haven't formally decided," I admitted. Over Christmas, Eddie offered me a junior management lead at Standish. It would be with the foundation first. I could set my hours and I'd report directly to him. But it was a smaller organization under the umbrella of Standish Enterprises, and it would let me work with funding charities and putting Standish resources to work in various communities.

It was—an impressive offer and a lot of work. I wasn't sure I was entirely qualified for it. Still, he promised me it would be a junior executive salary, nothing more than I'd earn if I were any other newly minted business degree college student.

"But I kind of want to do it. I like the idea of doing good things with the money and—it was through the foundation that I funded Rachel's grant to study overseas."

"I know," he said. "Pretty sure it's gonna be the perfect job for you, but I have a feeling you won't keep it part-time."

I grimaced. "I have to—at least at first. If I'm too tied up, I won't be able to work with you, and that's not acceptable."

His smile wrapped me up in a warm embrace. "Angel, we'll make the time. I told you, I'm content writing the music. It's actually been a lot of fun in some ways, now that I'm getting a feel for it."

Pride shimmered through me. "You're very good at it too. KC told me she was going to reach out to you about the tour they're thinking of putting together."

"They haven't done an album in a couple of years and their last one was just remixes of some of their older stuff." He looked thoughtful. "But they write a lot of their own music, so I'm not sure what I can offer them."

"We can work on that too—together. Cause, I'm a bit of an expert about their music."

Ian snorted. "And humble about it."

"Don't hate. We all have our talents."

We were still chuckling when we gathered up our jackets. Ian had to get to another class, and I was going back to the brownstone. He walked me to the subway, then, with a kiss and a brush of his gloved hand down my cheek, he turned to head back to school.

I turned over the album discussion and the Paris trip in my head. Then there was the foundation job.

Was I biting off more than I could chew with all of that? The guys liked to tease me about being an overachiever, but I *liked* to be busy. I *liked* doing stuff that helped others. But what if I couldn't balance everything?

I turned that over in my head all the way back to the brownstone. Jeremy was on his way out with Miss Abigail. She had on her little snow booties to protect her paws against the icy ground. She was also dressed in a waterproof windbreaker.

Snapping a picture of the pair in their matching outfits, I grinned at Jeremy. "Want some company?"

"Always, Miss Frankie," he said with an indulgent smile. "However, we are going to meet with Miss Bradshaw for some hot tea and sandwiches while she has a break."

"Well, I don't want to intrude on a date."

The fun thing about Jeremy was that he could reprimand in such an affectionate and stern tone that you wanted to thank him for it. "You are never an intrusion, Miss Frankie. Do you require some assistance? You look troubled."

"Probably overthinking," I admitted, glancing at the time on the phone. "I think I'm going to call my dad and see if he has a half-hour to tell me I'm being ridiculous."

Jeremy chuckled. "Well, if he does not, I will absolutely make time for you later. There is a proper stew for dinner this evening since you're all on different schedules today and tomorrow. There is fresh bread as well. I also restocked some of your favorites after the weekend."

"You're the best, Jeremy," I told him. "I'll stop holding you up. If you want to text when you're on the way back, I can start the kettle for you."

"That's very kind, Miss Frankie. I shall let you know." With that, he and Miss Abigail headed down the block toward the park. I loved that Jeremy seemed to be enjoying the time he spent with Ann. Would he want to move into their own place should this go further for them?

Shaking my head, I had to laugh at myself. Jeremy had been in Archie's life since he was a baby. He'd been in mine for eight years and we'd lived in the same place for four. Once upon a time, I wasn't sure how that was going to work out. Now, I couldn't imagine life without him.

We would cross that bridge when we got there. I wasn't above begging. I checked my messages after letting myself in and then fired one off to Hank. He answered almost immediately. Thirty minutes and he'd be done with office hours. He'd call me then.

A smile curved my lips as I took a deep breath of the fresh-baked bread and stew scents floating through the downstairs. Hank never made me feel like an imposition, he always answered promptly, and while he might not have the answers, it would help to talk to him.

I was soaking in the bath when he called back. The hot water and the jets had helped unknot muscles I hadn't even realized had tensed.

"Hey, Dad," I said, answering the phone before shifting to stretch one leg up to brace against the side. "That was faster than thirty minutes."

"I had five minutes left on office hours and no one in the hall, so I just closed the door." He sounded pleased with himself. "Sometimes, you just have to break the rules. Besides, I had a beautiful girl waiting for me to call her back."

Snickering, I shook my head.

"Too cheesy?" Not that he sounded like he cared.

"You can't do too cheesy." Even if I groaned, I wouldn't complain.

"Excellent, I love carte blanche permission. So, tell me, what's up with you?"

A sigh escaped me. "I've been thinking about going to see Eugene and Patience." Until I said the words aloud, I hadn't even realized how much that little nugget had been bouncing around in my head the last few months.

"They alright?" Hank was too good sometimes. Asking if they were alright was not just thoughtful but probably also a gauge of my reactions. "I don't think you've talked to Patience much the last couple of years."

"I haven't. I have exchanged a few letters with Eugene. He doesn't talk on the phone much—he says it's hard to hear without turning it up and he doesn't want Patience to overhear because he won't force me to talk to her."

Something truly thoughtful about him. Head back, I stared up at the ceiling. "But we've been planning the wedding…"

"And you aren't sure whether to invite them."

"No," I said. "I don't want to invite her." And I didn't. "I don't know that I can ever forgive her for setting Maddy up to be in a position to hurt Archie."

"To hurt you too," Hank added, and I shrugged even if he couldn't see me.

"Maddy wanted to kill him. She didn't care what happened to me since I wouldn't play along with the Eddie is my father nonsense."

"Sweetheart," Hank said on a sigh. "You're allowed to be hurt by your mother's choices. You don't have to defend them or try to be strong. Just like you're allowed to not trust Patience because of her choices."

I appreciated that thought. "But Archie said something a few months ago and I haven't been able to let it go." I traced my finger through the water, trying to sort my thoughts. "What if I never make an attempt and I regret it someday? They aren't young—hell, they seem positively ancient if you compare them to Grandpa Ted."

Maddy made me grow up too fast. It didn't really surprise me that she'd aged them too swiftly. It didn't help that they'd been older parents with her anyway.

"How about I go with you?" he offered and I frowned.

"You don't have to do that." Hank had very little to do with either of them. It wasn't like he and Maddy dated.

"Of course, I don't *have* to do it, but I want to be there for you. I wish my mom were still here so you could meet her. She would have adored you. Probably would have tried to spoil you rotten. Kelly's parents have asked about you a few times. They'd love to sign on as grandparents too."

"Have I ever mentioned how lucky you got with her?"

"Don't I know it," he said with a laugh. "I plan to never forget it, either. But I can definitely meet you in Connecticut if you want to see them. It might be easier for you to make some decisions if you look them in the eye. I have no doubt the boys would go with you, but—" He raised his voice a fraction on that last word. "If you aren't certain of them, you won't want to risk your boys in any way."

"I don't honestly want to expose you to them either," I admitted.

"Though Eugene's not so bad…"

"Look at it this way. We'll meet there and visit. If it's a bust, at least we get to go and have lunch somewhere together, so not a wasted trip. You can answer the questions you have in your head."

That would work. "You know, you're not the only lucky one. I think Kelly got a great deal when she met you."

"Oh, feel free to tell her that. I'll just be the one bringing her flowers and treating her like the queen she is."

I laughed. "I love you, Dad."

His sigh was worth the confession. "I love you too, sweetheart. Let me look at my schedule for the next couple of weeks, and I'll let you know what days would be best for me and see what we can figure out."

"I'd like that—I wanted to talk to you about the wedding too."

"Oof." He made the sound so dramatic. "You're growing up so fast. Not sure I'm ready for this talk."

"Sorry," I told him, not even remotely sorry. "We're all about the future here."

We talked for a few more minutes, then I needed to get out of the tub, and he needed to get moving to pick the twins up from school.

My phone started vibrating after I'd walked into the bedroom to find clothes. Archie's face popped up on the screen, and I grinned before hitting the answer.

"You know," I said by way of greeting. "I was just thinking about how lucky I am."

"Oh?" Intrigue filled his voice. "Tell me more. I'm about ten minutes away."

"Really?" He was early.

"Yep, started missing my beautiful babe and wanted to steal a few hours with her."

"So, what I hear you saying is that I shouldn't get dressed."

"I'll make it five, and don't you dare."

Grinning, I stripped off the towel to go hang it up. Tory gave me a bored look from the window seat and Tiddles abandoned the bed. My cats knew me well.

"I'll be the naked one in my room," I said as I wandered back to flop against the covers. "I might even get started while I wait…"

"You're killing me, Frankie. Don't stop." He made it home in under five minutes.

Chapter Eight
YES, PLEASE, SIR

IAN

Frankie and I ended up not making it out to the Hamptons house two weekends running because life got in the way—including a surprise visit from my parents. Not that I wasn't happy to see them, I just hadn't known they were coming to the city.

Mom joked that I would have made some excuse to not see them. Tempting as it was to agree with her, I did actually like them, even if they brought us brother fiancé shirts. Coop laughed and changed into his before we even went to dinner. Ass, but Mom enjoyed it.

Their visit included an ulterior motive, which I should have seen coming. Mom wanted to go dress shopping with Frankie. Panic flitted across Frankie's face, but Mom handled it fairly well—I thought, at least.

"We're not going to pick one out, but I thought it might be fun to help narrow the style down to find what you like. If you want more help than that, I'm all in. But I promise, this is more of let's just go window shopping, have tea, and make a day out of it."

"Okay," Frankie had said, cheering up. "That actually does sound like fun."

Mom swore to me before they went that she really did just want to spend the day with Frankie. "Sometimes, Ian," she'd scolded me. "I think you forget that we like that young lady."

True, but my need to protect her wasn't going away. "Well, have fun then and try not to scare her off from marrying us."

Her laughter tweaked my pride until she said, "Darling, nothing is scaring that girl off."

As it turned out, they spent two days out shopping and came home with a couple of outfits for Mom, some new ties for us, and a notebook full of ideas. All too soon, they were taking a train to Florida, where they were going on a cruise.

And the weekend after Valentine's, Frankie and I drove up to the house in the Hamptons. Archie asked *me* before we left if I minded him joining us before the weekend was out.

"Not Coop and Jake?" That surprised me.

"Jake's got a game and Coop's working this weekend." That was right. "Look, it's fine if you just want the time, but—call me curious, among other things."

I chuckled. "You're allowed. No, I don't mind. Give us the first night to ourselves, then come on up? However, don't tell her."

"Oh, I like surprises."

I was still laughing the next day as Frankie drove while I worked on the lyric sheet in front of me. "What's funny?"

"Just thinking about the guys," I told her the truth. "Jake said he'd get us some videos of any solid goals."

She made a face. "I felt bad when I told him I couldn't make it this weekend, but I promised to go to every single one between now and my birthday to make up for it."

My lips twitched. "There are only two games left, Angel."

"That's only if they don't get into the playoffs. Then there's a bunch more. So, I'll make it up to him. Besides, I've been to most of his games, and he said he could spare my good luck charm for the weekend cause clearly, you needed a muse, or you'd be done with that last song."

Oh, just for that— "I'll go to the games with you and keep you nice and warm."

She grinned. "Those are my favorite games. I like being cozy."

Yes, I knew. So did Jake. I flipped a mental middle finger. "Good. And I'm almost done with this song. I think I got the bridge I want. We can run through it at the house."

"Sweet! Can I get you to serenade me on the way there?" The playful batting of her eyes was absolutely unnecessary, but I totally sang for her, and on the third pass through it, she joined it.

Yep. That was the bridge.

By the time we got to the house, it was snowing. I loved that Frankie still lit up like a kid whenever the snow started. Then again, prior to our trip to Colorado senior year, the only snow she'd seen was always in Texas, which just didn't last long.

Another reason to stay in the northeast in my book. We all enjoyed the seasons, from the bright, colorful autumn to the white Christmases to the first blush of spring. We parked in the garage—another set of changes since Archie and Frankie took over the house. A shifting of the parking situation and expanding it to make sure if we were all up here, we could all park. There was an additional garage for guests.

"Go on," I told her, laughing as she danced out of the car. "I'll grab our bags and take them up. Then come find you."

To my enormous pleasure, she danced back to me and gave me a kiss before darting into the house. The staff—still took some getting used to remembering we had a staff of any kind—was kept pared down when we weren't here regularly. A housekeeper came in twice a week to clean, and when we planned on being here, she had the chef prep meals for us.

Sometimes they went shopping, though we were usually content to do that for ourselves. I'd called the day before with some requests. I left our guitars in the hall and then carried our bag up to the bedroom. We had plenty of clothes and toiletries here, but I brought a few toys from home.

Back downstairs, I glanced toward the French doors overlooking the patio. Frankie stood with her arms wide and her face tilted up toward the sky. Big fat flakes floated down where they glistened against her cheeks and her hair.

A grin pulled at my mouth. She loved the snow. We should get out here more often. It was quieter here. Less traffic. More space. And right now, just her and me.

In the fridge, I found the lasagna ready to be loaded into the oven. There were also two bottles of wine pulled, both her favorites.

The housekeeper left a note with the instructions for the other meals, all stored in the big refrigerator in the butler's pantry. The fact that the house *had* a butler's pantry entertained me.

She had also picked up the hot chocolate bombs from the shop in town. If we needed anything, her phone number was at the bottom, otherwise, just leave any mess, and she would take care of it on Tuesday if we didn't need her before then.

Turning the oven on to warm it up, I used the milk foamer on the espresso machine to super heat up the milk, then made her a nice spicy hot cocoa, just the way she liked it. Once I'd filled the tumblers and cleaned up after myself, I carried the tumblers out to the snow-coated patio.

Frankie turned at my arrival and bounced. "The forecast says we're going to get about a foot tonight. We could get more tomorrow. We could be trapped here… forever."

Her enthusiasm was rather contagious. "One, that's not a problem for me," I informed her as I pressed the hot cocoa tumbler into her hands and checked the temperature of her fingers. They were cool, but not cold. "Two, we're well-stocked since I think Allison stocked for it to be all five of us. And three…"

Since she was so close, I hooked an arm around her and pulled her to me for a kiss. Hints of coffee she'd had on the road, along with the rich decadence of the chocolate and a touch of spice, flavored her tongue.

All at once, I didn't give a damn about three anymore. Just the fact that I had her right there with me. It was nice when we got to carve out time for ourselves. Nicer still when it happened on the heels of everyone being busy.

One night a week, we made sure to have dinner together, all five of us, and one day on the weekends, we tried to spend together too. Didn't always work with our schedules, but the fact we made an effort just made all those days it did work out all the sweeter.

Reluctantly, I lifted my head and studied her flushed face. "It's getting colder out here."

"I know," she whispered. "A few more minutes? Then we can go up and put a fire in the bedroom. Or we can just make one in the living room—no one is here to see anything."

"Going to let me lay you out in front of the fire and have my way with you?"

"Yes, please, Sir." The breathless little catch in her voice undid me every time she whispered those words. It was the tone, coupled with the look in her eyes, and just the way she relaxed against me.

My angel.

Pressing my lips to her forehead, I held her to me. Then with a sigh, she turned her back to face the snow where she could lean against me and we could sip our hot chocolate.

"Ian?"

"Hmm?"

"This was a good idea. Thank you."

"I should be thanking you." Because until she'd said those three words, I hadn't realized how much I needed to steal us away and to have this time. We hadn't been to the club since before Christmas and there'd been no real time at home between the wedding, the holidays, and then bracing for the new year.

"You're welcome," she teased and I grinned. "What was three?"

"Hmm?"

"Earlier, you said three, but then you kissed me. Unless the kiss was three, that totally works."

Chuckling, I spread my hand against her abdomen and rubbed my cheek against her hat-covered hair. "Three, if we truly get snowed in, don't worry. Archie will come and get us." Or bring the guys, and we'd all hole up together.

"This is true. He's rather determined like that."

Yes, he was.

We lingered outside for another half-hour as the snowfall grew heavier. With the whole weekend ahead of us, there was no reason to hurry.

* * *

The next morning, I woke before she did and savored the way she slept, flat on her stomach, one hand on my chest and the other folded under her pillow. With care, I eased onto my side so I could study her. By the time we came in the night before, she'd been thoroughly chilled.

We retreated to the bedroom, lit the fire, and I'd put the lasagna in the oven to heat while she showered. When I came upstairs, I found her kneeling in front of the fire and our night pretty much just stayed in here.

It was more than just sex, it was taking care of her and soaking in her absolute trust. Of course, the sex was always amazing, and by the time we collapsed in the bed, I had ideas already brewing for today.

"You're staring," she murmured.

"I am," I agreed. "Shh, let me enjoy you."

She smiled, but her eyes didn't open. Ten minutes later, she said, "When you're done enjoying me—can I bribe you into getting us coffee?"

"You don't even need to bribe me," I promised, then kissed her bare shoulder. Her smile grew. "How are you feeling?"

"Sore in all the right places." A delightful answer. "Are we going to get to the music today?"

"Maybe." I chuckled. With care, I rolled her over and she lifted the lashes on those gorgeous green eyes. There were a series of little hickies across one of her breasts. I'd gotten just a little too enthusiastic. I pulled the sheet back as I ran my hand over her torso and down to her thighs. "Maybe we'll just stay in bed today. Except for when I get your coffee."

Her soft sigh was definitely *not* a complaint. Trailing kisses up her abdomen to her sternum and then to her chin, I hovered over her and smiled.

"Good morning, Angel." When she wrapped her arms around me, I settled my weight against her. Then tucked my face into the crook of her neck and blew a raspberry against her pulse point.

Laughter spilled out of her as I danced my fingers down her ribs, and then we were wrestling. Thank fuck for a huge bed. Considering we nearly went off the side of it.

Still laughing, I rolled off the bed and landed a light slap against her ass. "I'll go make your coffee, and then we'll work on music. Sound good?"

"It does, though—are you going to get me coffee like that?" At the sultry note, I glanced down at myself and then over at her, where she lay on her side, propped up on her elbow.

"Well, only if you promise to warm my dick up if it gets so cold it tries to fall off." The tease just rolled right out of me and Frankie's eyes lit up.

"Promise, I'll warm you right up."

"Then yes, ma'am," I continued with a wink. "Your naked coffee will be right with you."

Her laughter followed me down the stairs. Despite the joking about the cold, it was undeniably chilly down here. I managed to *not* turn into a popsicle. Not that it slowed her down when I came back, she settled right down on her knees in front of me at the fire and blew my fucking mind.

Totally worth a second trip to get her hot coffee since the first cup got cold.

When we moved to the studio to work, Frankie had a new idea. "Ian?"

"Hmm?"

I glanced up from the lyric sheet to where she stood wearing just my shirt. To be honest, I wasn't even sure she had panties on under that jersey. I couldn't wait to find out later.

"Think I can offer you a little challenge?"

I set the music on the holder on the piano and raised my brows. "You can offer me anything you want, Angel."

She grinned. "But will you do it?"

"Ahh," I said slowly. "Do you really want whatever it is?"

"Yes, please, sir." She was killing me in all the right ways.

"What do you want me to do?"

After directing me to settle on the bench, she opened my pajama bottoms and fisted my cock.

"Angel, I have no objections—"

"Shh," she scolded, then winked. "Please."

I mimed zipping my lips as she stroked me from base to tip. Sitting still took discipline. Then she answered my question about the panties when she straddled my lap and sank right down on my cock.

Her sigh echoed my own. Wrapping her arms around my neck, she shifted just a little and flexed around me. The urge to thrust upward had me bracing her ass. The heat of that soft skin against my thighs was a tease, whether I was still in pants or not.

"Okay," she said. "Now—I thought if you could play, we could work on that bridge."

"Like this?" Realization dawned. "Naughty, Angel."

She grinned slowly. "If you can play video games, Ian, I am almost certain you can play music."

"Almost certain?"

The challenge dripping off that statement sent a fresh pulse of heat right to my dick. The warm, velvet glove of her pussy wrapped around me was the absolute best kind of distraction.

"Hold on to me," I ordered, and she tightened her thighs and arms as I scooted us forward. Each bumping movement sent me surging up into her and she let out a huff. Her cheeks flushed and her eyes went a little shiny. "Good girl," I praised and she bit her lip. "You remember the bridge from the drive?"

"I do," she told me, though her voice was definitely on the heated side.

"Excellent." It took me a second to get my fingers onto the right keys and put my foot on the pedals. "Challenge accepted, Angel."

One thing neither of us considered was that each time I had to press a foot pedal, it lifted my hips a fraction and let me thrust gently, though a thrust all the same.

Four full passes on the whole song, bridge included, and we nailed it. "It's perfect," she whispered before her mouth found mine. We didn't even make it off the bench as I rocked her against my lap.

Rising, I took two steps to press her against the wall as I thrust my cock inside her, and she twisted her hips, writhing up to meet me. The frantic pace seemed almost too fast, but the orgasm threatened to spill out of me.

Her pussy spasmed around me a split-second later as she let out a soft cry and I came in a rush. Thankfully, the wall was right there, or we would have both ended up in a graceless heap on the floor.

With butterfly kisses, she helped me pull myself back together. Sweat dampened my forehead where I leaned it against hers and she smiled at me. "Was there a winner in that challenge?" I was more curious than anything.

Frankie laughed. "Yes. Us."

Boneless and far more relaxed, we eventually cleaned up and went back to work on the song. I wanted to make sure it wasn't just the buzz of impending pleasure that made it sound so good.

"I love it," she said.

"Yeah?" I glanced at her then back at the music. This song had been damn elusive. All the others had fallen into place—but this one was about the future, and I wanted it to be…

"It's full of hope and dreams, and it doesn't promise anything more than hard work and companionship. I love it," she repeated. "I love that it sounds like vows in some ways."

Oh.

"You caught that, huh?"

"I get your music, Ian. It's your love language. I know it took me a long time to hear what you were trying to say. But I know to listen now—I won't miss anything. Not again."

Wrapping an arm around her, I hugged her tight. "Keys and Kisses," I told her. "That's what I'm calling this one."

She smiled.

"The keys to your heart, the kisses you share, and the life you opened to all of us."

"The kisses you all gave me," she answered. "The keys you already had, and the life you all have given to me."

I chuckled. "It works."

"It does."

Leaning back, I took a moment to study her. "I have a surprise for you tonight."

"Another one?"

"Hmm… one I'm hoping you'll enjoy as much as the one you just gave me."

"Do you really want me to have this surprise?"

"Yes." Archie would want her to have it too.

"Then you just tell me what you need me to do."

Love filled me. "First, we're going through the whole list. I want to play them all and hear you sing. I want you to hear them with me. When we're done, we'll pick out what we want on the album."

That was our plan.

It took about three hours to get through all of them. We only paused to adjust a lyric or work through a particular refrain. Six months of work finalized in an afternoon.

Sure, we'd probably have more tweaks once the label got ahold of it. But we had a second album.

* * *

Archie texted that he would be there after dinner. I told him to come on up when he arrived. We showered after the studio time, then got a fire lit. Frankie ambled down to heat dinner while I had my shower.

We'd already changed the sheets on the bed. That was definitely a two-person job. We dined on the floor—no wine—though we kept it chilled for later.

"I'm going downstairs," I told her, gathering up the dishes. "Strip. On your knees in front of the fire. Eyes closed and just listen to the music."

"Yes, sir."

The commands settled me almost as much as they settled her. There were subtle eye hooks in the room. Archie had them added during the renovation. Anchors for where I could set up rope ties. There was also a private room for us off the main bedroom suite on those occasions that Frankie and I wanted to play alone.

I appreciated the attention to detail. I'd just finished the dishes when Archie came in. "See, I thought I was walking into something fun…"

"Oh," I told him. "You are. But I was waiting for you before I got started."

Surprise flickered across his face. "Yeah?"

"She's earned a surprise and a reward. You up for it?"

"Hell, yes."

Archie had actually come to the club with us a couple of times, both times he'd just observed. He was too much of a Dom himself to follow commands, but he did agree to suggestions if he ever joined us.

Lucky for him, tonight was the night.

Upstairs, I went into the bedroom a beat ahead of him and let him go into the bathroom to change. Frankie was right where I'd left her, her expression almost serene. When Archie came back out, I said, "Angel—open your eyes. Your surprise is here."

Chapter Nine

PLAY DATE

FRANKIE

My surprise was Archie. Delight curved through me when I opened my eyes to find him standing next to Ian. They were both shirtless—always nice—while Ian was still in loose pajama pants, Archie wore a pair of sweatpants. Just soaking up the heat from the fire and the soft music left me half-floating, particularly after a day when Ian and I spent equal amounts of time indulging our hedonistic sides while still getting work done.

Now, Archie was here.

"Hey Babe," he said, his slow grin as sinfully wicked as he could be. "I gotta say, I'm liking the welcome outfit. I should show up to surprise you more often."

I would love it if he would. He'd ventured with us to the club more than once. The second time, he'd been so hard after our scene, he had to have been uncomfortable. But he'd been more interested in making sure I was taken care of than letting me take care of him.

"I love when you surprise me," I said, then cast a look at Ian. Was this surprise also a playdate, or was he here just to watch again? Coop was far more the voyeur and loved coming to play with us, sometimes just to watch. Jake was the only one who didn't play as often, but he wasn't opposed to participating when Ian directed us all.

"Well, Angel, I told you this weekend was about us."

"Archie is part of us." I didn't even have to look at him to see the pleasure in Archie's eyes and expression. Sometimes, he forgot.

I suppose we all did. That was why we had to remind each other.

"Yes, he is." Approval radiated from Ian's voice. "He would very much like to play tonight."

Excitement spiked through my anticipation, and I couldn't suppress my shudder, from the tautness of my nipples to the goosebumps dancing over my arms. I wasn't remotely cold. If anything, a slow burn of want consumed me.

"Would you like to play with Archie, Angel?" The low light in the room kept Ian's eyes partially in shadow, but I had very little doubt they were dancing right now. He'd kept this surprise in his pocket all day. So good.

"I would love to play with Sir Archie," I answered, tilting my head. "May I play with Sir Archie, please, Sir Ian?"

The deepening curve of his lips and the fact Archie was already here answered my question, but I would wait. He'd told me to kneel and wait, and so far, there'd been no release from that instruction. Patience, in this case, would be amply rewarded.

"Well, Sir Ian," Archie drawled. "Do I get to play with our exquisite fiancée?"

"Oh, you definitely get to play," Ian told him. "Smartass."

"Dude, she's kneeling there all sweet and flushed and naked. You're lucky I'm still standing."

The urge to laugh bubbled up, but I swallowed it, even if I had difficulty keeping my lips from twitching.

"True, she is rather attractive like this." Then he gave Archie a teasing look. "Angel, present, please."

The command rolled over me, and I straightened my spine, spread my knees as I turned more fully to face them and turned my hands over to rest palms up on my thighs. The angle left nothing to the imagination. Even with the fire at my back, the air seemed far cooler against my pussy. Especially when they were both there watching me.

"Fuck," Archie practically exhaled the word. "How much play do we need?"

Chuckling, Ian gripped his shoulder then leaned in to murmur something in his ear. Shock stamped his face and his mouth fell open. I swore he pulled back a little and looked at Ian with more than a small amount of disbelief. They didn't say a word, just stared at each other, then Archie cut a glance toward me.

Curiosity roused, like a cat, to stretch and dig her claws into me as she yawned but then settled again. The heat, the security of being with them, and the awareness that Ian and Archie would both take care of me meant I didn't have to demand to know.

I'd find out.

"Yes," Archie said slowly. "I like that idea."

"Good man." Ian clapped him on the shoulder. "Go get comfortable." Then he glanced at me. "Be a good girl for Archie, Angel."

Thrill streaked through me.

"Do exactly what he says."

"Yes, sir." Not that I could contain my own smile. The rest of the world just fell away when we played out a scene, and this was no different. In fact, the world had been fading away all weekend. Sanding away the stress and the decisions, until it was just us and the music.

Us always included the guys, so Archie being here just added a rosey kind of glow to the hum vibrating through my system. Ian left the main bedroom while my attention was on Archie. He crossed to where I knelt on the floor. Tilting my head back, I stared up at him. With light fingers, he brushed my cheek.

"Let me know if I do this wrong," he said. "Even after all this time of watching you two, I don't quite have the magic 'understanding' that Bubba seems to get when he just looks at you and knows what you need."

"Sir Archie," I said, enjoying the way the firelight played in his dark eyes. "You know me. You love me." He glided two fingers to my lips. I kissed them gently, then drew them against my tongue and sucked his fingers. His abdomen tightened as the erection that his sweats had been hiding thickened as I stroked my tongue all around those fingers.

"I do love you," he whispered. The connection was always there, crackling away. It had been there for years, but the static that sometimes muted my understanding had long since burned out. Archie was every bit as much a part of me as Coop, Jake, and Ian. He didn't need Ian's understanding. He had his own. "As lovely as this is, I want this mouth wrapped around my cock and I want to feel your throat convulsing with each thrust."

A shiver of anticipation danced up my spine and my nipples tightened as if he'd caressed them. When he eased his fingers from my mouth, I licked my lips.

"Fuck," he said on a groan. "Do that again. Are you thinking about sucking me off? Do you like having your mouth full of my cock? Do you have any idea how hot you are right now?"

"Yes, sir." I couldn't resist teasing him, even if it earned me a swat or three. Especially if it earned me a swat or more. "I'm aching for you."

With impatient movements, he yanked his sweats down and then his cock was right there, thick, curved, hard, and straining as it glistened with pre-cum. There was something so intoxicating about Archie's sensuality. Maybe it was the fact that he'd been my first. Or maybe it was how open he'd always been. Or maybe it was simply Archie.

He fisted his cock and then rubbed it gently over my lips. The heat pouring off him was comparable to the heat against my back. Keeping my eyes on him, I parted my lips and relaxed my jaw. Salt and male and Archie on my tongue were the perfect aphrodisiac as he eased into my mouth. It was like he was afraid to thrust, or maybe he wanted to edge himself as much as me.

Holding me captive with his gaze, he glided over my tongue as I stroked it over him. The first drops of pre-cum I swiped away just added to the ache in my system. My pulse beat so loud it served as the metronome to his gentle thrust.

"Fuck, I love how hot your mouth is, Babe. I always have. I love fucking every single part of you."

Had I ever told him how much I loved that mouth of his? I used to think it should be illegal. Now, I couldn't imagine my life without it. Didn't want to. I closed my lips around his base as he pushed all the way to my throat. But I kept my gaze on him as I rubbed my nose against the tightening muscles of his abdomen.

Sometime over the last year, Archie's abs had been getting more and more defined. He worked out more. He had always been a runner. Always built lithe and athletic, but he'd put on more muscle. It was like all his edges had also been honed away, leaving only pure Archie behind. Every push of his hips shoved his cock into my throat, and I kept teasing the vein along the underside, alternating between sucking and stroking.

"I love fucking your mouth," Archie told me as he sank his hand into my hair. "Is your pussy soaked, waiting for me to fuck you there?"

I dipped my eyelashes in an affirmative. I couldn't very well answer around his dick, and I didn't cease the motions he encouraged as he guided me back and forth over his cock. Movement from behind sent a thrill through me as Ian appeared with red silk ropes in his hands. Oh, fuck yes. My pussy clenched in anticipation.

"Pay attention to Archie, Angel," he instructed. "I dare you to make him come."

Yes, sir.

I hollowed out my cheeks and sucked harder as I swallowed around him. The bump of Archie's tip against my throat triggered my gag reflex, but I kept swallowing until it passed.

"Fuck me," Archie swore and his fingers tightened, tugging my hair until my scalp lit up. Ian knelt behind me. The warmth of his legs against skin telling me that, like Archie, he'd shed his bottoms.

With light gestures, Ian moved my hands behind me, and then I gripped my forearms in a loose hold that pushed my chest forward and gave Archie full control over my head.

"Oh, look at those sweet tits all flushed and pink. Your nipples are so hard, Babe. Imagine what they're going to feel like when I suck on them."

I didn't really have to imagine, just the words conjured the motion and I clenched my inner muscles. Ian chuckled as he threaded the silk ties around my arms; the softness just added another layer of sensation to the seduction of teasing and using me. Even though the tension in my belly coiled ever tighter in anticipation, the rest of my body softened, and I took Archie so deep I was pressing my face into his belly. I couldn't breathe around it and the dance of spots came and went.

He didn't let me linger there on that edge too long. His nostrils flared as he watched me. I swore he didn't miss a single nuance of my expressions. Fingers flexing in my hair, he'd thrust in deep and my heart thundered the countdown, first five seconds, then ten. By the end, I would sway dizzily as he pulled back.

Ian worked the ties around me until he'd framed my breasts, pausing only long enough to tease the nipples with the rope, stroking it back and forth as I shuddered.

"Make him come, Angel," Ian whispered in my ear as he secured the ties behind me. I was rocking back and forth with Archie's thrusts. Ian's cock slid up and down against my ass, the faintest dribble of dampness betraying how turned on he was, and I reveled in it.

"Fuck, I am going to come," Archie swore. "I wanted to try that cockwarming, but she's so fucking sweet like this. That's it, Babe, just take my cock, take every inch of me."

His hips began to stutter and he tilted his head back, a stream of curses falling from his lips, and at the first pulse splashed against my throat, I relaxed my mouth and let him sit against my tongue.

There was something erotic as fuck just watching his expressions as his muscles flexed, and he came in a rush. "Holy shit," he whispered, dipping his gaze down as I kept my head tilted. Archie did like to keep it dirty, and I didn't swallow immediately; I let him see his release in my mouth. Even though tears sparked in my eyes, I held firm until he shuddered and then I swallowed.

A little salty and bitter, it was still him, and I savored every drop. With care, I lapped at his still twitching cock where it rested between my lips. His legs trembled and he pulled away before dropping to his knees and then his mouth slammed onto mine. I groaned as he chased the flavor of himself all around my tongue. He slid his hand from my hair so he could cup my face.

My nipples brushed against his chest and that just added a fresh wave to the desire already crashing through me. Ian's hand landed against my ass and the sting bumped me forward, but Archie steadied me, kissing me deeper as Ian massaged the heat into the cheek. Another series of light slaps followed; they alternated in force. I couldn't brace for any of them, and I didn't try.

Archie kissed the sounds right off my lips as I clenched at the emptiness in my pussy and dampness spread down my thighs. The heat of them framing me was an exhilaration as Ian lit my ass on fire but continued to soothe the burn. It left me aching for more.

"Shift over, Arch," Ian instructed, his voice a tangle of need and command as he wrapped his hand around the rope binding my arms. The intricate lacing kept the pressure from being too much anywhere but just seemed to frame me as he lifted me and helped me stand.

Archie let out a groan and then took my place on the thick rug. The softness of the fluff was just another tease against my skin. Wrapping his free hand around my throat, Ian tilted my head back, and his mouth closed over mine. The demand of his tongue seeking entry had me arching upward, though I couldn't move any further than he allowed.

Fingers skated up the inside of my thighs and then pressed my legs apart. A moment later, Archie's mouth closed over my clit, and I bucked at the sudden pressure and suction. I was so much more sensitive than I'd even realized. An orgasm crashed right through me and I screamed into Ian's mouth.

His soft chuckle as he kept me braced was delicious. Archie's tongue seemed to mimic Ian's as he thrust it against my entrance, pushing into me even as Ian sucked my tongue into his mouth. The rhythm alternated between them. Ian would ease up on the drunken kisses of pleasure as Archie would move to tormenting my clit and pushing his fingers into me.

Pleasure expanded through my chest as Archie lifted one of my legs to rest over his shoulder, and then I was leaning fully back into Ian as he devoured my mouth. The stroke of his fingers over my pulse just added more sensations to crash into me. Archie fucked me with both his fingers and his tongue until my earlier tears turned into full-on sobs as it went from pleasure to too much back to pleasure again.

Only when I was trembling uncontrollably did they ease up. "Shh," Ian murmured against my throat, rubbing his hand over my chest and down to my abdomen. The gentle petting turned firmer. Archie eased his fingers from me and helped lower me to the ground as he unhitched my leg.

I was still shaking as he maneuvered me right onto his very stiff, and erect once more, cock. The push of him into me had me spasming all over again.

"Open your eyes," Archie murmured, his voice a soft croon. "We're right here. It's okay—shhh…"

That's when it hit me that I was crying, and I blinked open my watery eyes to find Archie's face and Ian's right there. They were both hugging me.

"Hey, there she is," Ian whispered, smoothing a hand over my hair as Archie wiped the tears from my cheek. "There she is. Red or green, Angel?"

A wet laugh escaped me as I swallowed. The quaking was everywhere, and even forming words proved a little difficult. "Green."

"Yeah?" He studied me, weighing my answer as they kept hugging and petting me. The firm strokes of their palms over my skin and my muscles helped to quiet some of the violent shakings. More and more, I grew aware of the change in our positions, the thickness of Archie's cock where I was impaled on him. The soft hairs on his thighs tickled mine. The soft hair on Ian's arms brushed against my back as he shifted me forward. "I'm going to loosen this a little."

I wanted to argue that I was fine, but it was Ian's call. I nodded.

"That's my girl," Ian soothed even as Archie slid his hands down to cup my ass. The lift adjusted me and settled me more firmly on his cock. My inner walls spasmed, and we both let out a little hiss and his turned into a laugh.

"God, I love you," he told me, kissing away more of my tears. The silk ties loosened and nothing tugged at my shoulders or my arms at all. It was like they were there, but no more substantial than gossamer.

"I love you both," I answered him in between kisses as he teased my lips. "So much."

"We know," Ian soothed. "We know, Angel. Love you beyond all reason."

The next half hour—or maybe it was an hour—time seemed to lose all meaning as they were petting me. Archie's dick softened a fraction but remained stiff enough that he didn't slip free. They took turns kissing me. More than once, Ian pulled me back against him so Archie could massage and kiss my breasts.

They didn't tease or torment, only comforted and then Ian whispered against my mouth. "Still green, Angel?"

"So green," I promised. I never wanted to move from this position. The only thing that could make it better was if Coop and Jake were there.

"Ready for more?"

"Please," I implored him, lifting my still damp lashes even if the tears had long since ceased. "I need you."

His smile was so loving that it twisted my heart into tighter knots than he bound me in. "You have us—and you're about to have a whole lot more."

Exulted, I grinned at him in the few heartbeats before he shifted me forward, the action sinking me back onto Archie's cock, far more deeply. The wild spasms had eased and I wasn't quite so sensitive.

Still gripping the ropes, Ian kept me upright as he said, "Lay down, Arch, it's time."

"Yeah?" He nipped one of my nipples, the sting adding just an edge of pain to the haze of pleasure I basked in. "Good. Need you, Babe. Always."

As I clenched around him, his smile turned fierce, and then he and Ian adjusted their positions while keeping me steady. Archie on his back, me mounted on him and suspended partially by the harness of rope that Ian had created. Archie spread his legs, forcing mine wider, then Ian was behind us.

Oh yes, even before the press of his cock pushing at my entrance, easing his way in to join Archie's, I knew it was coming. The splintering pleasure of too much pressure and feeling them both inside me, together, bound just like we were, made spots dance in front of my eyes as he rocked forward. Beneath me, Archie's expression strained and sweat dotted his forehead.

"Breathe," Ian ordered, and I sucked in a breath. On my exhale, Ian pushed all the way in and the quivering returned. I wasn't alone this time, Archie's legs trembled beneath mine. "Good girl, so damn good for us. Take us like we were meant to be in you."

"She was," Archie said. The praise in their voices helped me adjust to the intensity of the pressure. It was just so much. "Made for us. Our girl. Our beautiful babe. And very soon, our wife…"

A groan spilled out of me as they began to rock, their pacing almost dead perfect as they pushed and pulled. Their praise wrapped around me like an embrace as they took turns kissing me, and it wasn't long before my orgasm tumbled me over and the world whited out totally. Too much. Too perfect. So them.

I roused to the gentle rub of Archie's hands along my right arm. The calluses on his fingers were in different spots from Ian's. Ian had my left hand in his and worked his thumbs against my palm. I floated between them, though I was definitely on a bed and not in the water.

"I can't get over it," Archie murmured. "There really is just something else when she lets go like that."

"Yep," Ian said. "She doesn't hold anything back. Arguably, I don't think she ever does—not anymore. She trusts us. But when we do a scene, or we play, she just lets everything else go and lets me carry everything for her. The decisions. The pleasure. The techniques. The releases are—breathtaking."

"The tears?" It was the first time the worry in his voice pierced through the drowsy pleasure wrapping around me. "Is that normal…?"

"Sometimes," Ian told him, and the confidence in his voice buoyed me. "Sometimes she needs to cry and it's not about sadness or pain, it's about stress relief. Those tears, though? I just think we overloaded her system and it was too much stimulation."

Archie's wicked chuckle pulled a smile from me. "It definitely was too much," I admitted. Oh, look, I could use my words.

"Hey," Ian said as they both turned their gazes up to me. I'd managed to flutter my eyes open and they were back in shorts for Archie and pajama bottoms for Ian. "You floated right away on us."

"Loved it. So full of you. Just perfect." I stretched, more like a cat than anything. I was warm everywhere. My ass was still heated from the earlier spanks, and my pussy was just—aching in all the best ways. My arms and shoulders were a little tight, but the massage was amazing. "Thank you."

"Thank you," Archie whispered, lifting my hand to kiss it. "I want to play more in the future—just need you to teach me the ropes—well, maybe not the ropes but definitely turning that beautiful ass pink."

I smiled at him. "If Sir Ian doesn't mind," I murmured. Not because I minded in the slightest, but the collar Ian had given me had been between us, and I wasn't wearing it right now but…

"We'll get him a charm for your collar," Ian suggested. "He does like giving them to you."

"Oh, fuck yes, excellent idea." Archie's grin grew and I sighed.

"You're staying, right, Arch?"

"Hell yes, I'm staying. We're having a snow day on Monday too."

Oh, that was nice.

"What about Jake and Coop?"

"They said we could keep you for the long weekend, but they get the next one." Ian's droll tone pulled fresh laughter from me.

"Yay. Then we can play tomorrow," I suggested. My lashes were getting so heavy. "Ian can teach you, and I'll be a very good girl."

"You already are," Ian murmured, then brushed a kiss to my lips. "Go to sleep, Angel. We'll be right here when you wake up."

I was already drifting back to sleep when Archie asked, "You really don't mind?"

"She's ours, Arch," Ian told him. "You're always welcome."

And they were mine.

Chapter Ten

SIS AND ME

COOP

Frankie and I were splitting up at the airport. She was heading for the international terminal and I was sticking with the domestic. "Call me when you land," I ordered as she wrapped her arms around me. "A whole week is going to seem like forever."

"You'll be fine," Frankie teased. "Rachel will send you all the pictures you could want."

"I know," I said with a sigh, gripping her tighter. "Send me updates in French. Get me all ready for your return."

Her laughter was a bright spark, but then I had to kiss her and let her go. She was going to be in Paris for nine days, well, seven considering a day there and a day back, but it really did feel like forever. "Tell your mom I said hi, and I love her."

"I will." I stared after her as she walked off, pulling one suitcase and one carry-on with her. I waited for her to glance back, knowing she would as soon as she got to the escalator. Her smile was permanently imprinted on my heart. When she mimed blowing me a kiss, I yucked it up by fumbling the catch, only to save it at the last second and then hugged it to myself.

With a playful roll of her eyes and a laugh, she disappeared as she took the escalator down. Fuck, I already missed her. I managed to make it through security and get to my gate before sending her a text though. The laughing faces she sent back made me smile. A week in Paris for her, five days in Texas for me.

Yeah, I'd much rather be in Paris with her, but she needed to check on Rachel personally. They definitely needed some girl time. In her absence, there hadn't been much in the way of girlfriends for her that weren't related to one of us in some way - from Kelly to my sister to her sister to Jake's sisters. Even Bubba's mom had taken time with her.

So yes, a hit of estrogen before she came back to the testosterone club. I spent most of my flight working on the last two case studies for class. We were six weeks-ish from graduation. A little over four weeks from when final projects were due and final exams would be taken.

I had an interview in two weeks with admissions for the master's program I wanted to attend. My gut knotted even thinking about it, so I just put it away. The next five days were helping Mom and Trina, mainly since Trina had been debating the whole college thing and why should she even bother?

I kind of wanted to hear her actual thoughts, not those communicated by Mom's frustration. Senior year was packed with crazy, but Mom was certain it was all about a boy. So—there was *that*. We landed all too soon.

Trina was waiting for me at baggage claim even though I had no baggage to pick up. Everything I'd brought with me fit in the carry-on and my backpack. She let out a little squeal and raced over to give me a hug. I picked the brat right up off the ground. She had gotten a little taller over the last four years. Not much taller. Still taller than Frankie, though. Her gray eyes were full of questions and drama, and so was her expression when I set her down.

"I am so glad you're here," she told me. "Maybe you can talk some sense into Mom."

"Yes," I agreed with her. "Because I've always been so successful at that."

"Don't be a jerk. I'm serious." She elbowed me and I threw an arm around her shoulders.

"I know you are, Sis," I said, giving her a squeeze.

"But you're already taking her side."

I cut her a look as we headed to the doors leading to the parking garage. "Yep, that's me. I'm Mom's little yes man. I *never* disagree with her. Ever."

"Asshole."

"Great," I said with a grin. "Now that we've settled that. Can we grab food on the way home, and you can fill me in on what's going on?"

"You buying?"

"Yes, Sis," I told her with a laugh. "I'm buying."

"Yes!" She did a little dance out from under my arm. The air was almost pleasant as we walked outside. Cool breeze, cool air, and no lingering humidity. Without a doubt too warm for the jacket I had on.

It wasn't until we got to Frankie's old Toyota Yaris that it hit me, Trina had been driving Frankie's car for a couple of years. Frankie had left it for her when we moved, and after we'd upgraded her to the new car, Archie and Jake had tinkered with it for her.

"You okay?" Trina stood at the driver's side door, keys in hand.

"Yeah," I said slowly. "I am." So many memories with this car. From Mr. Thorns to the stupid condoms—to kissing Frankie against the door of it; I had no idea how many times. It used to be her mom's car too. How often had we sat in the backseat arguing, picking on each other, or just laughing?

"You have a *weird* look on your face." She frowned, then she froze. "If you ever had sex in this car, you better lie to me."

I laughed. At her continued glare, I laughed harder and then put my bag in the backseat. "Just drive before I die of hunger."

My phone buzzed as I slid into the passenger seat. It was definitely ticking over my weird meter to be in this seat *without* Frankie behind the wheel. Frankie's message popped up on the screen, answering my *I'm here* message from when I landed. Her flight had been delayed a few hours, but they were getting ready to take off.

Ugh, she hadn't even left New York yet. That sucked.

I took a picture from the front seat and sent it to her.

She sent back nothing but hearts and I grinned.

"You two are so gross it's adorable," Trina informed me. "It's a good thing I like her. And you still haven't lied to me about the sex yet."

I laughed all over again. That particular train of thought was going to be entertaining as hell.

We popped through for burgers, fries, and shakes. Trina waited until we had food and were on our way back to Mom's before she filled me in. "Mom has a stick up her ass about college. I don't want to go. Not right away."

"Okay." I popped a fry in my mouth, chewed it thoughtfully and swallowed before asking, "What do you want to do?"

"Huh?"

"What. Do. You. Want. To. Do." I repeated each word, enunciating it clearly, cause you know, little sisters apparently don't listen.

She didn't answer right away, so I pulled out my burger and took a bite. Damn, that was good. I'd forgotten to grab lunch earlier because I wanted to get home in time to spend some time with Frankie and get laid before we went to the airport. Thankfully, she'd been all in on that. I was glad that she had booked a first-class ticket. That meant she could sleep on her flight and they'd feed her.

Hangry, sleepy Frankie was no fun.

"That's it?" Trina finally spluttered and pulled me back to the present. She wasn't even reaching for her food, just sipping her shake.

"Well, you haven't actually answered the question yet, so I don't know if that's it. I mean, I get that it's a Twitter and TikTok world these days, but I don't have like a twelve-second lip-sync to communicate in. I figured we'd just do this the old-fashioned way. Mom wants you to go to college. You *apparently* do not want to go to college. So—what do you want to do?"

Third time was hopefully the charm.

"I can't believe that's the only thing you're going to ask me." She shook her head.

Apparently not. "Well, should I ask something else? Cause you're avoiding that question like a pro."

"Don't psychoanalyze me." Nose wrinkled, she glared out the windshield.

"One, you're not that deep. Two, I'm not actually licensed to analyze anyone. Three, even if I was, you're family, and that's against most ethical rules."

"I'm not that *deep?*" The screech was so perfectly fourteen-year-old her that I had to bite my lip to keep from guffawing. God, she was so easy to needle. "You know, Frankie said all I had to do was actually talk about this, but I don't see why I should bother. No one wants to listen to me."

Frankie said.

"Well, since you're not actually talking about it, I don't know that you are bothering." I'd finished my burger and eyed hers in the bag. Nah, she needed to eat and I could get more at Mom's. "So, if you don't want to talk about what you want to do, why don't you want to go to college?"

"Does it matter?"

It really didn't until she got this defensive. Fortunately, no one was behind us. "Are you pregnant?"

Thankfully, I was ready for how hard she hit the brakes and jerked us over to the side of the road. Trina was a bit predictable. "What the fuck?"

"Okay, that's not a no," I informed her and met her gaze evenly. "If you don't want to discuss this with me, tell me you don't want to discuss it. But don't assume I'm taking sides or I'm here to give you hell, then ignore any attempt at me opening a dialogue with you. That was irritating as fuck when you were twelve. It's stupid at eighteen."

"I'm *not* pregnant." She practically spit the words.

"Excellent. Glad to hear it."

"Going to ask me if I'm a virgin next?"

"Nope." What I didn't know meant I didn't have to kill someone over. Besides, as irritating as it might be, she was an adult now. Be nice if she acted like it.

Suspicion fluttered across her face, and her eyes narrowed. Traffic blew past us as we sat there with the hazards on. "Just—nope?"

"That's what I said. I'm not playing coy with you, Trina. I don't want to know about your sex life. I would like to know about your plans for the future and why you're so hostile." I'd also like to know what you talked to Frankie about, but since she didn't tell me, I could assume it wasn't anything dangerous or violent.

Yet.

Frankie would keep her own counsel with our sisters. They trusted her. Jake and I both valued that trust they had in her. But she also wouldn't keep bad things from us, and she'd made that pointedly clear more than once. I trusted Frankie. I'd trust her on this right now.

After taking a long drink of her shake, Trina sighed, then flipped off her hazards and turned on her indicator. She checked traffic before she accelerated and got us back on the road. Cautioning myself to remain patient, I focused on the road while maintaining my own temper. Sometimes, Trina could be a real pain in the ass…

"I want to model."

I blinked.

"Last year, Rachel had me pose for her when I came up over the summer—before she went to Paris."

"I remember," I said slowly. "She was practicing different angles, and you volunteered for the shoot."

"Yeah, it was—fun. I had a really good time. She and Frankie picked out different outfits for me, and we made a whole girls' day out of it. She must have taken like nine hundred shots. Then before she went to Paris, she sent me the galleries and said I could use them for whatever I wanted. Just make sure to credit her. When I asked her what I could use them for, she put together a digital portfolio so I could see what it would be like."

"Okay. Rachel's good people."

"Coop, she made me look amazing. I mean, *really* amazing. I didn't even recognize myself in those photos. I've never been beautiful."

"Sis…"

"You don't count. You and Mom have to say I'm beautiful, cause you love me. Dad said I'm his little princess forever. But—I'm not super blonde or super busty or even supermodel tall. I've always been kind of average. Frankie's drop-dead gorgeous. Then there's Rachel, and she's got that classic old Hollywood look to her. Like Katherine Hepburn and Liz Taylor."

She definitely had Hepburn's attitude.

"Then there's KC and the Torched girls, which I still can't believe you guys all *know* and are friends with. They're all fabulous and so pretty. I'm—I'm just me."

Why was it so hard for girls to see how beautiful they were? Why did all girls have to go through this? I got what the literature said, but… this shit sucked. "But you're more than you in those pictures?"

"I'm pretty, and I'm mysterious and in some, I'm just fun. I kind of want to be that girl." She sighed, propping her head against her hand with her elbow next to the window. "It just—I looked so different. When I talked to Frankie about it, she said I already was that girl, or Rachel couldn't have brought it out with the camera."

"She's right."

Trina shot me a smile. "When I told her I wanted to try my hand at modeling, she said that she didn't know anything about that business except, you know, from television and the movies. That it was probably not easy and that it would be a lot of work with a good bit of rejection."

Look at Frankie, not sugar-coating it.

"That I could probably do whatever I wanted, but…" She let out a heavy sigh, so I waited her out. "But that I needed to have a plan. That if I were serious, she'd help me find an agent and look into what I needed to do."

That was my girl, trying to fix problems before they happened but also not promising something she couldn't deliver on.

"It would also be good to consider at least online courses or community college in the meantime, so I don't put all my eggs in one basket."

I grinned.

"Yes, your fiancée is really, really smart."

"Yes, she is. She's also an overachiever who believes in the people she loves. If she didn't think you stood a chance at any of that, she wouldn't encourage you."

"I thought the idea that I should go to school anyway said she didn't totally believe in me."

I chuckled. "No, hon, that's Frankie speak for always have a backup plan. You gotta remember how hard she worked all the way through high school. She might have money now, but she didn't have money back then. Having money hasn't really changed how she looks at the world. The time and energy she pours into everything is just—one hundred percent her. Sometimes, there's not enough to go around. She had plans and goals. She really wanted Harvard. She didn't get in. In the end, none of us went to our first pick school. Plans change. It doesn't mean we aren't enjoying it or having the time of our lives. She wants you to be successful. But she doesn't want you to be crushed or left hanging."

"That's really reasonable," Trina mumbled. The more the area around us grew familiar, the more I was falling back in time. The car. The area. Hell, we even drove right past the high school.

When had it gotten so small?

"So—how stupid am I that I kind of want to make the move to New York and see about breaking into modeling?"

"I don't think you're stupid at all," I told her honestly. "I'd ask how serious you were about it. How much research have you done? Do you know what you need to do? Um… is it like a job application thing? Or is it shopping those photos Rachel did? Or do you need an agent? Then…I'd ask how much are you going to be relying on Frankie and her contacts with Torched and the people she and Bubba know through

Bound Hearts."

"It's a lot," Trina confessed. "None of it is gonna be easy. There are a couple of agencies that actually offer training, but you have to audition—which sounds weird—but first, you send in the photos and if they like your look, they bring you in and do a test shoot. Then if you get past that, you can earn a spot. That's not a guarantee of work; you train, you do shoots, and there are all kinds of modeling."

"Okay." I rubbed a hand over my face. "Do you know what kind you want to do?"

"Not really," Trina said. "Part of me keeps expecting Mom to win this argument."

"It's impossible to win an argument if you don't know what you're arguing against," I pointed out, considering how non-responsive she'd been to me when I got in the car. "That said, Mom might actually have some ideas and knowledge to share."

"What does she know about modeling?"

"What do you?" I pointed out. "What do I? I mean, I can call Rachel, she might have some info for both of us, but the thing here is— it's not what Mom knows about this career—it's what she knows about life. It's what she knows about being an adult and being responsible for yourself. She isn't a psychologist. She understands on some levels what I'm doing, but it's never stopped her from trying to support me. Why not let her support you?"

"Because she won't." And there it was, the stubborn, dug-in pout. "She never approves of anything. Daddy always does, and then Mom always gets mad and tells me all the ways in which he is—"

"Stop," I said with a slice of my hand. "That argument doesn't work. One, we're not kids being yanked back and forth between our parents. You always take Dad's side because Dad will do absolutely *anything* to prove he loves you, even if it's a terrible idea. He will never be bad cop. He will always overindulge. It's who he is. You don't have to hate him for it or get mad at him. But the simple fact that he does that means Mom *has* to be bad cop. Or you go too far, Trina."

Mutiny crossed her face as we left the highway and the street lights flickered over her.

"It sucks," I said. "It always has. But you deciding you know what her answer will be before you even tell her anything—that's not fair either. Mom loves you. She shows it every day. She works. She feeds you. She clothes you. She makes sure you're getting a good education. She's backed you when you went out for cheer and dance. She found the money to help pay for extracurriculars. She never missed a school function unless she absolutely couldn't get out of work, and even when her life was falling apart, she made damn sure that ours didn't."

Trina blinked hard.

"Be mad at her for being tough on you and wanting the best for you and pushing you to be your best. Be mad at her for standing her ground and *not* letting you browbeat her into getting your way and loving you despite periodically going through phases of treating her like trash. But don't you *dare* decide what she will or won't say to you about a life plan you want to make while you think cutting her completely out is the thing to do."

Licking her lips, Trina sniffed. "You make me sound like a bitch."

"Well, if the shoe fits, Sis, wear it." I let that sit there in the silence between us. If she was going to erupt over it, better to do it *before* we got home. When she didn't, I glanced at her. She swiped at her cheeks. "Here's the thing…" I blew out a breath. "Mom loves you. I love you. Frankie loves you. If I can listen to what you want to do and Frankie can, and we can both offer our advice—why can't Mom?"

"Because what if I decide not to listen to her?"

"You're an adult. You can make that choice for yourself. You also have to understand that Mom doesn't have to support that choice. She can still love you and not give you the money to pay bills while you chase this."

"That's the same as making me do what she wants."

"Nope," I said. "It's the same as saying if you want something bad enough, you'll find a way. If you're looking at this as something Frankie and I will support you through, then yeah, I'll be there. Emotionally—always. Physically? When I can. Financially? Well, that's a discussion. One that will require a plan, and trust me, if you go to Frankie with this without a plan…" I shook my head and whistled.

Laughing through her tears, Trina sniffed again. "She kind of already told me not to bring it up again unless I had a plan."

That was my girl.

"You can ask for help," I reminded her. "But that's the thing—you have to ask. And to ask, you have to talk."

We turned into the parking lot of the apartments and a pang hit me. Frankie didn't live in that apartment on the corner anymore. Someone else probably lived there. Strangers. People who had no idea how we'd grown up here. Course, we might not be here that much longer either. Mom had hinted some about moving.

"Will you be there when I talk to Mom?" Trina asked *after* she pulled into the exact same spot Frankie had used for years. Fuck, this was gonna be a long few days.

"Thought you'd never ask," I said, then reached over to wipe away the last tear. "We're on your side. You know that, right?"

"Yeah," she said. "I do—just sometimes…"

"Sometimes it's hard. But that's why I'm the best big brother ever."

"You know—if you ever repeat this, I'll deny it."

"It's okay, Sis, you never have to say it. I know I'm the best."

I grinned at her and climbed out of the car. "Oh, and I never had sex with Frankie in here." I waited until she blew out a breath, then grinned wider. "Pretty sure Jake did, though." Then closed the door.

Chapter Eleven
LEGAL RECOURSE

FRANKIE

It seemed surreal to be turning in some of my last reports and projects for the year. Jake and I finished the final project for our history class a month earlier. Then we proceeded to just pick a whole host of historical-based movies so we could keep going cause it was fun. The guys teased us, but it didn't stop them from letting us pull historicals into movie night.

In a little over three weeks, I would no longer be a student. That was weirder than being engaged. I kept expecting to feel different somehow after the guys asked me to marry them. We were still us, however. The teasing and the rings were different. Different and adored. I loved where we were and I loved who we were.

Wedding planning aside, this year had just cemented us. I didn't want to be anywhere else. I wanted to be with Jake and Archie while they built a better engine. I wanted to be there with Coop while he got his master's degree. I loved seeing Jake and Archie repair their relationships with their fathers. I loved seeing Alicia put her family back together. I wanted to be there with Ian while he wrote music, whether it was for us or someone else.

I wanted *them* in my life, and I wanted to be in theirs. The marriage thing, though, I also wanted it to be legal. When Archie brought up the prenuptial agreement and presented it to all of us, I'd never seen so many slack-jaws. But it didn't surprise me. If anything, it just reminded me that I wasn't the only one in this family with this huge ass heart they kept talking about.

They were best friends, brothers, and they were all going to be my husbands, but they were also family to each other and to me. Our family. The fact Archie wanted everything to be community property so that we were all balanced and equals—it wasn't because he ever thought anyone was less. Rather, it was because he never wanted them to feel like they didn't bring the same things to the relationship.

I had zero trouble adding my finances to that. I wanted it all in. Financial commitment was nothing when they held my heart and my soul. So, the Standish Family Cooperative had been formed in its own way. That, in and of itself, had become one of the more amusing bits of teasing. We were all a part of Standish now. Just, *our* Standish.

"Thank you," I said to the driver after he pulled up outside the restaurant where Dominic Walsh waited just outside the doors. He straightened and put away his phone as I slid out of the car.

"Good afternoon, Frankie," he said, greeting me with his hand outstretched. I shook his hand before shifting my shoulder tote into a more comfortable position. "I could have come over to the brownstone, but I appreciate you meeting me here."

"You said you had court this morning, and I don't want to take up the rest of your day," I assured him. "I'm glad that court went well." I'd half-expected to be waiting for him because it was barely noon.

"Settled before the gavel dropped," he offered before opening the door for me.

"Congratulations," I told him as we made our way inside. "I hope—you know, good for you."

He chuckled. "Thank you. Two," he said to the hostess. "We have a reservation for Walsh."

The hostess smiled at him, her expression almost playful. "Of course, Mr. Walsh, if you and your party will follow me."

Dominic didn't even give her a second look as he motioned for me to go ahead of him. I followed her all the way to the table and she barely gave me a second look as she grinned at Dominic again.

"Can I get you a drink?"

"We're fine," I said when Dominic pulled out my chair for me. "If you'll give us a moment."

"Of course," she said slowly, then nodded to us. "If you need anything, Mr. Walsh, I'm Shannon."

"Thank you, Shannon." The immediate perfunctory response had me biting the inside of my lip as I took my seat and set the bag down next to my leg. Dominic didn't sit until the hostess left, then he let out a sigh before unbuttoning his suit jacket and taking his seat. Smoothing down his tie, he said, "Do you want wine? Or would you prefer coffee?"

"Coffee," I said. "Too early in the day for wine. But don't let me stop you."

"I'm working," he said, his expression easing. "Better to save cocktails until happy hour."

"Sounds like a good plan." We both glanced at our menus. I picked out the manicotti and garlic toast. He went for just a chicken alfredo. Once we had our coffees in front of us, I focused on him. "How are you?"

"I'm fine," he said with an easy smile that didn't quite reach his eyes. Somehow, I questioned whether he was fine or not. On the one hand, I did like Dominic and I was concerned. On the other—Rachel. "Actually, I should be asking you how you are. You're very close to graduation. Right?"

"Yep, couple more weeks. Commencement isn't until the first of May, but—it's crazy." My heart did that little fist bump with my ribs, and my stomach bottomed out like it did each time I thought about it. Coop would have wise words to describe the reaction, but to me, it felt like the high and the exhaustion after a grueling run.

I did it. Intellectually and physically, I knew I'd done it. I made it. But I'd been working toward this goal for so long that it was almost unbelievable that we were *there*. Coop had been accepted to Long Island University for his master's program, and he'd be attending classes on their Brooklyn campus. I was so damn excited for him.

"That's exciting," he said. "I hope you'll invite me to the ceremony."

"I don't think Rachel is coming back for it." While she was the sassy elephant in the room between us, it only seemed fair that he knew.

"Thank you for letting me know, but I would still like to attend for you and the guys. I feel like we've really gotten to know each other over the last few years."

We had.

"And while you have been withholding friendship out of loyalty to Rachel, which I respect, by the way, I do think of you as more than just a client. So, if you would be so inclined as to invite me, I would love to attend. No harm, no foul if not."

"Ugh," I said with a huff and rubbed a hand over my mouth. "That makes me feel like such an ass."

"Please, don't," he assured me before taking a sip of his coffee. "You have your reasons, and I respect them. You are a good friend, Frankie. This is one of the reasons I'd like to make you mine. But without opening that particular can of worms, I didn't ask for this meeting to talk about Rachel."

The touch of regret in his voice when he said her name twisted my heart. I bit my tongue against apologizing. She was my best friend. "No," I said slowly. "Sorry."

"You don't have to apologize," he said. "Although, I did want to talk to you because I think I have some good news *for* you."

"For me?"

"Yep, you mentioned before Christmas that one of the worries about getting married was the lack of a legal component to the ceremony."

"It's not so much just a legal component, but—I feel like they should have rights if something happens. I mean, we're talking about kids eventually and—I want to have rights where they are concerned. If there's an accident, if one of us ends up in the hospital, or when we have kids, they should all be fathers and all have rights where the kids are concerned. I know it sounds weird…" I was fumbling for this.

"You want security for them and for you," Dominic said, his expression gentle, but he paused as our food arrived. The waitress also brought us fresh glasses of ice water and neither of us wanted more coffee while we ate.

When we were alone again, I nodded. "I do want security for them. I never want one of them to be cut out of a decision that may need all of us to make. We're a family, and it's one thing for us to make those calls for ourselves, but what happens if we're sick or injured? I just—I don't want that to become a thing."

"I get it," he said with a gentle smile. "That's why I've been doing some research. Now, legally, you can't file for a marriage certificate with five people. The marriage contract is literally between two people. However, we might have some wiggle room to work a little magic—if you're willing to be flexible."

I perked up in the chair, excitement tingling in my belly. *Don't get too excited*, I cautioned myself. Hear him out. "I'm definitely interested in hearing what you've figured out."

"Okay, let's start with CNM," he said, straightening in the chair. "That's consensual non-monogamy. There's a very strong movement from the polyamorous side of things in this country. The big things to note are some of the legwork they've already done. Bigamy, for example, has been decriminalized in many states—not all. New York still has it listed in the penal code, but it requires a spouse—the person affected by the bigamy—to seek charges. Most of the time, it's not going to be pursued as an active criminal complaint."

Criminal…

"Bear with me, I have a reason for taking you down this rabbit hole." The caution helped, but at the same time, I couldn't help trying to swallow back the fear.

"Only four states have added civil unions and domestic partnerships to their anti-bigamy statutes. In almost all cases, the civil union, domestic partnership, or marriage is recognized as such based on the laws and statutes of where the marriage, partnership, or union took place." He glanced at me. "Following me?"

"If we get married in New York, we have to get married under the auspices of the statutes governing marriage here, but our marriage is recognized in another state because we were married here whether their laws would allow it or not?"

"Exactly. This *also* applies to civil unions and domestic partnerships. The technicalities get a little fuzzy in places, but we have a strong case. In the townships of Somerville and Cambridge, they have passed multiple-partner domestic partnership ordinances. Somerville was first, and Cambridge followed. There have been other towns and cities who have *also* begun to pass these ordinances, following their lead and requiring the domestic partnerships must fulfill six criteria."

Six?

"You must be at least eighteen years of age and mentally competent to execute a contract. You cannot have just terminated a domestic partnership in the last ninety days—unless it terminated because a partner died, and you cannot be related by blood closer than the state—in this case, Massachusetts—would allow for marriage." He ticked them off with his fingers. "Finally, you must be in 'a relationship of mutual support, caring, and commitment, and intend to remain in that relationship,' 'you must reside together,' and you must 'consider yourselves to be a family.'"

"That's it?" Holy shit.

"That's it—for Sommerville and Cambridge, MA. And for a little town called Freshtown here in New York—which passed that ordinance last summer." He grinned. "Now—this isn't a marriage, but it does confer legal protections often covered by marriage and civil unions. We would also add co-parenting as an agreement between you and medical powers of attorney for each of you—just to cover all our bases. This would allow you, as a group, to adopt all the children you produce—or in this case, the guys would all be able to adopt—because multi-parent homes are a fact of modern life. It takes a little finessing and a lot of paperwork—but then you have any ceremony you want."

Any ceremony we wanted.

My heart dipped and I leaned back in the chair. "Seriously? That's only three towns."

"Everything has to start somewhere. The more it's not contested and the more the anti-bigamy laws aren't enforced, you quietly and strategically change the flow of the stream. You're all adults, and you're all *consenting* adults. State anti-bigamy statutes may violate the Due Process Clause because individuals engaged in consensual non-monogamy are adults with the liberty to choose whom to form relationships with." He was so sober as he met my gaze. "It's imperfect, messy, and definitely going to take some hoop-jumping. If you all decide to legally change your names to one, we'll have more paperwork to fill out—but it's doable."

Blinking rapidly, I tried to wrap my mind around it. There was so much. The ceremony we were planning was for us and our families. There wouldn't be a typical marriage license for the officiant to sign. "Dominic—is there a chance this could hurt like Coop's chances for licensure? Or Archie's inheritance? Or Jake and Ian's work? I don't want someone to turn this on them."

"First, if any of them run into discrimination—we handle that on a case-by-case basis. You and Ian are semi-public figures through Bound Hearts, so could you get some notoriety on this? Probably. But as far as I'm aware, the world kind of already knows you have four boyfriends. Your social media manager has posted some tasteful images of the five of you together, as well as some fun shots of the proposal and from when they've come to your concerts."

"Yeah, but we've—we've tapered back, so I don't—"

"Do you know how many followers your Bound Hearts account has?"

I just stared at him. "To be honest, Dominic—high school kind of burnt me out on social media. The less I pay attention to it, the better. Andrea's a damn gift that she does so much of all that and just tells me what she needs from me."

He chuckled. "Fair, tell you what, you talk to your manager and your social media manager and let them know about the wedding and what you're planning—they'll keep you in the loop about how much exposure you want for it. Though—you might have people trying to crash the wedding."

I made a face. "Ugh, I should pay more attention to these things."

"Clearly, you don't have to because the machine is running wildly without you."

I exhaled. "Is it going to matter that we don't live in those locales?" Needing something firm to grab hold of, I dug into my manicotti.

"Well, I'll dig a little deeper on that, but I'm fairly certain we can set you up with a summer house there if you need one."

True. Archie would probably try to buy the town. My heart pounded madly. "My dad lives in Massachusetts."

"That could be useful," he said. "I think there's another town there, Arlington, that also has it on the books. Options."

I bit my lower lip, studying him. "Honest opinion—do you think this would work?"

"I think we can make it work. I wouldn't have brought this to you as a Hail Mary. This is too important to you. I've been investigating any number of ways to make this legally binding and protective of all five of you—including forming a limited corporation if necessary."

"A business?"

"Business entities get recognized as persons all the time, it's one way to do it, but you'd still need the power of attorneys and more. At the end of the day, marriage is a legal construct that confers some immunities and protections on the partners who enter into it. Pull aside the curtain of romance and religion and just look at the base facts—it's a contract. Contracts are not *exclusive* in this case in order to be binding and give you everything you need to provide security for you and your family."

Holy shit.

"Do you have paperwork or briefs or something? I need to walk the guys through this." I swore I was going to vibrate out of my seat. "Dominic, this is so much."

"Hey, you said you needed this. It's my job to make it happen for you if it is at all possible. It's not a done deal yet, but as I said—we will get there." Then he opened his case and pulled out a whole folder and handed it over to me. "Research, case law, and citations. Some of that is going to be a little dense…"

I flipped through it as he explained.

"There are also organizations that have been setting the stage for this. Statistics suggest that five to seven percent of families are multi-partner or involved in polyamorous relationships. So, we just build a strong foundation, and you guys have already done that."

Dominic had included a summary letter at the beginning, basically giving us line items of every opportunity he'd listed. This was above and beyond. It—it was giving me everything I'd wanted to give them.

"Thank you," I whispered, blinking back the tears. "I can't wait to show them this. Fair warning, Archie is probably going to call you."

"No problem," Dominic said with a chuckle. "I can handle him and Jake, and Coop, and Ian. Do I have your permission to speak to them about this discussion with regard to the attorney-client privilege?"

I grinned. "You absolutely have my permission to speak to them."

I went back through the paperwork, asking questions each time something else occurred to me. Dominic answered every single one patiently and had the waitress box up my lunch to take home when I gave up eating. He also ordered us more coffee.

It was mid-afternoon before we finished. Dominic walked me outside, where he waited with me for my car. Pivoting, I faced him. "I'm going to hug you, and I'm going to invite you to my wedding because you are a good friend."

I wanted to tell him more. I honestly did, but as I hugged him and he returned the affection lightly, I kept it to myself. Maybe the invitation to the wedding was enough. Because Rachel promised…

Mental fingers crossed.

"Talk soon?"

"Absolutely." He walked with me to the car when it pulled up and opened the back door for me. "Graduation?"

I laughed. "I'll send you a ticket."

He made a slight fist pump motion and then closed the car door. His expression sobered as the car pulled away. I sighed. I really did like Dominic.

Okay, Rachel, I said mentally. *Time for a little loving intervention. You did it to me, and now I'm going to do it to you.*

Here was hoping she loved me enough to forgive me for this.

Save
The Date
For The Wedding Of
Frankie, Archie, Coop,
Ian and Jake.
That Will Be Held On
Saturday
June 3rd
Ceremony to begin at
10 a.m.
Rose Garden
Trebek Inn
Freshtown
Join us for our happily ever
after...
Reception to Follow

Chapter Twelve

MR. SOMEBODY

ARCHIE

"**M**r. Archie," Jeremy said sternly as I continued setting the table. "This is highly irregular."

I snorted. "Irregular, Jere? Come on, if it's weird, I get it. But you and Ann—" At his narrow-eyed look, I did not sigh or make a face, I just corrected. "You and Ms. Bradshaw have been keeping company for more than a year. She's practically become a regular fixture around here. Frankie's right, we need to get to know her better."

Was bringing Frankie into play a totally underhanded move? Damn straight, and I'd play her every time. Jeremy did not like to disappoint her. Who could blame him? None of us did.

"Ann is a lovely woman, but her agreeing to see me—keeping company as you have so quaintly worded it—"

"Wait," I said, facing him. "What do you call it?"

"I do believe dating and friendship are the two words we've used to describe our relationship."

Gripping my chest, I feigned a heart attack. "Jere, are you guys f—"

"Don't. You. Dare." The reprimand was as effective as it had been when I was ten and he caught me stealing a motor out of the deep freezer.

"Now, Jere, I was just going to ask if you guys were having fun or getting serious. Give me *some* credit."

"Hmm-hmm," he hummed with a thoroughly reproachful look. "Mr. Archie, this is not something I am enjoying the teasing on."

Sobering, I finished setting the table as I said, "I'm sorry. Truly. Teasing you is second nature, but I'm not teasing you about your relationship so much as your response to my inviting her to lunch today. I thought it would be nice if we sat down—the three of us—and I got to know her a little."

The original plan was for Frankie to be here, but she and Hank were going to see Frankie's grandparents. I needed to do something, or I'd lose my mind, so with her blessing, I'd asked Ms. Bradshaw to join us. Even though she'd told us several times to call her Ann, Jeremy's sense of propriety was intense.

Miss Abigail sat on the floor, tail occasionally thumping as she canted her head back and forth while Jeremy and I spoke.

Contemplative frown firmly in place, Jeremy followed me back into the kitchen as I went to get the tumblers for water, cups for coffee or tea, and wine glasses on the off chance she indulged. He promptly plucked them from my hands and put them back up, selecting different drinkware.

"What has prompted this sudden urge to socialize with Ms. Bradshaw?"

"You care about her," I told him as I followed him out to the table. He corrected my settings, one at a time, as he put out the cups and glasses—no wine glasses. Noted. "You care about her enough that you spend a lot of time with her. You've gone on vacation together a couple of times." When he paused, hands on the back of a chair to study me, I added, "You're important to me. She's important to you."

"So, you feel like that makes her important to you?" Jeremy's tone seemed far too neutral.

"Jeremy, what did you say to me the day you met Frankie?"

"I said that young lady is very good for you, have a care with how you treat her."

I grinned. "Verbatim. Ms. Bradshaw is very good for you. I plan to have a care with how I treat her as well."

"You don't have to, Mr. Archie. I do enjoy Ms. Bradshaw's— Ann's company very much. We have lunch a couple of times a week, we go for walks as often as we are both free and I have, upon occasion, taken her out for dinner. But I won't allow the relationship to interfere with my responsibilities here." With that, he returned to the kitchen.

"Jeremy…" I followed him as he checked the oven warmer where I'd set the bread and then the pots where the linguine and the sauce were waiting.

"You did not cook this."

At the short declaration, I laughed. "No, I promise, I didn't even touch anything unless Frankie told me to. She fixed this before she left to take the train to Connecticut."

"Oh." Surprise flickered over Jeremy's face.

"Hey, after the last stove—which was *not* my fault—I gave you my word, I wouldn't do anything again without supervision, and I've behaved. All explosions are now purely limited to the shop in Brooklyn."

At the tightening of his brows, I lifted my hands.

"I have not detonated anything in over a year…" Geez, blow up one stove. Okay, three. But who was counting? "The point is, I wanted—you know, we wanted to do a nice lunch. Frankie even went to the trouble of fixing it."

Manipulative? Maybe a little.

"So you would feel safe in eating it, and probably to make sure I didn't blow up the kitchen."

Jeremy chuckled softly and shook his head. The amusement left me flat-footed. It was hardly the first time I'd earned a genuine laugh from him, but still… "My boy," Jeremy said as he closed the distance between us. He gripped my arms firmly and then patted my shoulder. "This is more than enough. I appreciate the efforts. I do. If this is your way of telling me that I am free to leave you and pursue whatever it is that you believe I might want to pursue…"

What the fuck? No, I didn't want him to go. I wanted to make sure she was good enough and get to know her so if she moved in—

It took me a minute to realize Jeremy had gone quiet, a faint but very real smirk on his lips.

"Jere, that's really not nice," I pointed out, then raked a hand through my hair.

"I will have you know, Mr. Archie, it is every bit as nice as you deciding to have a tête-á-tête with Ann without warning me ahead of time. If I'd understood your concerns, I would have absolutely made these arrangements."

I sagged and leaned against the wall. "You're not planning on leaving?"

"Unless you and Miss Frankie, along with Mr. Bubba, Mr. Coop, and Mr. Jake, have decided you no longer require or desire my services—"

"No, none of us want you to go. Even Frankie says you're family." Yes, please, pay attention to my use of Frankie and do not abandon us. "Jere, you've been the glue helping us get through the last four years. You look after us, the brownstone—you've been handling the coordination of the renovations for the house in Hamptons. You're the man who has the trains running on time—I get if you want more of a life than this, and I respect that." My gut sank. "But I truly did just want to get to know her cause, you know—she might be spending more time here, with us."

"Entirely possible," Jeremy told me. He checked his watch. "When is Ann arriving for this meeting?"

I glanced at the clock on the wall. "We have thirty-five minutes. She's pretty prompt."

"Yes, she is." Pride shining in his eyes. "Give me one moment." He stepped back to the food and made some adjustments, and I just shut up. He obviously didn't want the food to go bad, and I respected that.

A soft furred head butted against my hand, and I glanced down at Miss Abigail. She gave me a soulful look so I scratched her gently between the ears.

"Very good, thank you for waiting. Let us step over to my rooms and have a drink, shall we?"

His room.

To have a drink.

On automatic pilot, I followed him, with Miss Abigail keeping us company. He had a very nice set of rooms, a sitting room with a library and office off of it, a television with a pair of chairs and a sofa—that apparently now belonged to Miss Abigail because she hopped right up on it and curled up on a blanket that lay over it.

Jeremy went to the bar and poured out two glasses of scotch. It had been a while since I'd had the good stuff, and I gave Jeremy two bottles every Christmas. I had since the first year I found out he liked it—when I was seven.

His scandalized reaction had cemented my desire to always find a way to get it for him. Grandpa Ted had always come through for me. A pang hit at that memory; a pang and a smile. At least I could take care of it myself these days.

"Have a seat," Jeremy said as he passed me a glass, and I perched on the edge of one of the armchairs. To be perfectly honest, this was weird. We should have rescheduled it to when Frankie could be here.

"This feels an awful lot like I'm in trouble," I admitted. "Except I'm in my twenties, and this is alcohol."

I glanced at him, and his dry look communicated more than most people's three-minute oratories.

"Okay, fair point. Alcohol has never been on the banned list."

"Largely because you were always a clever boy. If it was permitted, then I could monitor it and hopefully avoid anything catastrophic. You were also a very determined young man when you put your mind to it."

"I hope I still am," I admitted.

"Mr. Archie…" He paused, then took a sip of his drink before saying, "Archie, if you're worried that I want to leave—I don't. I actually rather enjoy looking after all of you. Did I expect that at some point you wouldn't have any further need for me? Well—yes."

When I would have opened my mouth to say something, he stopped me with just a look.

"For the moment, I am being informal because I believe your concerns are rooted in the abandonment you still associate with your parents. You and Mr. Edward have come a long way in the last few years. Your affection for Frankie has softened you and made you stronger, while he has begun to put himself back together after that horrid woman."

My jaw didn't drop, but I didn't think I'd ever heard Jeremy refer to Maddy in those terms before.

"I always had an opinion," he reminded me. "The point is, it is natural for a young man to grow up and to not need the adult figures in their life as much. You don't. Whether you recognize it or not, you have grown up—remarkably well for someone so determined to destroy just about everything in the name of figuring out how it works."

I laughed. "It's just deconstruction."

"Well, it does have its limits where charm is concerned. However, the point is, Miss Frankie is good for you. Those young men you bonded with as friends are good for you. I've watched all of you grow the last few years, remarkable, capable young people filled with compassion, more than your fair share of mischief, and the commitment to each other that is extraordinary. Personally, I think you could have proposed to that young woman sooner, but I also recognize that none of you needed it to know where you were going to be. You proposed when you were all ready to take that step."

It was more than a little uncomfortable to be the recipient of such blunt praise. But I didn't interrupt.

"While you don't need me as you once did, you do still need me." Jeremy nodded to my glass, and I took a mouthful and it helped to steady my nerves. "You do. Miss Frankie does. She certainly needs me to keep you boys in line when you get to be too much. But the others do to their different extents. So, while I don't think you need me day in and day out—I know you still need me here."

"Jere, it's not just about need," I said. "I want you here. *We* do." No doubt in my mind what Frankie would say. "But I also know I shouldn't be selfish with you. I can't—think of a time in my life when you dated before. Since you and Ms. Bradshaw truly seemed to have hit it off—I wanted to be there for you too."

"Young man, you have always been supportive. While my

personal life was never something for you to worry about, you never knew about my socializing because I didn't allow it anywhere near you."

I grimaced. "That's not entirely fair to you, I mean—you're allowed to have a life."

"I do have a life—the one I have here. With the young men that I have helped raise and the young woman they adore. The family who thought enough of my perceived loneliness and went in search of a puppy so I could have company."

We both glanced at Miss Abigail.

She watched us somewhat adoringly. Well, she watched Jeremy and I grin. "That was Frankie."

"Of course, it was," Jeremy said with a chuckle as he swirled his drink. "Truth be told, she was right. I have enjoyed Miss Abigail's company so much. I have enjoyed watching all of you with her. Miss Abigail is also why Ms. Bradshaw and I began talking in the first place."

That, I hadn't realized.

"So, Archie…"

"Jere, not gonna lie, that sounds weird. Yet, I don't hate it."

He laughed, then shook his head. "Do not get used to it. You have been Mr. Archie to me since you were a baby, and you always will be. I think, however, from time to time, we can sit and have a drink and talk to each other. Particularly if either of us gets concerned about the other no longer requiring our presence."

Raising my glass, I reached over, and he tapped his to it, then we both knocked back the scotch. It went down smooth and left a trail of warmth through me.

"Now," Jeremy said. "Let us finish getting lunch ready for Ann. We can enjoy the meal and any future invitations you will extend through me, yes?"

"I solemnly swear. But I'm pretty sure Frankie wants to give her an invitation to the wedding."

We rose, and he nodded. "She asked me would I like to bring her as my plus one. Since I plan to make sure everything goes off without a hitch, I did ask her if she would mind being abandoned for half the event, and Ms. Bradshaw has volunteered to assist me."

Oh.

"Jere you—"

He gave me a stern look, and I paused. Right. Shut up, Archie.

"That's amazing, Jere. I know Frankie and the guys are gonna appreciate your help. I'm good at the big events, but with school and everything else…"

He nodded. Of course, he did. He knew.

Thankfully, the lunch was nowhere near as awkward as it could have been. Ann Bradshaw was every bit as charming and intelligent as she seemed. It made sense; she'd earned Jeremy's attention. Miss Abigail joined us for lunch, though she slept on her bed on the floor while we ate.

We talked about school, the wedding, future plans, and I mentioned possibly moving to the house in the Hamptons permanently—when Coop finished his master's. Or maybe elsewhere. For the foreseeable future, the brownstone would remain our home.

That pleased her, and I caught the look they gave each other. Not long after, I excused myself to take the dishes to the kitchen while Jeremy and Ms. Bradshaw went for a walk. Coop was in the upstairs living room when I got up there, his book open but discarded on the coffee table and a game controller in hand.

"Is it safe to go down now?"

"You could have come down and joined us," I told him as I slumped onto the sofa. He thrust a second game controller at me.

"And interrupt what had to be some quality and very

uncomfortable bonding time with Jeremy and his new squeeze?" He shot me a look. "No, thank you."

I flipped him a middle finger and waited for him to die, and then restarted it in two-player mode. "Bite me. She's actually a nice lady."

"Yep," Coop said. "You think Jeremy would see anyone who wasn't nice?"

"Okay, smartass, Frankie wanted to have a sit-down and get to know her too."

"I know she did, but she was also worried about you, and she wanted to put your concerns to rest as much as she wanted to make sure that this chick was good enough for Jeremy."

I chased after him through the winding roads and traps as we floored our respective cars. That made sense, Frankie was always looking after us. Abruptly, I stopped accelerating and blinked. Shit— Coop was going to win if I didn't get it together. He still won, but he didn't cream me. I came in a respectable third, all things being equal.

"You forget what you were doing?" Coop asked.

"It just occurred to me that Frankie set me up."

"It's called handling you," Coop corrected. "Sounds better."

"Not really," I said, then laughed as I shook my head. She'd set me up, got me all ready for it, and then—yeah, her leaving hadn't been planned, but she had picked up on my worry.

"Feels good, doesn't it?" Coop said as he picked up his soda and took a drink.

"That she cares?" I nodded. "Yeah. It does. Okay—round two, I'm going to kick your ass."

"You can try, Arch," Coop said. "But you will never best my superior skill and big stick."

I groaned, but I didn't miss the starter this time as I floored it past him. "It's not the size of the stick but if you know how to use it."

He cut in front of me. "So sad for you that I can do both."
We were still at it and laughing when Jake got home.
And we were still tied, dammit.

Chapter Thirteen

IF I COULD

FRANKIE

Hank stood on the platform, waiting for me, when my train arrived. The simple joy warming me at his smile and the way he lifted his chin when he spotted me in the window still caught me off-guard, no matter how often I saw it.

Not even a week earlier, I'd said something to my therapist about wondering why it still surprised me that he loved me or that the guys did. I *knew* they did, so why would it feel like that so often? She'd countered with a question, "Does it feel like a *surprise* so often? Or are you just happy that you can feel their love so strongly?"

Pretty sure it was a little bit of the former and a lot of the latter. It definitely left me with food for thought, then and now. I packed up my laptop and slid it away as we approached. When the train came to a stop, I got up and headed for the exit. Hank was right there as I stepped off.

"There's my girl," he said by way of greeting, scooping me up into a hug. I laughed as I returned the hug. Dressed in a light jacket, baseball cap, and sporting a new beard, Hank looked more like a student than a professor.

"Hi, Dad," I said against his ear before pulling back to kiss his cheek. He set me down, then wrapped an arm around my shoulders to direct me away from the train and the flow of people stepping off. "Thanks for coming down to meet me."

"My pleasure," he said. "Sorry for the short notice. I had meetings canceled, and you were free, so this seemed like a good time."

"It's a great time," I told him as we made our way out to the parking lot. "I mean, honestly, I think I'd be nervous any time we went. But I called Eugene before I headed to the train station and he sounded happy that we were coming for a 'late lunch,' as he put it."

"Good." Hank opened the passenger door for me. "Want me to put your bag in the backseat?"

"Thanks." I handed it to him and rolled my head around as I glanced at the area. Winter still lingered, though spring was pushing its way through. My birthday was a week away. So weird to even think about that, when my attention was far more focused on getting through finals.

"Hey," he said as he circled to the driver's side. "You don't have to go and see them. No one will hold it against you. If they do? You send them to me. I'll take care of it."

I grinned. "It's not that, as much as I've wrestled with this—it's the right thing for me to do. Archie made a good argument. And if this doesn't work out, well, then I know I tried."

"Sounds like a plan."

Once we were in, he started the car and pulled up the directions that he'd apparently already programmed in. "How are you doing? Classes are winding down for you, right?"

"Yes," he told me with an easy glance before turning out of the lot and following the directions. We weren't that far from Blue Ivy, but we didn't have time to stop there. Plus, I wasn't even sure if KC was there right now or not. We hadn't talked since the last zoom call about Ian's latest songs for them.

Those conversations were insane but fun.

"Wow, don't overwhelm me with data there, Dad. I wouldn't want you to spill all your secrets at once."

He snorted. "Sorry, sweetheart. It's mostly finals and spending the last couple of weeks getting last-minute papers, makeup work, and arguing with college students who do not have it together."

I winced.

"That said, I wasn't thinking about that so much as thinking that you're graduating in a few weeks and a few weeks after that, you're getting married."

Oh, that was a way to get my stomach in knots. "Well, if it's any consolation, you have a few more years before Alec reaches high school graduation."

"Ha!" He shook his head. "That does not make me feel better. Just—" Then he broke off with another shake of his head. "Don't mind me."

"Dad… what?" It was getting easier to say it more and more. I thought of him as Dad every bit as much as I did Hank these days. Sometimes more. I liked that I could call him Dad. I liked it even more that I liked being able to call him that.

"It's depressing," he admitted. "You don't need depressing right now. We might get enough of that with—" Then he edited himself again and hushed.

"Well, one, you're my dad, so I don't think they call it depressing so much as nostalgic."

"No, it's depressing," he corrected me. "I feel like I just found you. I met you right before you graduated from high school. You were grown. Done. And now, you're grown again. Just—reminds me of how much I missed."

I blinked rapidly at the level of emotion in his voice. My chest tightened. He wasn't wrong. Not really. "I feel the same way," I admitted. "Sometimes—I think about the stuff. Father's Day was just another day growing up. I think I was six when I first realized we didn't celebrate it."

Coop had been trying to make something for his dad and wanted my help. I couldn't figure out why.

"I'm sorry we missed all that stuff too. But—not anymore. You know?"

Hank gave me a misty smile. "See, here I was trying not to be depressing, and you're just making me want to cry."

I laughed. "Sorry?"

"Don't be sorry. I still have that first Father's Day card you sent."

I cringed a little. The guys had helped me pick it out. That June had been just us, between the island, Paris, then later London, and performing with Torched. It had been a magical time. Still, I'd wanted to send him a card. So… yeah, I picked out a totally cheesy Dad's first Father's Day card.

Even if it hadn't remotely been *his* first.

"Yes, not anymore," he told me. "Which brings us to the wedding…"

"Actually, graduation is next. Don't rush the wedding. We still have more to do before we're done with getting ready for that."

"I thought you got the dress and booked the venue."

"We did, but that's not everything," I reminded him. The area was getting more familiar. The first time I drove down here, it had been with Archie. "It also brings us to the part of the ceremony that I've been kind of chicken to talk to you about."

"You can talk to me about anything." I loved the confidence. I really did.

"You know we're not having a traditional wedding."

"No, really? Me inheriting four sons-in-law wasn't supposed to be my first clue."

I swatted him for that, and he laughed along with me. "You have been amazing in your support, even when you didn't totally understand us."

"Frankie," he said as we came to a light. "They love you. That was clear from the first day I met you. Every interaction I've had with them since only reaffirms that. You are quite literally the center of their world. I had no idea who you were when I met you, only that you were my kid and I wanted to know you. The young woman I've gotten to know? She's quirky, intelligent, an overachiever, compassionate to a fault, a little too indulgent where her younger siblings are concerned, and quite possibly one of my favorite people."

"Quite possibly?"

"Well, I didn't want all the compliments to go to your head."

I chuckled. "Good call."

"My point is—I love you. Whatever it is, whatever quirky new thing we're throwing at the wedding—I'm here for it. Just—promise me that it's kid-friendly."

Fresh laughter burst out of me, and I had to wipe the second wave of tears from my eyes, only these were far more humorous. "It's definitely kid-friendly. It's, hopefully, dad-friendly too. Just—I don't want anyone to give me away. I know that's kind of a tradition but…"

"But I wasn't there when you were growing up."

"No, that's not it. I meant it when I said I don't want anyone to give me away. I want to go to them, the way I always have. Just as me.

They chose me, but I also chose them. It took us a long time to get to this part. We had a lot of battles and misunderstandings along the way. I nearly lost my friendship with them because I got mad."

Not that they were willing to let me go, but I had refused to talk to them after finding out what they'd done. I shut them out. I walled myself away. If they hadn't been so stubborn in not letting me close that door—

"The point is, we made it. We survived a lot. And I want to honor the fact that we chose each other. I want you there, and I want Kelly and the kids. I want the whole family. Even if it's enormous now." I made a face, and he slowed as we turned onto the last street leading to Patience and Eugene's home. The house where my mother grew up. "I want you to join us, but I don't want to be given away."

"The father-daughter dance?"

I laughed. "All yours, I promise."

"Yes." He made a little fist pump, then pulled to a stop at the entryway to their drive. "I never want to give you away either," he said. "I do want to be there. I want to be in your life. Although I also kind of want to threaten them, but they outnumber me."

I giggled.

"So, let's do this—you give yourself to whoever you want to, and you guys choose each other. They know that I'm always in your corner. Even if the unthinkable were to happen and you were wrong."

"Oh, come on…" I gave him a playful shove.

"True. You would never be wrong." Then he winked.

That went so much better than I'd worried it would. Of course it did. Hank was a great guy. Then we both sort of sobered and stared at the house as we followed the drive to the circle in front of the *huge* stone mansion. To be honest, Archie's place was big. The house in the Hamptons was big.

Hell, the *brownstone* was big. None of them intimidated me the way this place did. It was just—*sad.*

"She grew up here, huh?" He pulled up to park next to the still broken fountain. I frowned at it. There were weeds creeping up along the cracks. The hedges had gotten thicker than the last time I was here, and they didn't look shaped or lush, just overgrown. No, not overgrown. That wasn't the right word. They looked neglected.

"Yeah," I said as I unbuckled my seatbelt. "Looks fun, doesn't it?"

"Looks a lot like something out of a murder mystery," he admitted and then grimaced. "Sorry."

"No, nothing to be sorry about. It definitely looks like that." I shook my head. It looked less somehow than my first visit. Maybe because the people it housed weren't such mysteries anymore, or perhaps it was just that my feelings regarding them were so incredibly complicated.

The air was chilly, not quite a frost to it but definitely cooler than we'd had in the city or even at the train station. I folded my arms, kind of wishing I'd brought a heavier jacket as I stared at the front door. Eugene knew I was coming. I hadn't mentioned Patience. Hadn't asked if she'd be here.

There was a real possibility I would run into her. While I'd barely had two words to rub together for her since Maddy's funeral, I wrestled with the unease from potentially seeing her.

Glancing across the car, I met Hank's gaze, where he waited for me. No judgment reflected in his eyes, just a reserved kind of patience. Squaring my shoulders, I unfolded my arms. "Shall we?"

He grinned. "Absolutely."

At the front door, I rang the bell. We didn't have to wait long before an older Asian woman wearing scrubs answered the door. My heart immediately plummeted. A nurse? But her smile appeared almost instantly.

"You must be Francesca."

God help me. "Frankie," I said in the same breath with Hank and I threw him a grateful grin.

"Sorry, your grandfather calls you both. Come in, come in. He's been excited since he got the call. He even wanted to put on a new sweater."

Inside, the house seemed dark, despite the curtains being thrown open on many of the windows. There was a faint—musty odor—like no one lived here, and that tugged at my heart too.

"Thank you," I said. "This is my dad, Hank."

"Jackson," he added as he held out his hand. "Hank Jackson."

She gripped it easily, and I automatically held out my own because he was right, that was the polite thing to do. "I'm sorry, I don't know your name."

"Well, now why would you?" She gave me what I would call a maternal look along with a warm smile. "I'm Leslie Chao. I'm your grandfather's day nurse and physical therapist. He's in a feisty mood today."

Why did he have a physical therapist? A dozen questions hovered on my tongue as I followed Leslie to the sun porch where we'd met Patience and him before—well, when it had been Archie and me. I pulled off my jacket as we stepped out.

"Was that her—oh!" He rose from the chair where he'd been working on what looked like a crossword puzzle. "There you are! You're here. Now, didn't I tell you I had the prettiest granddaughter?"

He gave Leslie a look like she'd been arguing with him. I hesitated a moment when Leslie motioned for me to stay still, but Eugene was already making his way over to me, moving with far more spryness than he'd had the last time I saw him.

With a grin that could only be described as playful, he clapped his hands as he walked toward us. "Shocked?"

I didn't want to be rude. Then he was clasping my hands in his weathered ones and squeezing them gently.

"You can be honest, I looked like hell the last time we saw each other. But I'm getting in my steps every day, and Leslie here kicks me solidly in the tuckus when I get lazy. I'm practically twenty years younger."

I had no idea what I'd been expecting, really, but this was not it at all.

"Can an old man possibly get a hug, or are we not there yet?"

An echo of the words I'd thrown at Patience that last time and sadness gripped me. It didn't seem like it had been long ago, yet he'd changed so much. I hated to say for the better, but there was color in his cheeks and a glint of mischief in his eyes. The man he'd been before had been broken and so damaged.

"You may absolutely have a hug," I told him, and relief softened his expression as I gripped him gently for fear of hurting him. But his embrace was fierce, and he patted my back before releasing me.

"Mr. Jackson," he said, holding out a hand to Hank.

"Hank, please, Mr. Grayson—"

"Then you must call me Eugene," he said as they shook hands. "No formalities here, right, Leslie?"

"Absolutely," she said with an amused smile and a shake of her head. "I'm just going to let Carol know your guests are here and she can bring out lunch when you're ready."

"Excellent. You should pull up a chair and join us. I'm sure my Frankie would love to hear all your horror stories about what a tyrant I am."

"I'm pretty certain your granddaughter did not come all this way to talk to me. Now, behave." She made a shooing motion, then cast a quick smile at us. "See? Feisty."

I laughed, and when Eugene offered his arm, I took it. Hank took my jacket and then we moved back over to the table where Eugene was set up.

"I've got iced tea out here. Perfectly terrible stuff, but if you mix it with lemonade, it's like a legal cocktail that the doctor doesn't yell at you about." He poured drinks for us both, and then as soon as we were settled, he said, "Before we get too deep into the weeds, because I am so glad you're here, I wanted you to know that Patience is upstairs. I asked her to give us at least an hour to visit before joining us. Then I also informed her that if you did not want to see her, we would not force the issue."

I was torn between amusement about the drinks and the sinking reality that he'd already handled the grandmother I was on the fence about seeing. Coming here was absolutely the right thing. I glanced over at Hank and he gave me a small, almost encouraging smile.

Pretty sure it was encouraging. So, I gathered up my courage and leaned forward. "I don't mind seeing her," I said. "I am also really glad I came to see you. Before you get her to come down—can you tell me how you are? Really?"

"Ugh," he said with a faint huff of disgust. "You want to discuss my health."

"To be fair, Eugene," Hank said, lifting his glass. "You look pretty damn good compared to the last time we saw you." Well, that was one way to cut right to the heart of the matter.

"Yes," he said with a sigh. "I had a bit of a heart issue." He raised a gnarled hand when my smile faded. "Don't you start. The heart issue wasn't the heart attack I'd had before. This was more of a bad valve. They replaced it. My ticker's a lot stronger now. That was apparently the source of all the problems."

"Why didn't you tell me?"

"Well, at first it was. I didn't think it was all that serious. Then the surgery was done, and I was getting better, so why worry you?" Then he lifted his hands. "And ultimately, we caused you a lot of pain, Frankie. I didn't want to be the source of any more. You made your feelings clear at her funeral, and you were right. Patience took it hard, you know, Maddy's death. Had a bit of a breakdown. It was good for her, I think. She's healing—slowly. We both are. It's a process…"

Those were some very familiar words.

"So, each day, we do a little more. She works out here with her flowers. I do my crossword puzzles. We walk. We talk. We spend time together. Losing Ted was a blow, especially coming only a few months after Maddy."

They hadn't come to the funeral, though, and I thought that might be out of respect for Eddie. Or maybe just to not cause him any more grief.

Or had that been when he'd had his surgery.

Archie was right, I would have regretted not seeing them. "I'm glad to hear that. I want to hear it all, and I have a lot to tell you too." I glanced at Hank and there it was, that steady encouragement. "Maybe we should invite Patience down now."

"Oh, hell no," Eugene said. "This is my hour. I'm going to enjoy it. I never get to know things before she does."

I burst out laughing and he grinned.

"Well," I said, blowing out a breath. "In that case…"

We were going to be there for a while, but I was looking forward to it.

Finally.

Chapter Fourteen
WONDERFUL WORLD

JAKE

I was going over the preflight, headset on, and my attention almost wholly focused on the controls in front of me. In the seat next to me, Frankie watched patiently with her fingers linked together. Amusement flickered in the curve of her smile. The sweet scent of her shampoo wreathed us in the comfortable confines of the cockpit.

The fact that I'd helped her with washing her hair before we'd driven to the airfield danced in the back of my mind. Waking up to Frankie, showering with her, laughing over breakfast, or just sitting with her feet propped in my lap while she read on her phone, and I worked on designs—living with Frankie was the best.

Done, I checked with the tower to get clearance to taxi to a runway. They sent me to the third runway, the farthest from where the plane would hangar, but it would be fun to drive there. "Ready?"

The nerves were real. Not for the flight. I could handle the plane. I'd done a half-dozen solo flights before I'd even considered bringing her up with me. Then waited out the winter for the best conditions. Finishing the last of our finals made this an ideal time to "celebrate."

"Always," she said in a tone so indulgent. I leaned over and kissed her soundly before I got us in motion. She laughed, caressing my cheek before I pulled back. "What was that for?"

"Do I need a reason to kiss the most beautiful girl in the world?"

Frankie's laughter deepened and she shook her head. "But I was asking about why you gave me one…"

"You're lucky I have to fly, Baby Girl."

"I am lucky," she agreed. She linked her fingers again and stared out the window ahead, though the weight of her gaze seemed to return to me again and again. "Not just because you *have* to fly."

Yep. I was a sap. But I was a happy sap, and the rest of the world could kiss my ass if they didn't get it. Once we reached the assigned runway, I radioed the tower for clearance. The smaller airport meant we didn't have to wait long.

Frankie let out a little whoop when I glanced over at her.

"Seatbelt on?"

"Aye aye, Captain." Her teasing grin quieted my own nerves. "Take me up into the sky, Jake."

The hint of wildness in her grin took me back to that jump the previous summer. Skydiving turned out to be something she loved. We'd done it a couple of more times. We planned to do it more over the summer, as time permitted. But today? Today we weren't jumping out of the plane.

Mental fingers crossed, I let the tower know I was taking off and waited for their acknowledgment before I accelerated. This was the moment that always sent my blood pounding and my pulse racing. Acceleration plus lift, then we were airborne. The loud rumble of the wheels speeding over the tarmac fell away and I kept the throttle and yoke steady with one eye on the controls and the rest of my focus on the air in front of us.

I didn't want too steep a climb, but I did want to get us to our cruising altitude as we angled up and away from the small Long Island airport where I'd been learning to fly for the past couple of years.

Frankie let out another whoop and I laughed. She came through clearly on the headset, even if it did add a bit of mechanical click to it. "Like that, do you?"

"Yes," she said, the grin echoing in her words. "This is better than a rollercoaster."

"You don't like rollercoasters."

Her laughter washed over me. "Well, I love you. So this trip was already well and above any of them."

I groaned. "You talk to Hank too much. Now you're delivering the dad jokes." But I was grinning. Cause as dad jokes went, it was awfully funny. As we began to level out, I glanced over to find her grinning wildly as she looked out the windows. "How are you doing, Baby Girl?"

"This is—amazing. I mean, I still remember my very first plane ride. This is so much better—noisier, but better."

I chuckled. "That's why we have the headphones on. So we don't have to yell."

"How do you come down from this? I mean, you've been doing this for a while, and I know exactly how thrilled you are, but this is—"

"I know," I told her. "I keep wondering why I waited so long to learn. Then I remember, you know—money for lessons and being old enough. At the same time, I can't imagine going back to when I couldn't do this."

"Do you have to get more flight hours to qualify to fly the private planes?"

I snorted. "Different jet classification and yes. But I'll get there eventually. The whole point of learning is to not only test engines in real life but to have a feel for what I know they can do."

"You won't take an engine up that you don't know is safe, right?"

"Don't worry, Baby Girl. We have a whole list of things to go through before we do anything live and in the field."

Her lips compressed and her knuckles whitened for a moment.

"I promise," I told her. "We're a long way off from that kind of testing. Right now, it's all about the learning, studying, and applying what I know to what I understand."

"Thank you. I just love you guys so much…"

"Right back atcha, Baby Girl. Right back atcha. Okay—what do you want to see? Coast? Mountains?"

"Freshtown," she said and I grinned.

"Freshtown, it is." I adjusted our flight path and radioed in the changes to take us northeast. It might be almost two hours by car from the city, but it wasn't that far considering the flight.

"Can you believe we're about to graduate?"

"Can you believe Coop is willingly going to keep going to school without you?" I countered. I was ready to graduate. Beyond ready. Arch and I had both discussed possible master's studies, but if we did it, that would be down the road. What we wanted to do now was far more practical in application. Theory was great, but we had enough work and enough plans to keep us busy for a while.

"Oh, now I kind of feel sad that he will," she murmured and I chuckled.

"Don't you dare think you need to enroll in a graduate program just because Coop is. One, he'd be appalled, and we all know exactly how hard you've worked. Two, you're planning two careers already, you do not need a third." I sucked in a deep breath and fisted my temper. Why was I yelling at her? Was I yelling? No. I just… "Three? I want you to enjoy your success and meet the challenges you've already set for yourself, meet and enjoy them, without piling more on. Please."

I tacked that last word on because she really didn't need to be yelled at. If Frankie decided she needed a damn doctorate, we'd back her up and find a way to make it work.

"I know, I'm an overachiever—it just—it hit me that you were right. Coop and I have been going to school together since kindergarten, and suddenly he'll be going to go to classes and I won't. *But…*" She layered emphasis on that word. "I'm not just going to go sign up willy-nilly to take a class because he is. Though—I might make you do one of those online history courses with me for fun."

She tweaked me and I deserved it. "We can do that," I agreed. "Sorry, Baby Girl. I worry."

"I know," she said, casting another smile my way before looking back at the landscape below. "It's hard not to worry about each other. That's what we do."

Agreed. "Still feeling good about inviting Eugene and Patience to graduation?"

"Eh…Eugene yes. Patience—maybe. Eugene's—he's so different now. It's like this huge weight is off of him, and I don't know what I expected when Dad and I went to see him, but…" She spread her hands. "He just seems happier. Patience, too, for that matter. The last time I saw them at the funeral, Patience especially, she was so angry and hurting and lashing out. Not this time, though. I figured this would be a test run for whether I invited them to the wedding."

That seemed reasonable. "Cause of Eddie?"

"And Archie—and you guys and me. I don't want people at our wedding who are going to be throwing vitriol or anger. I had enough of that from Maddy. She's dead and buried. I'd like to leave her there."

The element of pain that crept into her voice would never not make me want to deliver a beat down to every single person who made her feel that way. But you couldn't beat the shit out of a ghost. "No one is going to mess up that day. Not for you. Not for us. I mean, I'm starting to get why Archie keeps leaning toward elopement. Maybe we should consider it."

What did we need, really? But the five of us? Based on what Dominic said, we could sign some papers and file them. Then we'd have all the legal rights we needed and tax protections. Though that was a little strange to think about—the kind of money Archie and Frankie had… the kind of money they would continue to earn, along with Bubba and hopefully me and Coop? Yeah, we had some tax considerations.

"No," Frankie said, her voice soft but firm. "I want to shout it from the rooftops. I want to have pictures and memories from that day. I want to look back on anniversaries and tell goofy stories about how we tried to feed each other cake, and you smooshed Coop's face in it and then got Archie and we nearly had a food fight."

"That's oddly specific."

"Tell me it won't go down just like that." The dare in her voice made me laugh. "The point is, I want it for us and for me. I want to stand up there and tell everyone we love and everyone who loves us that we're committed to this relationship. That we're a family. That we're where we want to be."

"Fuck, I love you," I told her. "And if that's what you want, Baby Girl, then we'll shout it from the damn rooftops. I'll tattoo it on my dick if you want."

Her snort echoed over the mic. "You'd tattoo your dick when you won't pierce it?"

"Piercing isn't sounding as bad as it used to. But yeah, I'd tattoo it if that was what you needed. Though it doesn't really declare it to the world, not that I'm opposed to strutting out there in the buff."

She pressed her hands to her mouth, laughing. "Oh my god, I want to say yes just to see if you'd do it, but I don't know how long your dick would need to heal afterward and the wedding is in two months."

"Two months—might be cutting it close." I winked at her when she shot me another one of those gorgeous grins. "We're almost there."

She leaned forward. From this height, we wouldn't get a lot of detail, but we could see the roof through the trees and where it parted around the open field and rose gardens—an outdoor wedding in June.

Man, it better not rain. Then again…

Frankie would probably just laugh and we could dance in it.

"I love this," she said. The words were softer but still carried over the mic. "I love that we're going to get married there."

"You and Bubba, both said it was gorgeous, and that was before we drove up to see it."

"We had a wonderful weekend there, never did get to go back, and I still can't believe Archie rented out the whole place."

"Oh, yes, you can," I countered. "It's Archie."

"Yeah, it is. Plenty of room for family, friends, and then all ours before we go to…"

"Go where?" I teased. The wedding location was Frankie's choice. The honeymoon was ours.

"Not even a hint or a clue?"

"Nope. You won't get it out of me, so don't try to charm me with your beauty or sweetness. The honeymoon is planned. We'll go. We'll have an amazing time kicking off the rest of our lives together. Before you bring up packing, we've got that covered. Not that you need to be dressed at all."

"Yes, I'm sure you and the guys will have no problems with me getting on or off a plane completely nude." Dry and sarcastic, just how I liked my baby girl.

"Well, you can fly in my plane nude anytime you want. Like I said, nothing to worry about."

Despite her protests here and there, she really hadn't poked at us about where we were going. No, we'd discussed everything from the menu, which Jeremy was in charge, to the kind of cake to how formal we wanted to be and if we were writing our own vows. From the music to the ceremony to the wording we wanted the officiator to use—that had all been a joint effort.

"Do you think Sara is going to get you guys "Brother Husband" shirts next?" The question pulled me right back to the present, and I laughed as she grinned. "And would you wear them?"

"Hell yes, I'd wear it. Brother Husbands sounds pretty damn good, my soon-to-be wife."

No lie. That sounded even better.

Chapter Fifteen

100 YEARS

FRANKIE

Commencement took place at Yankee Stadium. The guys were stoked. NYU's colors? Purple. Talk about a high school flashback. The caps and gowns were gorgeous. I was half-tempted to go hunting for our caps and gowns from high school, but I literally had no idea where they were.

The morning of, we got ready. Coop wore a t-shirt and shorts under his gown. Ian went for a nice shirt and jeans. Archie debated a suit and tie, then just went for casual with a polo and slacks. Jake had to change his shirt twice because each time he came down, Jeremy found something wrong with it.

I got ready on a video call with Rachel. She wasn't coming. I hated that she wouldn't be here, but she promised that if she ever walked—I'd get the invitation.

"Love you," I said as we hung up and she blew me a kiss.

"Love you, too. Knock 'em dead."

As tempting as it was to give her hell if she missed my wedding, I wouldn't. She was finding herself. Finding her life and her choices. The last several months in Paris had been good for her. And she had helped me find the perfect wedding dress. It was long before I went to Paris, but the guys hadn't—and wouldn't—see it until our wedding day.

She even found me the perfect shoes. They were to be my something new.

"Frankie," Coop bellowed from downstairs. "Let's go, some of us aren't born naturally beautiful and we're ready."

"Bite me," I called back cheerfully before grabbing my cap and heading for the stairs.

"Bare it—"

"If you finish that statement, Mr. Cooper, you and I will be having a very long discussion about decorum that will not entertain Mr. Jake nearly as much as he thinks it will."

I grinned when I got to the last step. "Aww, Jeremy. Cut him some slack. He's getting up there in years. You know he's the second oldest and all that. All those finals really wracked his brains."

Coop's not-so-surreptitious middle finger toward me from behind Jeremy's back made me grin. I winked at him and he chuckled.

"At least one of you knows how to dress appropriately for the occasion." He sounded and looked quite stern. A feature of his personality when he was stressed. This was a big day for him too.

Pausing to press a kiss to his cheek, I said, "It's a big day, Jeremy. You look great. Will you take pictures with us later?"

I was only in a dress because Kelly warned me that Hank would want a thousand pictures, and the sundress was actually a perfect match for our robes. I wore sandals instead of heels, and I had on my charm bracelet, my necklace, and my rings—all of them from the engagement rings to the Larimar ring Coop got me in Martinique to the class ring Jake presented me during Christmas in our senior year.

"I would very much enjoy that, Miss Frankie," Jeremy said, then nodded. "The car will be here in five minutes. Miss Abigail, come." He led the lab back to her crate, which was in his room. I was glad he was coming with us. I kind of wished Miss Abigail could come.

"You handle him really well," Archie said in a mock stage whisper as he slid up next to me and pressed a kiss to the corner of my mouth. I appreciated the care, I'd just gotten the gloss on, but I had more if I needed to reapply it.

"Did you talk to Rachel?" Ian asked, his deep blue eyes knowing.

"Yeah, I knew she wasn't coming. I guess a part of me hoped that there would be this last-minute change of plans. And," I continued holding a hand up to Coop. "Before you ask, I didn't check to see if she would make the wedding. If she's here, she's the maid of honor—if she can't make it, well, I'll have a host of bridesmaids."

Because I really couldn't see anyone else in that position.

"It's going to be fine, Beautiful," Coop soothed, some of the playfulness draining away. Fingers linked with mine, he tugged me to him and dipped his head to kiss me. Still light, good boy.

"I think we look pretty good," Jake commented. "If I do say so myself."

"Picture," Archie ordered, and we huddled together with Jake holding his phone up and away from us. It was a selfie, but it was adorable.

"Shall I take a few before we go?" Jeremy's absolute dry tone was a thing of legend. He took a few of us with my phone. I got a few with him and Arch. All of which we would share to our cloud drive.

"Selfie with us, Jeremy? We'll do a proper photo later, I promise. But you're an honorary grad here. We would not have gotten through the last four years without you."

"True," Archie agreed. "We'd have had to live on a diet of takeout, soda, and beer."

Ian laughed. "Frankie would have objected to that much beer. Especially between Jake and Coop."

Oh, there was a story we did not need to re-live like ever. However, I did need to buy a new lace bra at some point. I filed that away for now. "Hush, before we scare Jeremy off."

Thankfully, he chuckled and we huddled again, this time with Ian and Jake framing us. They both took shots with their phones so we could go with the best angle.

"All right," Archie said, clapping his hands. "Caps, everyone, it's time to go and gradumacate."

Jeremy's mood must have buoyed because he didn't even call Archie on the mispronunciation. Or maybe he was just so used to us that he was letting it go. We were still laughing when the car arrived. Jeremy intended to take a separate car, but nope, we insisted he ride with us.

While he conceded, he took the front passenger seat instead of the back. Probably safer, because we cranked up the music and sang all the way there. It was ridiculous, fun, and so relaxed. The drive on the buses to graduation for high school had been so—fraught and stressful.

This just wasn't.

"Hey," Coop murmured, bumping my foot with his. "What are you thinking about?"

"Just—this is kind of anticlimactic in some ways. This is what we've been working toward for the last four years, and at the same time—it's like just a check on the list to the rest of our lives."

"Profound," Archie offered, threading his fingers with mine. "Disappointed?"

"Not even a little bit. I've loved my classes, even the ones that made me crazy. I've loved living with you guys and building our lives together." I caught Ian's eyes and grinned. "I loved recording our first album and now getting ready to really record our second. It's been—a life. I love my life. I love that we have done all of this together, and we're going to keep on doing this together."

"Couldn't imagine my life without all of you," Jake confessed.

"Oh, Hell, you're gonna get sappy on us." Coop pressed a hand to his chest. "I'm the one emotionally in touch with myself. You're supposed to be the hot-headed jock."

"Who can still kick your ass," Jake said drily, though the corners of his mouth twitched.

"Thankfully," Ian said, raising his voice a little. "We don't have to worry about any of that, because we're all stuck with each other."

"Forever," Archie elongated the word as he tacked it on, wicked grin firmly in place.

"That makes me happy." Great, now *I* was getting emotional. I blinked my eyes rapidly. "If you guys make me cry, you're going to have to help me with my makeup."

Ian pressed a kiss to my temple and Archie squeezed my hand. Coop and Jake each kept a foot pressed to mine. "Crank up the music, Jake," Ian said. "No tears today."

Oh, there would probably be tears today. There were going to be many moms in attendance. Moms. Dads. Siblings. Grandparents. Jeremy. It wasn't long before we were in a queue of cars moving through the parking lots. Jeremy wouldn't be sitting with us, but we left him where he could join Eddie and the others as they came in.

Honestly, we hadn't coordinated seats for them. I wasn't sure I wanted Eddie to have to deal with my grandparents today, but Dad promised he'd run interference if necessary. Out in that sea of people, they were all arriving.

Nineteen thousand students would be graduating. That was the number, which was why we were having it at Yankee Stadium. "You know," I said. "We really need to come back here for a baseball game."

"Yes," Jake said solemnly. "That's exactly what we need to do."

I grinned. "Who am I, and what have I done with your Frankie?"

"Wasn't going to ask," he said. "Just gonna take you out to sports."

Once we got there, though, it was a sea of students. While the all-school commencement was open to everyone who qualified to graduate, we didn't have to walk. Representatives of our various colleges would be chosen to accept on behalf of our class. It also meant we could sit together, which I was rather fond of.

This was so different from high school.

Not sure I'd label it as better, but I was excited. Course, as we made our way to our seats, I was stunned by just how packed this place was. Nineteen thousand students and a whole lot of family.

With the sun shining down and a strong breeze—thankfully—we made our way to our seats, our caps firmly in place. You couldn't tell what any of us were wearing beneath the gowns. I was still glad I opted for sandals. The pre-show included a video with interviews from various graduating students and a listing of accomplishments.

When Ian's face popped up on the jumbotron, I blinked. He was talking about Bound Hearts, and they even featured a clip from one of our shows. I swung wide eyes at him and he gave me a little shrug and a grin. "I didn't know if they would use it."

Archie popped up in another clip with Jake, but it was just a snapshot of a presentation they'd done. Another clip of Coop was featured in the montage, with him coming out of the community center he'd been working at for the last year. When my face popped up, I did another double-take. But it was of Rachel and I both standing not far from the doors to her dorm. That had to have been that first year we were here.

Did I look like a baby, or was that just me?

By the time they did the parade of the faculty and our honorary guest speaker came out, I was ready to be done. Except the former first lady of the United States was up there, discussing the value not just of education but application. I found myself leaning forward as she talked about the role education had played in her life. How each signpost along the road to the future was a chance to further ourselves.

Goals, like life, could be ever-changing and fluid. One thing she had learned, the one item she had taken with her from elementary to high school to college to graduate school and beyond—every single day was an opportunity. You didn't have to be in school to strive to learn more. You didn't have to be enrolled to always be a student.

Life was for living, learning, and growing. Look around you, she instructed. Look at the people sitting next to you. The people in front of you. The people behind you. These were the people who were on the same journey as you. Sometimes those paths intertwined, sometimes they diverted, but we could always learn from each other. That the best education came from living our lives to the best of our capabilities.

The words resonated with me. Mainly because my path was thoroughly and utterly intertwined with my four best friends. I swore there must be pollen in the air or something because my eyes got watery, but when she finally congratulated us and encouraged us to keep growing, no matter where life took us, the tears really did fall.

"Five bucks," Coop said as he kissed the side of my head and his hand found mine. I laughed through my tears cause Archie just shook his head and promised to pay him later. I didn't even care what the bet was about.

Two hours after the ceremony began, we were officially graduates.

While they didn't want us throwing our hats in the air, we did it anyway to the roar of the guests and families who cheered us on. It was freeing. Coop swung me around in a hug before passing me over to

Archie, then Jake, and finally Ian. When we pulled together in a hug—all of us—I had to blink back more tears. It was crazy and the best.

Course, nothing prepared me for the afterparty. Everyone had come, including Patience and Eugene. I broke away from the guys to see them. Eugene beamed, his eyes shining as he gave me a hug, and Patience murmured her congratulations in a worried voice, and it wasn't until I recognized the wariness in her eyes that I realized she expected to be rejected.

Regret was a horrible, bitter medicine that curdled in the stomach. I didn't want any more regrets. I didn't want any more pain. We'd all had enough of that. So, I hugged her and she froze briefly then, with a slight hesitation I understood, and she returned the hug.

"Thank you," I said, when I pulled back a little, glancing from one to the other. "For coming, for wanting to be here—for trying."

"Thank you for having us, young lady. I told Leslie we'd have the prettiest granddaughter out there. I was right, wasn't I?" He motioned to Leslie, who was standing not far behind them.

"I didn't even see you, I'm sorry."

"Don't worry about it, hon. Let your grandfather brag. It's what Eugene likes to do. And he's right, you're very lovely."

"Mr. Grayson," Eddie said from behind me and I went still. "Mrs. Grayson."

"Dad," Archie said in a quiet voice and I swore my heart fisted. Would they be able to handle it?

"Edward," Eugene said as he glanced past me. Then with a gentle, if awkward, pat on my shoulder, he stepped around me and held out his hand.

I caught Patience's compressed lips and frozen expression, then turned to meet Archie's gaze. He was as worried about this as I was. Even with all the people moving around us, I didn't really register those sounds.

"It's good to see you," Eugene was saying and I honed in on that. "I wanted to give you my condolences about Ted, and we," he continued, with a glance back at Patience before focusing on Eddie again, "wanted to apologize for our last meeting."

"I appreciate that, and no apologies are necessary," Eddie told him, and like Eugene, he also glanced at Patience. "Feelings and tempers were all running high, and I understood then like I understand now. I just—I wanted to tell you how proud of Frankie we all are. You have an exceptional granddaughter."

"Yes," Patience said, seeming to find her voice. "She is wonderful and… we understand that you have been looking out for her." I was holding my breath as Patience gave me a small smile. "I know you avoided bringing him up while you were there, but your father mentioned it to us when we talked to him about coming today."

Oh boy.

I hadn't realized that.

Eugene nodded. "He's very proud of you too. We all are." Then he focused on Eddie again. "I heard you offered her a job."

"I have," Eddie said, the corner of his mouth quirking. "She's kept me on the hook for a bit, insisting that she needed to graduate before she took any permanent steps going forward. I think that's a well-reasoned and thought-out plan. I've enjoyed mentoring her and Archie."

What. The. Fuck. Was. Happening. Right. Now.

From the look on Archie's face, he didn't know either.

"We're terrifying the children," Patience said abruptly and then turned to me. "Edward came up to see us last month when we called him. He didn't have to after how I behaved, but he did. We had a long conversation—all three of us. Our issues with each other were never supposed to be your burden to carry. I'm sorry for any part that I played.

Part of apologizing in front of you is so that you could see we are making an attempt—genuinely"

Eugene let out a gentle huff. "We are sorry, and yes, we did talk to Edward. We want to be a part of your life. How ever way you'll have us, and Henry—Hank, sorry. He was very clear that you and Archie, as well as those other young men are very much a fact. Which meant we had to get on board or get out of the way."

"We're a little behind," Patience continued. "But we'd like to get on board. If you'll let us."

That was when the real tears came and when I hugged Patience this time, she returned the grip with a fierceness she'd never shown before.

"I'm so sorry," she whispered against my ear. "For all of it. I know we can't start over from the beginning, but maybe we can just go from here?"

"I'd like that," I admitted. "I really would." Then Eugene gave me a hug and I tried to wipe away the tears without making a mess. Hank handed me a handkerchief a split-second ahead of Eddie and I laughed at them.

"I don't know whether to scold you or hug you."

"You can do both," Hank promised me, and I threw my arms around him for a hug. The guys were there, I caught them checking on me and when I cast them watery smiles, they answered with chin lifts, nods, and knowing grins. "I'd do anything for you," Hank said as he pulled back. "This was something I could do. I could say the things they needed to hear and that you needed them to hear. You deserve everything. Won't always be easy, but if I can go to bat for you, be damn sure I will."

This was what it was like to have a family. It took forever to sort us all out for photos until Bill and Klara took over. With military precision, they got us sorted out and then we took photos with each family. With us. As a group. With individuals. Until Chloe announced she was going to die of hunger if we had to take one more photo.

Honestly, same little sister. Though Eugene and Patience were tired, so they begged off from a huge meal to go to their hotel. But I promised to visit with them the next day and have lunch before they headed back to Connecticut.

Eddie waited with us while I got them into a car, and after I waved them off, I turned to look at the guys. We'd talked about this—all of us. I just hadn't formally informed Eddie. So, since this was a day for emotions and new starts, I said, "if you can wait for me until after July— I'd like to accept that job. Officially."

"Yes." Eddie mimed a fist pump and I raised my eyebrows.

"Dad," Archie deadpanned. "Please don't do that again."

Laughter and tears. It really was a perfect day.

Chapter Sixteen

OUR GIRL

COOP

"**W**hy are we wearing waistcoats again?" They were more Archie's thing. I was not a suit guy.

"Archie won the bet," Jake said as he came out of the bathroom wiping his hands. "You got that?" His was on, and all he needed was his jacket. Even his tie was straight.

"I did not win a bet," Archie corrected from where he stood in front of the mirror in the suite, fixing his tie. "These worked out the best with the dove gray suits."

"Dove gray," Bubba chuckled as he walked out of the other bedroom. "You'd think it would have a different name." Like Jake, he was all ready except for his jacket

We'd gone with our own colors for the waistcoats and ties. Red for Archie. Purple for Jake. Green for me. Dark blue for Bubba. Everything else we had on would match, from the gray slacks to the dress coats to the white shirts underneath.

Archie's dad had gotten us all watches. Weird present, but whatever. They were expensive watches and they matched. Okay, not weird. It was actually thoughtful of Eddie. Just unexpected.

"Why would it have a different name?" Archie asked. "The gray is a softer color, but it's an outdoor wedding in the morning. Besides, Frankie liked it."

Which pretty much summed up any tiebreaker ever. I fixed my tie and then glanced at Jake. "Is it straight?"

"Yep." He cocked his head to the side and then reached over to fix part of the knot. "Now it is."

"How are we doing on time?" Archie asked.

"We're good." Jake glanced at his watch. "Dominic is supposed to be here by now, though. Right?"

"He texted," Bubba said as he picked up his guitar case and set it on the coffee table. "He was going by Frankie's suite first to drop off a gift, then coming up here."

"What the fuck kind of gift did he get Frankie?" Archie's entire demeanor shifted and I chuckled, which yanked his attention to me. "Why are you laughing about it?"

"Cause we're not in school and we don't have to chase the other boys off. Trust that she wants us and nothing he has to offer or is bringing her has anything to do with stealing her."

Jake snorted. "I haven't had a good fight in a while."

"If you get into one today, you are explaining it to her." I patted his shoulder as Bubba just shook his head. Before the argument could go anywhere else, there was a knock at the door. "Oh look, someone's here."

Archie got the door first and he yanked it open. Dominic Walsh, dressed in a light-colored suit, said, "I come in peace and bearing gifts."

"How's Frankie doing?" I asked before he could incite Archie or

Jake. I swore the guy really did like to wave a red flag at the bull that was them.

"She seemed good." A smile crossed his face. "She also signed everything, so—I'm here to collect your signatures, gentlemen, then I'll take care of all the final filings."

"Hmm." Archie stepped to the side and let him in. We all moved to the chairs and the pair of sofas that framed the conversation area of the suite's sitting room. "You didn't have any trouble with the LLC requests?"

"Nope. That's taken care of, which means all tax considerations will be folded under that umbrella. It also means any new contracts for Bound Hearts or the division of Standish-Benton Engineering will have to be folded under that heading as well. Essentially, each of you will be a signing agent for the LLC."

"In English?" I asked. Frankie had been a part of the language on the contracts, and I absolutely trusted her judgment, but I still wanted to at least distill it down to something that made sense to the individual.

"Base facts," Dominic said as he set out five folders. One for each of us. "The Standish-Jackson Family LLC pools all of your financial holdings under the LLC, for which each of you is a full partner and has signing rights. All joint property will be transferred into the LLC, meaning you are all equal title holders to each piece of property established under it."

"It also provides a tax shelter for our assets and income."

"Exactly," Dominic said. "That's the first three pages. The next three are the domestic partnership agreements tying all five of you together in a domestic partnership under Freshtown statutes. This will extend all co-parenting to each of you in the event of offspring. Then we have the medical power of attorneys, granting each of you full rights to make medical calls and to visit in the hospital."

Offspring. I snorted. What a way to phrase it. I picked up my folder and flipped through each page. Each page had little sticky notes color-coded for where we had to sign and initial.

"The last set of pages are the legal name changes you requested. Once everything else is filed, I will submit these. It will probably take six to ten weeks before you will get everything back, at which time you can then update your licenses and passports."

Amongst all the stuff at the end was also another sheet, this was a—

"Holy shit, Arch," Jake said. "Are you sure about this?"

JAKE

"I told you I was when I told you about the prenup. This just finalizes it. A joint account that we all have access to and full signing rights on. Frankie moved her funds last week when I did. You guys can drop in yours when you want or not, we will all still have our own bank accounts too, but this will be where we pull for anything joint—like homes, vehicles, vacations…"

Fuck, that was a lot of zeroes. But Archie had been very clear that he was all in. *We* were all in. Since Frankie's signature graced every single page, I added mine. We traded folders as we each signed our way through them.

"And that," Dominic said after he checked them, "is that. Congratulations."

Since he offered his hand, I was the first to shake it. Then Coop, Bubba, and finally Archie. "You are staying for the wedding, right?" I didn't really like the guy, but he had come through and his research had settled some issues Frankie had that I hadn't even thought or worried about.

"That's the plan."

I nodded. "Then we'll see you down there."

Once he was gone, I looked at the guys. "Well, Mr. Standish," I said to Archie. "You still sure about this?"

"Mr. Standish-Benton, I absolutely am." He grinned. "Along with Mr. Standish-Brennen, and Mr. Standish-Rhys."

Yeah, that was weird.

Course, weird had become our brand.

Archie was at the bar and pouring champagne into the glasses. "One each and not a drop more until the party this afternoon. But I thought we owed it to ourselves to celebrate making this shit work."

I couldn't really say he was wrong. After he handed out the glasses, he raised his and said, "To the last five years and to the three years before that. I can't imagine a better group of brother boyfriends, fiancés, or husbands."

Bubba chuckled. "To a friendship that lets us fuckup but never lets us get away with it and which we can always count on to have our backs and kick us in the ass—at the same time if necessary."

I thought it would be a strain to come up with the words, but no, they were right there. "I told you guys five years ago that I was in. That if she wanted all of us, I was fine with it. I was fine with it being *us*. We've had our moments." I met Archie's gaze. "We've had our challenges. I don't doubt we won't have them in the future, but if I'm going to have any team at my back, you guys are the ones I want."

That left Coop. "And you call me the sap. To Frankie, because she's the glue that brought us together and for whom we will do anything."

Our glasses clinked as we toasted. Then drank. If I were going to get emotional with anyone, it would be these assholes.

"How we doing on time?" Archie asked and Bubba glanced at his watch again.

"Thirty minutes."

Fuck. My stomach dropped. It was like I'd gone too steep a climb and we needed to level out.

"Nervous?" Coop asked.

"Yes," I admitted. "And no. It's like the feeling I get right before a big game."

"Nerves," Bubba said. "A little stage fright thrown in. Only, this is a hell of a lot more important than a game."

Yes, it was. "You guys got your vows?" I'd been having trouble with mine.

"Right here," Archie said, tapping his head. Coop and Bubba both nodded, and I made as if to pat my jacket pocket where there was no slip of paper with the vows on it that I hadn't written yet.

The champagne helped. Some. But that jittery feeling increased. I moved away from them to glance out the windows. The old inn was a real find. Apparently, Bubba had stolen away with Frankie up here for his birthday that first summer after we moved into the brownstone.

Good place.

The rose garden and the gazebo were perfect. The sun shone, the sky was a perfect shade of blue, and there was barely even a cirrus cloud to break it up.

"Are we still planning on the wedding night here? Or did we want to head to the airport early?"

That had been the only item we'd gone back and forth on. Archie had voted to go early, and we could do the wedding night on the plane. Bubba voted here because we had no idea how late the reception would run, but I didn't think anyone would begrudge us disappearing early.

Coop abstained entirely. As long as the wedding night was with Frankie, he didn't much care where we spent it. Honestly, I didn't disagree, but...

"You want to get out of here," Bubba said, looking at me, and I shrugged.

"It's not that I don't like the place. I do—I think we should make a point of coming back here again, but not with every single member of our rather extensive familial networks, complete with nosy sisters and pushy younger brothers. Not to mention the whole dad bromance thing is getting kind of weird."

"Kind of?" Coop said with a grin. "I think it's hilarious that your dads and their dads are all getting along. Just leave mine out of it. I heard them all betting on grandparent names last night before I came up."

Grandparent names?"

"For real?" Bubba said with a groan and then scrubbed a hand over his face.

Yeah, I was with him on that.

"Oh, Eddie was pretty confident he would get his pick of the name *after* Hank. Apparently, Hank is definitely in pole position." The exasperated amusement made me laugh, but Archie just shook his head.

"Look, as long as they harass each other and not us," he suggested. "Let them do it. Kids are at least three or four years away."

"You know," I told him. "That doesn't seem as long as it sounds like." Honestly, she was going to be so damn beautiful. I kind of couldn't wait for that part. To see her get all big-breasted and swollen abdomen. Not that she didn't have the prettiest titties, but pregnancy was supposed to make them bigger.

"You're totally picturing her pregnant right now," Coop said, amusement in his eyes and his voice. "Aren't you?"

"Yeah," I admitted. Couldn't help it. The image snuck in every now and then. Had for over a year. I was content to wait, but when it was time?

Hell. Yes.

IAN

Picturing her pregnant? Had I? I could admit to that. I let Coop rib Jake while I went to get water. We had another fifteen minutes, and then we'd head down. Asking the dads to give us the morning had been a solid plan. At the hour mark, we split up to head out to see our respective families.

The photographer would be doing candids throughout the ceremony. We'd skipped all posed photographs except for the wedding shot itself—that one we wanted to keep. Jake and I found our dads downstairs having a drink. Klara, Alicia, and my mother were nowhere to be found.

"Please tell me that all the women didn't descend on Frankie," I said, and Dad chuckled at me.

"Don't worry, they had breakfast with her early on before it was time to get dressed, and right after that, they were all hustled out. I think the only one still up there was Hank—" Dad paused. "Nope. He's not there, he is now with Kelly."

I turned to see Frankie's dad and stepmom coming into the lounge with their boys. Hank gave us a wave and nodded to Dad.

"Come on," Dad said, giving me a firm shoulder pat. "Let's take a walk."

"We're due to start in thirty-five minutes." It was just a warning.

"Don't worry, I won't let you be late for your wedding."

I wasn't worried. Nothing was allowed to mess up this day. Coop was coming down the stairs with his mother and sister. Archie was near the main doors with Eddie and a guy I didn't recognize. Leaving them to their conversations, Dad and I headed out to a wide, shaded veranda.

The air coming from the mountains was blowing in cool. It was the perfect kind of breeze for the sunny warmth of the morning.

"How you doing?" Dad asked as we walked.

"I'm good." Better than good, really. "This feels like a big deal and nothing at all."

"Good."

I blinked and glanced at him. "Good?"

"That's how it should feel. Panic is somewhat normal. It's the question of are you doing the right thing? But this relationship is one you've been committed to for a long time."

This was true. "I had my moments." I could admit that. "When we went to Dallas and had the conversation, I began to second guess everything."

Shouldn't have done that. Or maybe I needed to in order to get out of my own way so we could be here.

Together.

"The truth is, each time we've run into a challenge, they're all the ones I lean on, and in turn, they lean on us. It works. I like that we can surround Frankie and protect her." Then I grinned. "I like that she protects and looks after us. She pushes us to be better at tackling challenges we might not have otherwise. It's good."

"I'm really glad to hear that," he said. "Now, I have a bit of wisdom for you."

"Yes, sir?" I kind of knew this was coming. It was one of the rights of passage. At least none of the parents had gotten on us about being too young to get married or settling down. That was one thing we'd all done already.

Picked each other. Moved in with each other. Worked and shaped our lives around each other.

Getting married was all about setting the table for the future and making sure everyone, ourselves included, understood the seriousness of our commitment.

The big reason to get married? We wanted it. We wanted her.

"Your mother and I have been married for close to thirty years. The secret to our success? It's simple. If we disagree or fight, the person it's the most important to, wins."

I raised my brows.

"Sounds strange, I'm sure. But it works. There are some things that are just far more important to Sara than they are to me. Some things are more important to me than to her. So, when it comes down to fighting or just letting the person it's more important to win, we always default to the latter."

Chuckling, I turned that over in my head. In some ways, we already did that. "You told me this before, I think."

"Probably," Dad said, amused. "But it's good advice and worth repeating. Course, how the five of you decide who it's most important to—well, I won't even begin to assume."

Which was even better. "Thanks, Dad."

I wrapped my arms around him for an embrace, and he patted my back. "Always, my boy. Always. Oh, and one last thing…"

Oh boy. "That is?"

"I convinced your mother to not aggravate you for a grandchild until at least your fifth anniversary." He patted my shoulder. "You're welcome."

Laughing, I reached up to fix my tie as guests began to make their way out of the inn and toward the garden.

One glance at my watch was all it took to confirm.

It was time.

ARCHIE

"Archie," Dad said when my watch alarm went off. It was time to get into position. Guests were making their way out. Coop passed with a glance at his watch and I nodded.

"What's up?"

"Just—wanted to say how proud I am of you. All of you, but you especially."

"I keep thinking we're going to hit the point that doesn't feel or sound weird," I admitted. "But thank you. Not just for saying it, but for being supportive. For looking in on her grandparents and making peace with them somehow."

"That was more Hank than me, I accept their right to hate me, but they don't. They really do want to let the past go and they want a chance to have Frankie in their lives. Makes me miss Dad, though."

"I miss him every day." I touched my waistcoat, where the pocket watch rested securely. "Still feels like all I have to do is pick up the phone and call him. But it gets easier. I can almost hear him."

Dad chuckled. "So can I. He'd be giving me a firm look and a wag of his finger. 'That's enough of being maudlin on the sprout's wedding day.'"

Fuck. "Yeah, that definitely sounds like him."

"Well, he would probably give you some kind of sage advice about how a happy wife leads to a happy life. I'm not that sage, so I'm just going to tell you—don't give up. Trust your gut and don't give up."

"I think I can handle that."

"Excellent." Then he pulled out an envelope from his pocket and I groaned.

"Dad…"

"Ah," he said, holding it up. "This isn't a check. However, I did make some purchases for you and Frankie in your names. And a few tidy investments."

"Okay. Then what is it?"

"It's the deed to the house on Long Island. Not a wedding present, since Dad wanted you to have it, but I made sure it was in all your names as promised."

"Thank you," I said as I took it. "I know you were planning to make sure we have it and we're still not using it full time for a while yet. Just—a house to get away and maybe to have the whole family for Thanksgiving again."

Dad grinned. "I'd like that, and there's Jeremy. Time to go."

It definitely was. I put the deed away and grinned at Jeremy. He looked quite good in his dove gray suit. He and Miss Abigail would be standing up with us. We couldn't decide on a better best man than Jeremy for all of us.

Leaving Dad to head outside with the guests, I headed toward Jeremy. "You need to get into position," Jeremy said, checking his watch. "We're definitely moving on time. The bridesmaids are already down here and ready."

I turned to look, but at Jeremy's cluck, I laughed and headed out. The rose garden had five pathways leading to the gazebo in the center. That was where we would be exchanging our vows.

Jeremy and Miss Abigail would make their way to the gazebo after the bridesmaids. Frankie had joked that Jeremy could be her best man too because, in truth, the only other people we would ask were each other.

The music playing shifted to the song that would begin the slow processional for the bridesmaids. It was kind of funny that she only had three. Becca and Louisa had begged off of doing it. Blake, however, was all in, as was Trina.

Chloe was definitely out there. Blake and Trina wore dresses that matched their brother's waistcoats. Chloe had on a deep blue one to match Bubba. But the garter I'd left Frankie with her lingerie was red for mine, so that worked just fine.

We had about a hundred guests. A small wedding, or so we'd been told. But I didn't want a bunch of strangers. Having a few members of the Standish board present was enough. This was our wedding with our friends and family.

Chloe was the first one down the aisle, then Trina, followed by Blake. From where I stood, I had a good view. The music changed. Not quite the wedding march yet, though I had joked we should really change it up, but Frankie liked the standard.

Jeremy started forward, and I grinned. He wasn't alone. Rachel moved alongside him, looking all kinds of elegant. Definitely a sight for sore eyes, and hell yes. Made me wonder if she was the present Dominic had to drop off with Frankie before he came to see us.

Didn't really matter. The important thing was that Rachel was here.

Now the day would be perfect for Frankie.

Chapter Seventeen
BECAUSE YOU LOVED ME

FRANKIE

The knock on the door pulled me out of the calm I'd been trying to gather to myself. I'd been surrounded by mothers, sisters, and friends. Patience had even come in and offered me a bracelet for something old, and even though I had the coin from Hank's mother, I took it for my something borrowed.

That seemed to make her happy. Hair done and cosmetics fixed, I promised to call if I needed help getting ready, but I really just wanted a few minutes to myself.

"Yes?"

"It's Dominic," he called. "I brought you a little something and the papers for you to sign."

Hadn't I already signed them?

Dressed in the robe, I moved to the door and pulled it open. Only it wasn't Dominic standing there but a sight for sore eyes.

"Rach…"

"Hey, babe," she said with a slow grin, and when I threw my arms around her, she hugged me back. "I got this," she was saying over my shoulder. "Go on."

I barely caught Dominic's smile as he winked at me then he was striding away. I all but dragged Rachel into the room with me. "You're here!"

She laughed. "I am! And you're getting married in less than an hour. What do you need?"

I didn't need anything that wasn't here now. "Your dress…"

Then she was pulling off the jacket, and I stared at the pretty gold dress she wore. "Yellow roses," she reminded me. "They're for friendship. I really love the choice."

I loved her too. All at once, I went misty-eyed and Rachel gave me a brusque look. "Nope. No messing up the cosmetics. Come on, let's do this."

Just like that, Rachel took over.

"Do we like your hair like this, or do we want to do something different?"

I laughed. With a question like that—" What do you think?"

"I think I got here just in time."

As it was, she only changed it a little. Loosening it from the updo and pulling it over one shoulder.

"No veil, right?"

"Nope," I said. "And no tiara. The moms were all trying to talk me into one."

"Eh, a tiara isn't enough for a queen. You'd need a crown."

I laughed. "I got you. That's even better."

"Don't you dare make us cry. I need to save this smudge-proof test for when we're in the ceremony."

Soon as my hair was fixed, I pulled off the robe and she gave me a low whistle of appreciation.

"I gotta give it to Rich Boy, his taste in lace is…" She made a chef's kiss. "The red garter is a nice touch."

I turned to show her the four charms on the side of my panties. "I like these." A plane. A guitar. A Greek capital letter for psi. And the gold A from my very first date with Archie.

"Those are adorable. Okay. You can definitely keep Rich Boy." At my expression, she laughed. "I know, you're keeping all of them. But let's get you in that wedding dress. I'm kind of excited to see it for real since I've only seen it on video calls."

I didn't tweak her about it. She'd come all this way for the wedding, and I didn't know if she'd called Dominic or he'd called her. Right now, I wouldn't push.

Selfishly, I was just glad she was here.

The dress was a strapless, bodice-hugging number with little lace roses embroidered or stitched into the bodice. It had just been perfect when I'd seen it. Then, trying it on for the first time felt like a "me" moment.

The skirt was made of several different layers of silk, satin, and tulle. It had lift, kind of like a ballgown but was also light enough for me to raise. As I stepped into it, Rachel helped pull it up until it hugged my bust, then she buttoned up the dozen or so fine buttons on my back.

The bodice itself contained fine boning so it would hug my frame and stay in place. As snug as it was though, it didn't suffocate me. In fact, what I loved about it was the confidence to not worry about a nip slip.

While a fun thought for later, now was *not* the time. I kept a hand pressed against my stomach to keep the butterflies contained because when she finished, she leaned over my shoulder to look.

"You look like a damn fairy tale princess. Where are your shoes?"

I pointed to the bright white sneakers and Rachel laughed.

"I can't even give you a hard time for those," she teased. "Cause they are so you. Come here, Cinderella." In nothing flat, she had my shoes on and laced up.

For jewelry, I kept it simple. A pearl necklace that Eddie had given me from his mother. A pair of pale blue earrings from Kelly, because she wanted something blue. The borrowed bracelet from Patience—also pearls. Must have been a generational thing. The coin was tucked into a small pocket sewn into the bodice of the dress.

"You look amazing."

"So do you," I told her. I really did love the golden yellow dress, and I had absolutely picked it out for the roses hidden in the lace trim. It was a perfect summer's day dress on top of that, and Rachel looked like a million bucks. "Thank you for coming."

"Wouldn't have missed it," she said, holding up four fingers. "Scout's honor."

"I don't think that's the scouting symbol."

"Were you ever a scout?" she challenged, and I laughed.

"I'll take your word for it."

"All right, where's the bouquet?"

Ten minutes later, we made our way down a back set of stairs, away from the guests and the guys. It was time for them to already be outside. When we reached the doors that would lead to the main path to the garden, Jeremy and Miss Abigail were there.

"Hey, Jere," Rachel said. "It's good to see you."

"And you, Miss Rachel. You look lovely."

"I think you look pretty snappy yourself. Are you my escort for this?"

"So it would seem. One moment." He swapped Miss Abigail to his other side, then offered her his arm. "You look stunning, Miss Frankie.

Those boys had better be good to you."

"They already are," I told him, grinning. "Besides, you'll be there to whip them into shape."

"Yes, I will."

Then the music changed, and the pair of them, along with Miss Abigail, headed out next. Closing my eyes, I took a deep breath. My bouquet was a combination of roses—an exact match to all the ones Rachel had sent me as Mr. Thorns. The guys picked it out, a reminder that she had also opened their eyes with the act.

Something we'd all needed.

When the Wedding March began, I stepped out the doors as the hotel employees swung them open, and I began my walk down the aisle. Well, it was down the steps to the path, then toward the center of the garden itself.

I loved the fact I had sneakers on, because I didn't stumble once. Although my heart had fisted at the sight of the guys walking toward me. They moved in damn near perfect sync.

I caught the smiles coming my way from Kelly and Hank. Alec and Craig were sitting with them. Becca and Louisa leaned forward in their seats. Carly sat with her date, the guy she'd been seeing for the last year and who'd won Coop's approval.

Mostly because he made his mom happy.

Alicia, Bill, and Klara were beaming. Not far from Hank, Patience and Eugene had spots with Eddie. Leslie, the nurse, was here too. Andrea, our social media manager, had made it, and so had Lauren, our sound engineer.

So many people from here, from Texas, Standish proper, and the music business. There were even a couple of guys from the hockey team and the community center where Coop worked. KC and the girls couldn't make it, but they'd sent huge presents and promised to see us over the summer.

Even as aware of them as I was and as delighted as I was about my best friend being there, it was the guys I couldn't take my gaze off. Fortunately, their approach kept them in my line of sight with the barest turn of my head.

Our ordained minister waited in the shade of the gazebo as we stepped up and the five of us circled her. I'd met her during some of our research into domestic partnerships and polyamory in the state.

She agreed to perform the ceremony after meeting with all of us, and I rather liked her. Straightforward, direct, and a little biting with the wit.

"Today, we are gathered in this beautiful rose garden on this stunning summer day to celebrate the commitment of Archie, Coop, Frankie, Ian, and Jake. These five friends, and make no mistake, they are friends first and have become a family. They share their passion, their devotion, and most of all, their respect and loyalty for each other.

"Building a family is no easy feat. Often, we think of family as the group we are born into. But family is not just blood. It's heart. It's soul. Through the five of you, you bind all of your families into one larger one. A community. What is a community but a great family that supports the one in the center? The heart of this particular community.

"As one who understands the heart wants what the heart wants, I also know that this is no easy task to make such a devoted pledge to each other. For Frankie, who will be taking on four husbands, and for the four husbands who have cemented their brotherhood in their shared devotion for their future wife—we are all here for you. That is what it means to come together today to celebrate and witness your love."

I swore I wouldn't cry. I swore I wouldn't. But out here, surrounded by the rich, vibrant scent of the roses and staring at the guys who loved me so much they'd been fighting for me from the beginning—it was damn hard not to cry.

"We decided to do our vows in the order in which we proposed," Coop said, and a ripple of laughter went through the guests. "It may seem like such a little thing to decide what order to go in, but for us, it's about supporting each other and not fighting over who has the most right to be at your side. We all have that right. We all want to be there."

Coop held me transfixed with his gray-green eyes.

"Today, I'm marrying my best friend. I'm marrying the girl who was never afraid to pop life right in the nose when it dared to take her on. I'm marrying the girl who defended me on the playground and later kicked me in the ass when I needed it."

More laughter and my grin was so wide it hurt my face.

"I'm marrying the girl I promised to marry when we were five years old, and she said yes between the swings and the slide. Frankie, you're my best friend, my lover, my champion, and my heart. Everything I am, is yours, Beautiful. Well, except for the part that keeps these knuckleheads in touch with their deeper feelings."

Jake thumped him and I laughed through my tears. It was so perfect.

Then Jake focused on me, his pale blue eyes alive with so much emotion.

"I promise you that I will always care, always fight to connect, to be there to comfort you and celebrate you. No matter what life brings, we will cherish the time together and I will support you—all of you—through everything that entails.

"Frankie, I am so lucky to have found someone who embraces all that I am, and enriches me by pushing and challenging me to be better. I can't wait to continue this adventure with you. To build our dreams and chase our goals. I am so excited for this future we're making.

"Baby Girl, you're my best friend, my lover, my partner, and my heart. Everything I am, everything I will be—it's yours and theirs. I promise to always defend you and this family. Period."

So somber and serious, my heart stretched out, wanting to encompass them all.

"Angel," Ian took the step inward toward me. "I chose you the day I met you. I saw you sitting there in class, and all I could think was, will she look at me with the smile she had when she walked in? Every single day you've shared that smile with me has been the best. I choose you now, who you are inside and out.

"I promise to laugh with you in good times and in bad. I will endure with you when the road gets hard. I will always respect you as Frankie, my heart, my best friend, my muse. I promise to love you always. And I will always have their backs, my brother boyfriends, as Mom decided to dub them and then the name stuck."

The guys laughed and so did our guests.

"My promise to all of us and to you. This is our family. We don't need to be anything more than who we are."

The tears had won out. They trickled down my cheeks and I couldn't stop them.

"Frankie," Archie said. "You know me, I wanted to hire a skywriter for this part, maybe a hot air balloon, or some performance artists to take this totally over the top in telling you how much I love you."

The fact Coop actually rolled his eyes told me that there had actually *been* a discussion. God, I loved them so much.

"But I know you love to hear me talk…"

That dirty mouth could not show up in mixed company, but the devilish twinkle in his eyes promised me he was thinking it. I licked my lips, tasting the gloss and the tears.

"So, I have to tell you—I fell in love with *you*. With your qualities, with your big ass heart, as Jake likes to call it, and with how you look at life. With how no matter what, you pick yourself up, and you keep on going. With how you choose kindness when I would fight. With how you will fight to protect those you love.

"I know that sometimes we're so different, but your needs, your interests, and your desires—they are so important to me. This family we've built together, the ups, and the downs, whether it was my stubbornness or yours or theirs, there is literally no one else that I want to have my back than you and these three idiots."

I giggled as Ian just shook his head, but they were all smiling.

"I promise to give you all of me. To always talk to you and to listen. To be kind and honest and trust you all no matter what. You are my best friend, my soulmate, my other half—you are the sunshine I never knew I needed, and now I can't live without you."

God, the tears just wouldn't stop. "You're my reason," I whispered. "All of you are my reason. You were my reason then, and you're my reason now, and I know you're my reason tomorrow and every other day that follows. You are my best friends. My protectors. My defenders. My champions.

"You have always fought for me, even when I didn't understand what you were doing. You were there for me in some of the worst times and never left me alone. If I was drowning, you jumped into the water and kept my head up. When I needed help to climb, you were there. When I needed all of you…"

I swallowed, looking at them one after the other.

"You didn't make me choose. You said I could love you all. That you would love me regardless. You have cherished me, kept your promises, and built a life with me that is so full, and so beautiful, that I can't wait to see what we do next. It's always *us*, none of us are alone.

"You have made me happier than you could ever imagine. Your

love fills me with strength. No matter what life throws at us, I know we'll be together. I love you all so much. I will always love you, and wherever you go, I will be there at your sides because that is where I'm supposed to be."

"Come here, Baby Girl," Jake said as I was half-sobbing and then I crashed into them. They formed a much tighter circle around me until they were all hugging me.

For a moment, they were all I could feel and hear. They were my heart. My breath. Coop found my hand and gripped it. Archie pressed a kiss behind my ear. Ian wrapped a hand around my nape, and Jake pressed his lips to mine.

"I would like to say that we might be rushing ahead a little, but what you five have sworn to today, let no one challenge or try to destroy. By the power you have vested in me, I pronounce you—"

"Wait!" Chloe shouted and I pulled back a little, still sniffling as I turned to my little sister. "You guys forgot the rings. You can't do the husbands and wife thing without your rings."

Jeremy and Rachel were both giving us fairly misty-eyed smiles, so I just grinned. "You're absolutely right. We need the rings."

Thankfully, Jeremy had brought the case with all five simple gold bands. I refused to replace a single one of my engagement rings, so a simple gold band would go with them. That was that. They would each get one too.

Archie opened the box, and I took my time putting one ring on each of them and then kissing them to seal the deal, and when I was done, they slid my gold band into place.

Maybe a little unorthodox, but this was our day. As one, we looked at our minister, who glanced at Chloe. "All good now?"

"Yes!"

"Excellent, then by the power you have vested in me, I pronounce you husbands and wife. May your life be ever blessed."

I collapsed into Coop, who picked me up and then kissed me again. The tears were still flowing, but so was the happiness. This was the day I'd never realized I'd always been dreaming of. But it wasn't about the day, I didn't think it ever had been.

It was always about my guys.

My brother *husbands*.

I was so getting them shirts if Sara hadn't already.

Chapter Eighteen
IT HAD TO BE YOU

FRANKIE

Hank whirled me around on the dance floor inside the ballroom. The doors were all thrown open so that we could be inside or out. The perfect weather of the morning extended into the afternoon. Sunshine, cool breezes and big fans made the dancing fun.

"You make a beautiful bride." While he was all smiles now, his eyes had been damp earlier when he came up to congratulate us.

"Thanks, Dad." I was still a little stuffed up from my own crying. Rachel had worked wonders to help me fix my makeup after, and she'd had to fix her own. I would never be a pretty crier. I got too blotchy and my nose was too stuffed.

I glanced over to where she and Dominic danced and kept my mental fingers crossed for her.

"Also," Hank continued, his smile taking on a more mischievous quality. "I need to pass you a message."

"From?"

"From your husbands, of course." I swore his eyes were practically twinkling. "You see, they want to escape with you early, and they have come up with the perfect plan."

Laughter bubbled up through me as Hank twirled me around again. He kept dancing me away from the others and I, for one, remained thrilled that I had on sneakers rather than heels. As much as I'd been on my feet since putting on this dress, and it was over three hours after the ceremony now, I was pretty sure I'd be hobbling if I were in heels.

"I can't wait to hear this plan."

"I thought you'd be on board," Hank said. "Kelly slipped up to your suite about an hour ago and packed your bag. So, everything you need is already in a suitcase. It would be better for you to change out of the dress before you make your escape, but that would probably tip our hand."

Understood.

"In roughly fifteen minutes, you'll excuse yourself to go to the restroom. Rachel already knows what is going on. While you're out of the room, Eddie and I are going to begin a toast off and get the other dads engaged. That will buy you all a window to make it out to the car Jeremy has arranged."

Oh…

"And then you're off for your honeymoon. Don't worry about anything. Eddie and I have your grandparents, Jeremy has the house and the cats, and you will be off celebrating your nuptials with your husbands, doing absolutely nothing that would potentially scar me for life just thinking about."

I threw my head back and laughed. "I love you, Dad."

We paused in the dance for him to hug me tight. "I love you, too."

We'd already cut the cake, done the toasts, and I'd had a dance with each of my husbands. We'd even done a group dance, too—though when they changed it to the chicken dance, Coop fled.

Goofball.

Right on cue, when he glanced at his watch, I moved over to Rachel, who gave Dominic a nod. "Go," he said. "I got this."

Arm in arm, Rachel and I made our way out of the ballroom and down the hall to the restroom. This one was blocked off from the public with a little rope and sign.

"Someone has been planning this," I commented when I found that not only was the bathroom closed off, but there was already a change of clothes waiting for me.

Rachel chuckled as she began unbuttoning my dress. The moment it loosened, I took in a deep breath. I hadn't even realized how tight it was until it was released.

"You've been sweating," she commented as it fell down and I stepped out. I had been. With all the dancing, in and out of the sun, there was a hint of red on my shoulders. Not a real sunburn, because I had actually used sunscreen. "Go ahead and change all the way, I'll take care of getting the dress to Jeremy, and he'll get it to the cleaners."

"Oh, wait—I need to get the coin." I didn't take it out often or wear it many places, but it was essential to me. Once I had it freed, I pulled open the bag to find a sundress inside of it. Light and airy.

It was also much cooler to put on for my legs and my chest after the wedding dress.

"Change the shoes?" I glanced down at my sneakers. They were a little grass-stained in a couple of places, but I wasn't worried about that.

"Should be sandals in there," Rachel said as she picked up the dress and hung it carefully. "I mean, the shoes you have on are totally on-brand. So do what you want."

The minute I pulled them off and stood on the cold tile, I groaned. Yeah, my feet were sore. Socks came off next then I was in sandals.

Rachel stuffed them in another bag, and then I shed the pearls and the earrings. One set would go back to Kelly and the bracelet to my grandmother.

Only after I was fully ready for my escape did I face Rachel again. "Thank you for coming—I know I could have done it without you, but I didn't want to."

"Sorry I kept you on the hook so long about whether I would come or not," she said. "I have a lot to tell you—ahh, before you ask. Not right now. This is like three bottles of wine and sitting outside, alone, for girl talk. We'll make time for it. Right now, we need to get you out of here and into the car so you can run away with those men who love you so much."

I hugged her and she gripped me back just a fiercely. "I love you, bitch," I whispered.

"I love you more," she countered. "Bitch."

We were both laughing as we let go, and then I did one more check of my hair and cosmetics in the mirror before glancing at the rings that filled one full section of my left hand's ring finger.

The wedding rings themselves were inscribed, but we hadn't shared that with anyone. They all read: Love. Loyalty. Family.

Our personal family motto.

Rachel hung up the dress and then opened the bathroom door. Dominic stood outside, waiting, or like he was guarding. "I've got a clear path for us."

She nodded then glanced at me. "Let's go. Chop-chop."

I followed them out. Instead of heading toward the ballroom again, we continued through the wing where the bathroom had been located. Then we passed a large kitchen and a staff area before we slipped outside. We'd come out literally on the opposite side of the building from where we needed to be.

"Rach, your heels," I said because there was no sidewalk path.

"Yeah," she said with a wrinkle of her nose. "I can handle it barefoot." She tugged off the shoes. "Let's go."

Dominic chuckled, and he caught her hand and cupped her elbow over the uneven ground as we circled the building. The drive that led up to the main building came into view as a limo glided up toward the round in front of it.

"That," he said, "will be your ride."

Excitement threaded through me as I spotted Coop sauntering out the front doors in a baseball cap, t-shirt, shorts, and a pair of sunglasses. He looked like he should be on a beach in Bermuda instead of upstate New York.

Jake and Ian came from the opposite side of the building. They had bags with them. The driver was out and had the trunk open by the time we got there.

"Thanks, man," Coop said to Dominic, shaking his hand and then holding his arms out to Rachel. "Get over here and get a hug."

She laughed, and to my surprise, as well as delight, she gave each of the guys a hug. Though we were missing one husband.

"You guys need to get out of here. We're not going to be able to delay them all for long. With four of you already missing, I'll bet they figure it out soon."

"I'll call you when I come back," I promised her and got one last hug before I slid into the limo. The guys were right behind me and Jake tugged me over into his lap. "What about Arch?"

"He's coming," Ian assured me as he rubbed a hand up and down my calf. "He wanted to do a little something over the top to cement the distraction so that by the time they notice we're gone…"

Coop grinned. "Frankie—look out the window behind us."

I twisted in Jake's lap and then let out a gasp at the balloons—so many of them. There had to be a hundred hot air balloons, all brightly colored and some of them with huge banners hanging from them.

They all read—*We love Frankie Standish. Ours forever.*

Tears burned in my eyes, the name thing hadn't been so much a debate but a way to cement our ties to each other. I didn't want Curtis anymore. Jackson had never truly been my last name. Grayson had too much baggage. That left Standish, and with the company, it just seemed to be the way to go. So, each of the guys had added Standish to their last name, but they would still be Rhys, Brennen, and Benton—they'd just also be Standishes.

The funny part was while he'd tried to play it cool, it made Archie so damn happy that I thought he would bust. That was what had firmed it up for the guys. It just wasn't as important to them. When it came to kids, we'd make the decision that was right for us at the time.

Until then, we were the Standishes. Period.

A door opened, and then Archie was there, jogging down the steps to slide into the limo and onto the seat next to Coop. Unlike the guys, he hadn't changed out of his suit, but he had loosened his tie on the way out.

"Babe," he said with an appreciative smile. "Tell me you saved me my present."

With a bit of squirming, I shifted to sit between Jake and Ian, then propped my right foot on Archie's leg. Coop snorted a laugh as Archie snaked his hand up under my dress and then hooked his fingers into the garter.

"You love me," Archie said with a happy grin before peeling the garter down and off.

"She loves all of us, dork," Coop commented, but he teased his fingers over my calf. "Do you have a present up here for me?"

"Her panties stay on," Ian said in a firm voice, and I wasn't the only one going "*awww*." At my imploring look, Ian kissed me. "Sorry, Angel. We decided we're traveling first rather than wedding night first, so—" He gave the guys a look. "Panties on."

I pouted, then grinned. "Just because my panties stay on, doesn't mean we can't have some fun."

He groaned. "You are a bad girl."

"Yes, but you like me when I'm bad, and I'm good." Then with a little wiggle, I worked my way down to the floor and helped Ian open his shorts. Two and a half hours later, my jaw was a little sore, but I was pretty proud of how melted they all were.

I also hadn't asked any questions about our destination. Though, I didn't miss that Archie had my passport. We were flying on a private jet, which meant different departure procedures.

At the jet itself, Archie picked me up and carried me up the steps like we were going over the threshold. It was adorable. But the wonderful thing was, this plane had a bedroom. One Archie availed himself of to change as soon as we were on board.

Sadly, my panties were still on and remained on through pre-flight, takeoff, and then during the serving of our dinner. It was way later in the day than I realized. We had champagne, steak, baked potatoes, and our wedding cake for dessert. I didn't even ask how they got it here.

Laughter filled the meal. It wasn't long, belly full and with the champagne in my system, before I was getting sleepy.

"Come on, Beautiful," Coop said, tugging me to my feet. "We can get some sleep. It's been a long week."

"Worth it," Jake said. "But Coop's right, Baby Girl, go get some sleep."

Even though I'd been kind of hoping for something more than sleep, I yawned my way through brushing my teeth. It was just Coop and I when I stripped out of everything and just climbed into the bed naked.

He was down to his boxers and wrapped around me.

The engines lulled me, but then Coop slid his fingers between my thighs and began to work his thumb against my clit. A little moan escaped me as he increased the pressure. He traced kisses along my throat, then tugged on my ear as he worked me right up to the edge.

There was no edging or hesitation. When the first wave of the orgasm hit and I began to cry out, he kissed the sound from my lips as he continued to plunge his fingers into me. Eventually, he petted me down as I shuddered against him.

"Now," Coop said, kissing me again, his tongue teasing mine for a few seconds before he lifted his head to clean his fingers off with his tongue. Fuck, that was hot. "You can get some sleep."

As much as I might have wanted to have played, he wasn't wrong. Wrapped up in Coop, I was out like a light.

I woke up to the heat of a tongue between my legs, teasing and stroking as—oh, Jake—yes, that was Jake licking me up like I was his favorite treat. My nipples were already peaked and aching as he pursued my orgasm with a kind of relentlessness that left me squirming.

It wasn't until I came on his tongue, half-screaming, that he shifted on the bed. "Good morning, Baby Girl," Jake said in a husky whisper as he crawled up my body. Then his mouth was on mine, and all I could taste was my own release.

The rock of his hips teased his cock against my pussy, then with one hard shift, he pushed inside. I was already sensitive and aching for him. We didn't need words as he stroked his hands up and down my body, his thrusts gaining in force until I was on the edge of an orgasm all over again.

"Fuck, that's so hawt," Coop said as I caught him watching us from the open bathroom door, and then my orgasm crashed over me as Jake's hips stuttered. The first warm rush of his release just lit me up.

We lay trembling for a moment, panting and overwhelmed. As soon as Jake shifted, Coop took his place. He thrust into me, fucking right through Jake's cum. The piercing just added to the sensual torment as my pussy spasmed around him.

Every rock of his hips pushed me up the bed, but Coop kept his arms hooked under me, his hands cupping my shoulders and keeping me there. I thrashed against the stimulation. So much.

Too much.

Then I was screaming for real this time as Coop shoved me right over the edge. I dug my nails into his back as I clung to him, and he filled me all over again. Body arched, I ground against him as Jake laughed next to me.

It took me a while to float down from the spiraling sensations and focus on him. The plane's bedroom had more light in it than when we'd gone to sleep. I didn't even know what time it was and I didn't care.

Boneless, warm, and loved, I only cared that I was with the four people I loved most in the whole world. "Where's Archie and Ian?"

"Napping out front," Jake said, rolling on his side. "We've got to land soon to refuel, but we have time to shower. Then you can go back to sleep if you want."

"Or have breakfast," Coop suggested. He was still buried inside me, his cock twitching whenever my pussy spasmed around. "Coffee, tea… me."

Jake snorted. "She's had you quite a bit. Pretty sure the other husbands would like their chance to consummate."

The bickering was familiar and comforting. I half-tuned them out as they snarked back and forth. Husbands. I had four husbands. Our family, which had been ours for years, was officially "official."

Eventually, I let them help me out of bed and into the shower. It was too small to fit all of us, but they kept me company while I washed up and I did the same while they did. After, dressed only in a t-shirt and nothing else, I went out to the chairs to buckle in as we came in to land—somewhere.

I didn't even ask. Just waited until we took off again to slide into Ian's lap and kiss him. Five minutes later, he was on his feet and carrying me back into the bedroom. Behind him, Coop and Jake high-fived, but I caught Archie's private little smile and wink.

Yep. These were my guys.

As it turned out, Archie played a little hard to get, and I was okay with it, especially when I realized where we were going for our honeymoon. Quite literally, the other side of the world, to the private island owned by friends of Archie's grandfather.

"It's ours for the month," he said as the yacht sliced through the water on the way to the island. We hadn't been back since that first summer after high school graduation.

Now we were here after college graduation. There was some symmetry in that.

I was dressed in a bikini and sarong, I'd had a hat, but the wind kept pulling at it so I'd put it away. For now, I trusted the sunscreen to keep the burn away and the sunglasses to deal with the glare.

We were all up on the deck as the little green speck in the distance grew larger. Excitement spilled in my blood. This was—perfect. We'd start married life together far away from anyone and anything that could bother us. We'd get time to just be *us* before we had to get back to real life, work, school, and more.

"I love this," I told Archie and he pressed a kiss to my shoulder.

"Yeah? I hoped you would. We debated a lot of different places to go, almost said we could go back to the house in Texas for a month, no one would think to look for us there, or the cabin in Colorado. But then I remembered the island, the isolation, the privacy—you walking around topless all the time…"

I laughed. "I'd walk around fully nude, but I'm not a fan of sand in my asscrack."

"Agreed, we'll keep the full nudity to the house and the deck." He wrapped an arm around me and spread his hand out over my abdomen. "Our wife gets to do whatever she wants for the next month, and whoever she wants…" I cocked an eyebrow at him.

"Really?" I shifted and ground my bikini-clad ass against his groin. The hardness of his dick was impossible to miss. "Think you can fuck me right up against this rail with the crew right here?"

"Mrs. Standish," Archie said in a voice so full of mock scandal it had my thighs clenching. "You might make me come in my pants if you keep talking like that."

"Then shut up and fuck me, Mr. Standish. I'm aching for you."

He nipped at my ear and then shifted until his back was entirely against mine. "Hey, guys," Archie said over his shoulder. "Give us some cover?"

I didn't even look because I trusted them to handle everything.

"As for you," Archie said, sliding his hand up to pinch my nipple through the bikini top. "Hands on that railing and hold on, this is gonna be hard and fast, Babe."

"Promises, promises," I said on a gasp, but I did as I was told and held onto the rail. I hadn't even heard him open his shorts as he tugged my bikini bottoms to the side and then pushed into me in one hard thrust.

Eyes on the island ahead, I held on as Archie pounded away into my pussy and worked his fingers against my clit. Not screaming took everything I had, and when I floated down, aware of how soaked he'd left me, I caught Ian watching me with a smile.

Yeah, I wasn't putting on clothes for the rest of the month. I'd get an excellent tan and a really fierce workout.

But we'd also kick off our life the way we wanted it to be—together.

Chapter Nineteen

THREE YEARS AFTER THE WEDDING

FRANKIE

Our next tour stop was Atlanta, but we had a week off after that to fly back to New York for Coop's graduation from his master's program. Backstage in our dressing room, I sat with my feet up as Ian went over a new set of chords for one of our songs.

With the second album, we'd done a much shorter tour, but every single show had been sold out. So, the following summer, we'd done surprise pop-ups at different music festivals. For this tour, we agreed to a longer one with more dates, but we had to have regular breaks to go home.

Coop was finishing up his final year in graduate studies. He wouldn't be able to fly out and meet us much without risking his grades. Jake and Archie were deep in a redesign phase on the test engine they'd been building and rebuilding.

They were so excited for the first aerodynamics tests coming later in the summer. I missed them.

"We'll see them soon," Ian said, his voice soothing. "I know you hate being on the road and away from them."

"Was I sighing again?" I'd been reading messages on my phone. Coop was in a final right now, and I kept checking to see if he was out.

Archie had sent me some very lovely dirty pictures as rewards for the equally dirty ones I'd had Ian take of me so I could send them to them. Three years of marriage, and I was still crazy for them.

All of them.

"A little, you get that little frown right here." He touched a finger to the spot between my brows. With a gentle stroke, he eased some of the tension. "And it's been almost six weeks, but we go home tomorrow, and we're there for ten days."

"I thought we only got six," I said, twisting in the seat.

"Nope, I told the guys we needed a longer break than that. We've got six more months on and off the road. The third album is doing amazing. Don't get me wrong, I'm happy about it, but come Thanksgiving? We're going home and not leaving for at least a year."

God, that sounded good. "I'm just glad Eddie doesn't mind me working from the road. Though I feel bad that he has to pick up all the funding meetings that I can't go to."

The foundation work turned out to be so much more fulfilling than I ever imagined. Investments for charities and then building funds for scholarships for different organizations—it was amazing. I also campaigned and got other companies invested.

"Bound Hearts is great publicity for the charity work the Standish Foundation does," Ian reminded me. We'd donated twenty percent of our tour and album profits directly to the foundation's charities and music programs. "You get on conference calls every day that you're needed."

I did, but still… my phone buzzed, and I flipped messages from Coop's to Chloe's. I still couldn't believe she was a sophomore in high school. Alec would graduate—next year? Ugh, I was losing track.

The history questions cracked me up. Chloe's least favorite class was one of my favorites. But as long as she did the reading and tried to keep up, I would help her. I answered the first two questions, and then she popped up again with a request to go video chat.

"Chloe wants me to video chat her," I said over my shoulder, and Ian lifted his chin then glanced at the clock. "We have just under an hour and you still need to eat. Talk to her, and I'll go grab food for us."

"You're the best," I told him as he set the guitar aside and rose.

"I do try," he said with a chuckle before kissing me. "Don't let her talk you into going up to Boston on our break. She loves to play the baby sister card."

Did she ever.

"I got this." As soon as he was out, I called her. She answered on the first ring and pressed a finger to her lips as she moved through the house.

I didn't stare at her as she walked because that bobbing always made me feel vaguely motion sick. Finally, a door closed, and she huffed out a breath. "I didn't expect you to call so quickly."

"Mic and equipment checks are in an hour," I told her. "So I won't be free for long. What's up?"

"You know, it's a little weird when I remember you're like a rock star and shit."

I snorted. "I'm not a rock star, I'm just a singer and part of a duo. We happen to have a great time. What's up?"

"Still sounds like a rock star to me. So—" She elongated the word. "Is your tour bringing you to Boston at any point?"

"Not this time, as far as I can remember. We actually added some European dates and a few in Canada, though." That was weird enough.

"Damn. What about somewhere within driving distance to

Boston?"

"Chloe," I said, firming my tone. If I wasn't careful, she would wander all around the point for a half hour before she got to it. The last couple of years, she'd gotten awful about coming out with what she wanted sideways.

Asking if we were busy before asking what she wanted. It almost felt like verbal traps, and I felt bad for calling her on it the first time. The second time? Not so much. By the third time, I'd figured it out.

I loved her. But I would only indulge her so far. Apparently, the method worked because Dad and Kelly asked me to keep it up.

"There's a boy, and he loves your music. He thinks you're hot, which is weird, but my friends all told him you're my sister." She wrinkled her nose. "He asked if I could get us tickets to see you."

Oh. Fuck.

I pinched the bridge of my nose. "We don't have any shows on the upper east coast." If she really wanted, I could fly *her* down to see one of our shows, but I wasn't bringing her whole friend group and a boy.

"It's stupid, I know. He's cute, and I like him—but I thought if I could prove you really are my sister…"

"Sweetheart, you have pictures of us. If that's not enough for him, it's not about proving I'm your sister, it's about what you can do *for* him." Which made him a dick. "That's *not* okay."

The heaviness in her sigh tugged at me. "I kind of knew that," she admitted. "I was hoping you wouldn't agree…"

"Oh, sweetheart." Leaning forward, I studied her on the phone's tiny screen. "You deserve so much better than that. Tell me you know that."

Chloe flung herself down on a bed. "I do. Maggie said he's an arrogant ass who knows how pretty he is. But that's the problem—he is pretty."

"Well, if he isn't pretty on the inside, then I don't care what he looks like on the outside." I still couldn't believe he told her *I* was hot. Who did that? "Want me to ask Jake to drive up?" Or I could call Alec.

Though the *adult* thing to do would be to call Kelly and Dad and let them know. I was on the fence, though…

"No, I'll handle it. Because you're right, and so is Maggie." Another sigh. "When are you coming up to see us?"

"We'll be home for Thanksgiving," I promised. "Then Ian and I are taking a longer break. We may have to do a handful of shows as makeups in the spring, but we'll be home for the rest of winter."

"Frankie, it's *May*."

"I know. We agreed to a longer tour schedule this time with a lot of breaks. Ian's music is taking off, and we're going to open for a few bands in the fall. So—ask Dad and Kelly when would be a good time for me to fly you guys out to meet us somewhere. Then you can come to a show."

"Oh my god! You are the best!" The squeal hit an uncomfortable decibel level, but by the time Ian got back, Chloe and I were off the phone and I was back to stalking Coop's text messages to see if he'd even opened them yet.

The scent of bacon hit me and my stomach growled. Bouncing up, I threw my arms around him, and Ian picked me right up as he kicked the door closed behind him.

"What's the matter, Angel?"

"Nothing, I'm just glad that when you guys were dicks it was never about using me to get to someone else."

His eyes narrowed. "Someone making life hard for Chloe?"

"Someone is gonna regret it," I told him as he set me down. He'd gotten us BLTs and fries. There were bottles of water too. As much as I liked soda, we had a couple of long sets, and we needed all the hydration possible.

After I filled Ian in on the little punk who thought I was *hawt* and his challenge to Chloe, Ian looked thoughtful. "Yeah, you're right. Definitely a punk. Feels weird to be thinking about kicking a sophomore's ass, though."

I laughed. "It feels weird to think about high school at all." Three years after college, seven years after high school. Sometimes, it felt like an entirely different life. "Still, Craig is his age, I could sic him on the guy, but Dad and Kelly would probably prefer a more peaceful resolution."

After stuffing another French fry in my mouth, I jumped when my phone buzzed. I wiped my fingers off on my jeans and then grabbed my phone.

Message from Coop. Yes!

Ian sat forward as I swiped it open. The message was short and to the point, but I raised my fists and gave a whoop.

"He did it!!"

Laughing, Ian snapped a photo of me as I did a happy dance. He'd been presenting his Master's thesis today. Granted, it wasn't the doctoral, but it was the final component he needed to graduate with honors. Then he would be taking the state licensing test.

Our boy was going to be a psychologist.

I blew a kiss at the phone as Ian held it up, an indulgent look on his face. Yes, he was recording me. No, I didn't care.

"I am so proud of you," I said to the phone screen. "You kicked ass. You're going to be the best Dr. Standish-Brennen *ever,* and when I get home, you get anything you want from me as your reward."

"Hey," Ian said. "Why don't I get that deal?"

I grinned at him because he was just playing. "You get me every night on the road. You gotta leave them something."

"This is true," he said with a wink. Then he turned the camera to face him. "Frankie's right, man. This is excellent. Save the celebration dinner for us, and we'll be home in thirty-six hours."

Wrapping my arms around Ian's neck from behind, I stared into the camera. "I miss you guys, and I love you."

Ian ended the video and sent it, then dragged me around to sit in his lap. "You know we can change this tour—"

"No," I said with a shake of my head. "We talked about this. All of us. I do miss them. I hate being on the road without them, but I also love being on the road with you. You guys want me to give up the IUD in a couple of years, so this may be the last time we really have the time to just go and do it. We put enough breaks in."

The IUD conversation happened the past Christmas. Jake asked, then it led to a discussion. Coop still needed to get his licensing, and he wanted time to settle into his career. Ian and I were nearly done with the new album. This was the perfect transition year, particularly when we'd been planning a shorter tour, to begin with.

"We don't have to keep any time frame you're not ready for," he reminded me, and I nuzzled a kiss to his lips. Like Jake, he'd grown a beard the last year or so. It was so soft that when I kissed him, it didn't leave a beard burn, but it definitely tickled.

"First, I wouldn't have agreed at all if I didn't like the idea. I'm still a little scared because what do I know about being a mom? And at the same time, I do know all the things *not* to do." I traced my finger over his lips. "Second, there's no guarantee we're getting pregnant right out of the gate. But I figure we'll have lots of fun trying."

Ian chuckled. "We're still gambling to see who gets first?"

I shrugged. "You guys came up with that one." Each of them wanted to father at least one, that was what we'd discussed. So, at least four kids. That seemed like a lot, but I also loved the idea of growing our family.

So, the first time trying to get pregnant meant everyone got an equal shot. Second time, bio-daddy number one would be stuck wearing condoms.

"I love you," I whispered to him, and he cupped my face. "You know that, right?"

"I do," Ian told me. This time when he kissed me, it was gentle and sweet, it left me sighing into his lips. All too soon came the knock for equipment check. Then we'd have to get ready to perform.

My phone vibrated, and so did Ian's, the message from Coop made him laugh.

"I'll let you take care of sucking his dick, if you don't mind, Angel."

Nope, I didn't mind at all.

Chapter Twenty
FIVE YEARS AFTER THE WEDDING

FRANKIE

August

I sat on the floor in the bathroom, my head back to look up at the ceiling while Coop checked his watch. At least the tile was cool, it felt great. Especially after throwing up my guts when I caught the scent of coffee.

How was that fair? Coffee had turned on me. Or had I turned on coffee? Archie slipped into the bathroom with a glass of cold water and a Sprite. Oh, that sounded good. I'd already rinsed my mouth out.

After a sip of the water, I took the can and pressed it to my flushed face. This *sucked*. "I'm probably sick," I pointed out.

"Maybe," Coop said easily with another glance at his watch. "But we've been trying for months."

Enthusiastically and with great zest. The guys had taken it all as a personal challenge. I could honestly say that my stress levels were almost nonexistent with all of the endorphins they kept flooding my system with, well, endorphins and far more.

The ice-cold can was so nice against my face. After a couple of minutes, I popped the lid and took a sip. Then braced for whether my stomach would object. I had to be sick. Why would I suddenly react to *coffee,* of all things? Coffee was life's blood. It was what made the world go round.

"Two pink lines," Coop announced.

"Fuck," I swore, and both of them jerked their gazes to me.

"Babe," Archie said as he slid down to sit next to me.

"It's the coffee," Coop said gently, understanding in his voice even if there was a hint of laughter in his eyes.

"That's not fair," I mumbled, leaning my head onto Archie's shoulder. "I need my coffee. Why turn me off coffee?"

They must really love me because neither of them laughed. However, they did want me to make a doctor's appointment.

Poor Ian was in California when I got the results, but we called him as soon as Jake got back from the store run. Apparently, he'd gone for more tests.

"Guys, we don't need multiple when we are actually trying." It was hard not to adore them. While I didn't want to wake Ian up, Archie just gave me a look.

"Fuck that, trust me. He'll want to be woken up for this."

He absolutely wanted to be woken up. "I'm getting on the next flight back, Angel."

"You still have meetings…"

"And they will still be here," he said in a tone that brooked no arguments. "Or not. I actually don't care. I want to be there. Hey, Arch, do you think…"

"Already on it, man. Go ahead and start packing." Archie left the room with his own cell phone at his ear.

Coop nuzzled a kiss to the top of my head as I curled into his side.

"When is your appointment?" Ian asked, though it sounded like he was already moving around to pack.

"I haven't made it yet. We wanted to call you first. Well, actually, I was going to let you sleep, but the guys said you'd want to be woken up for this."

"They were right." Oh, he sounded testy.

"In my defense, I threw up because of coffee." Even the thought of it was making me squeamish. "So, I'm going to plead on how thinking straight is off the table right now."

His warm laughter buoyed me, even as he said, "I'm sorry, Angel, that sucks."

"It really does."

Jake and Coop were great; they waited until after Ian said he was on the way to the airport to laugh at my plaintive complaint. Next up, we called the doctor, and when they weren't open yet, Archie was all set to bug the poor woman at home. We could wait an hour.

All grumbling aside, they were adorable. Coop couldn't take the day, though. In fact, none of us really could, but Archie didn't care. He and Jake weren't leaving. Coop promised to check-in and I moved my meetings to remote.

It was late afternoon before I could see the doctor anyway, and I was at the appointment with Jake while Archie went to pick up Ian. A blood test and an exam later, she confirmed that I was pregnant. Better news, it wasn't ectopic.

We got pamphlets, a series of appointments, as well as a list of screenings and tests, along with when we would need to do them. From the moment we removed the IUD, this had definitely been the plan, and I still found myself a little on the dazed side.

Jeremy was the one who suggested we wait until the end of the first trimester to tell anyone else. That seemed reasonable. The guys were alternating between excited and cautious.

First point of concern, the brownstone had a lot of stairs. Thankfully, while they debated any alterations, Miss Abigail came to lay next to me on the sofa and rested her head on my lap. What was even funnier was that Tiddles had also ventured down to the living room level, where he curled up on my other side. The cats and Miss Abigail had long since come to a peace accord.

Since Doctor Felucca thought I was closer to six weeks than eight weeks, that put my due date sometime in late April. It also meant I probably got pregnant in June. That seemed *apropos.* June remained our month.

October

The meeting took most of the day, but it was a big one. It was the end of the year fundraising review and year-ahead outlook. We had to lock in dates for the following calendar year, not only for future fundraising dinners and parties but also for disbursements, scholarships, and endowments.

Honestly, in the last few years, this meeting was probably the most grueling of the year for Foundation work, but it was also my favorite. I had to haggle with the representatives of the board and the various committees to get them to agree with our proposals.

So far, my best had been fifty percent. That was the year prior. I'd gotten fifty percent of our proposals and almost sixty-eight percent of the investments I'd been looking for by the end of the day.

It made me feel like a champion. As it was though today, I was having a hard time staying focused on the numbers and the dry recitation of the effects a recession in the European Union would have on our coming year. It was the opening salvos of financial chess.

Fuck, it was boring me to death. I was having a hard time sitting still, and my mind kept wandering back to waking up sandwiched between Jake and Coop that morning. I'd been more than a little horny, and we were all late by the time we finished.

The fact that I could still *feel* them three hours later suggested I should have scratched the itch, but I found myself wondering how quickly we could wrap this up. When we neared the lunch hour, and we were not any closer to where I wanted to be, I had to resist the urge to scream.

As soon as we called it for lunch, I excused myself to go to my office. I didn't really like eating with everyone else right now. Most of the queasiness had passed, even with the smell of coffee—thankfully. Though decaf was not my favorite, it was legit better than nothing.

"Hey, Babe," said a wildly welcome voice as soon as I pushed my office door open.

"Archie…" Relief and desire swarmed through me in equal measures. Leaning back against the door to close it, I turned the lock before crossing to where Archie was rising from the chair in front of my desk.

While he wore a suit, I barely noticed that just that he was here, and then his mouth was on mine and I arched into the kiss. The aching need unfurling in me turned into a forest fire. My breasts had begun to hurt in the past couple of weeks, but this wasn't the same thing.

"Damn, Babe," he breathed in between kisses. "Remind me to bring you lunch more often."

I pushed his jacket off his shoulders. "I don't want food," I told him, and his eyes gleamed as he leaned back to study me.

"Babe, don't you have that all-day—"

"I don't care," I said fervently. "We have ninety minutes for lunch, and I know just what you can do in half that time…"

I swore my pussy clenched just thinking about it. Archie nodded. "Take this skirt off and the shirt. Fuck knows I'll rip it."

He didn't have to tell me twice. I rarely got this dressed up for work, only for the important meetings. The skirt was a little tight and not all that comfortable anyway. I stepped right out of it and laid it neatly over the back of a chair before sliding off my jacket and blouse.

Archie backed up to the sofa and stripped with the kind of efficiency that let me enjoy the way he moved. There was a new scar on him, one I always checked whenever his shirt came off. He'd long since ceased scolding me for checking.

An accident at the shop had sliced him with shrapnel. It looked far worse than it had been, but that scar always reminded me that he was still here with me.

I was soaking my panties, but I left them in place, cause Archie tended to like tearing them off himself. I swore it was why he always bought me the lace ones. Easier to rip.

Sitting down, Archie ran his hand up and down his cock. Hands on my hips, I licked my lips as I watched him teasing himself. There were already drops of pre-cum on the angry red tip.

"I'm not the only one aching."

"Babe, my dick has been your biggest fan for fifteen years. He's always aching for you."

Laughter swelled up within me. "I'm so damn horny," I admitted and his grin grew. "I can't make up my mind whether I want to suck you off, have you eat me out, climb on you over there and ride you until we can't see or…"

Touching my tongue to the top of my lip, I turned to bend over my desk. The wood was cool against my flushed skin. I wiggled my ass in invitation. The warmth of him brushed over me a second before his hand landed on my ass. The spank was so mild; he could do so much more.

"How badly do you want it, Babe?" The hot lick of desire rippled over me at the teasing words. "Tell me how you want me."

"I need your cock, Archie. I want you to just fucking slam into me, give me everything, and fuck me right here—" I didn't get to finish the plea as he gave me exactly what I asked for. He yanked my panties to the side and filled me right the hell up.

Dragging my ass back some, he gripped my hips. "Hold onto the desk, Babe, and tell me if this hurts."

"Yes, sir," I promised, already half-ready to come just from the rock of his cock through my slick folds. Every push knocked him a little deeper in me. The cool temperature difference between the desk and my skin just added to the sweet torment on my nipples.

Then Archie flexed his hands on my hips and railed into me with a kind of ferocity that had me gasping. When he slid his hand around to tease my clit, I came in a rush. Only the fact that we were in the office kept me from screaming.

At least the first time. He held me steady as I shook and trembled through the first orgasm, his heavy cock resting inside me. Then when I began to calm, he fucked me all over again.

Sometime around the third orgasm, we moved back to the sofa, and I climbed on top of him. He let me have control until we were both a shaking, trembling mess.

"Feel better?" His breathing was a harsh echo of mine, but the soothing warmth of his hands stroking my back helped to quiet some of the storm.

"So much better, but give me a minute, and then I'm going to suck you off."

He laughed. "Babe, you don't have to do that."

I lifted my head and glared at him, but it was hard to stay mad when he was so damn edible. "I want to—" I was still convulsing around him, and it was hard to explain how much I wanted or why I wanted it so badly, but we had another hour and five minutes.

We made the most of it, even if I did go back to that meeting without any panties on.

Worth it.

December

Between the wildness of my libido and the holidays, the guys and I were enjoying the snow holiday to ourselves. Well, that, and the fifty-some odd presents that came in for baby-to-be. I'd finally begun to show a baby bump, much to Jake's exultation.

He found a dozen reasons a day to cup my tummy, to pet it. Ian had taken to serenading the baby bump, which was one of my favorite things. Archie and Coop also took turns reading to the bump.

When Archie pulled out manuals on engineering and basic electrical connectivity, I'd stared at him and he shrugged.

"Jake talks about hockey regularly, and Bubba's always singing to him/her; you have Coop for the grounded actual fairy tales and stuff. Besides, Dad is insisting it's never too early to expand the mind."

"And you like reading journals and articles to the baby."

"And I like reading them," he agreed. I just went back to my own book as he resumed his reading.

It was—amazing and endearing. We weren't planning on moving from the brownstone for at least another year. Though he had his license, Coop was spending the first three years working under the supervision of other psychologists. In thirteen months, he'd finish that contract and we could look at seriously relocating to Long Island.

That meant we needed a nursery here. Coop and Ian both gave up their rooms and Archie had the wall knocked out between them. I thought we could just split my room in half, but the guys had all taken to sleeping up here more and more. They rarely used their own rooms. So, we transformed the new larger space into a nursery with a closet and changing table.

The guys painted it a gorgeous sky blue and added clouds. There was even a plane hidden away up there. The decorations ranged from animals to vehicles to musical instruments.

Nothing gender-specific. Pink had never been my favorite color, but I didn't want all blue or all pink or even the more gender neutrals of all green. I wanted colorful, thoughtful, and personality-filled.

Not that the baby would care at first. Everything I'd read said the first few months the baby would need *us* more than anything else. I couldn't wait to meet him or her. The doctor who had done the ultrasound, she knew.

We voted three to two to wait.

Poor Jake and Archie, it was killing them, but they'd agreed that the majority ruled on this one, and it wasn't until we voted that it even occurred to me I kind of wanted to be surprised.

"Next time," I promised them, and they'd both brightened up. "Next time, we'll find out early." I mean, I was the swing vote. Coop and Ian had only laughed.

Still, it was getting closer every day, and I couldn't wait to meet them.

February

My back ached, and the baby was tap dancing on my bladder. With a lot more ease than my ungainly body suggested, I slid out of bed and headed to the bathroom. I swore I had to pee like every other hour.

It was ridiculous. Needed to go somewhere? Go to the bathroom and tinkle before leaving. As soon as I got there, find a bathroom, because I'd need to tinkle again. It was hard to explain to the guys how awful it was to need to pee so badly, and then it was just all drip, drip, drip.

I was starting to wonder if the bump had left me anything remotely resembling a bladder anymore.

Ian was sitting up when I came back out of the bathroom, and I sighed. "Sorry," I whispered. I was too achy to lay back down, so he got up and brushed a kiss to my head. Jake and Coop were still out. Archie wasn't in here, but maybe he had crashed in his room.

No, we found him downstairs in the kitchen with work spread out on the dining table. He gave us a guilty look when we came down. "Crap, did I wake you up?"

"The bump," Ian and I said at the same time. As it was, I didn't want to sit but needed to pace. In a little while, the bump would settle, but currently, they were acting like I had trampolines instead of internal organs.

Archie fixed me tea while I paced, then he and Ian discussed the engine issues that Jake and Archie had been having.

"Anthony?" I suggested.

They both paused to glance at me. "Not bad, not loving it though," Archie said. "What about Andrew?"

"Could be—I dunno—Archibald?" Ian suggested, and we both

gave him a look, but he raised his hands. The decision to name our children with the initial of their biological father was an idea that I'd just clung to. I liked it. They were all the dads. They were all excited and doing their various reading.

They'd be great fathers. They took turns going to appointments with me. Someone was always around if I needed assistance. I never had to get up in the middle of the night alone. When I got horny—they'd even taken to tag-teaming to give everyone time to recover.

They were *hilarious* when they talked about going for the gold. Still, it was nice that they took my needs so seriously. We had "I" names and "C" names. The J names weren't being as cooperative, though I did love the name Jennifer. The guys weren't as fond. The "A" names were proving a lot harder than I imagined.

Baby Bump, I said mentally as I continued to pace in time with their bouncing. *You need to settle down because you have more energy than all of us.*

It would be a bit yet. Eight, maybe nine weeks. We were firmly in the third trimester. The doctor promised to do the paternity test immediately after the birth. Bump would have a day or two just being Bump, but then we had to have a name ready.

March

Jake worked his thumbs into my lower spine, and I wanted to cry. It felt so damn good. We'd finally found the secret to letting me get more sleep. Bump settled right down as soon as one of them had a hand on my stomach. Especially if they talked to the bump while they did it.

Granted, I slept better with their hands on me too. "Right there," I said with a groan as he found a particularly stubborn muscle.

"You did too much today," he said in a gentle, if accusing tone. "Aren't you supposed to be cutting back at the office?"

"Today was the day for me to hand off a few of my responsibilities," I admitted. "Eddie came in to supervise, and trust me, he was fussier than you guys about the number of breaks. But it also made the day last so much longer."

And I hadn't had the heart to tell Eddie he was making it worse. The man had been over the moon from the day we told him. I swore, he and Hank had found even more reasons to bond as they took bets on which of them could get the baby's sex out of us.

So far, neither was winning. Archie suspected that his dad would bribe our obstetrician, so he got a promise out of him to *not* do that.

They were insane.

"He means well," Jake said gruffly.

"I know. And your mom called this morning. They're working out a calendar so they can all come for various weeks that will give us backup with the baby."

Jake chuckled. "Mom's dying to come and take care of you. So are Carly and Sara. I have a feeling they would have been here already if they didn't think it would be smothering."

I laughed. "First grandchild," I said. "They are going to be insufferable."

"In the best way," Jake agreed as he eased me back to lay against him. Arms wrapped around me, he settled his palms on my belly and began to rub in gentle circles. "Now, Bump is going to nap, and so are you. Dinner will be another hour."

He didn't have to tell me twice.

"You guys are going to be the best fathers," I told him as I yawned. "You already are."

Best fathers.
Best husbands.
Best friends.

Chapter Twenty-One

ALMOST SIX YEARS AFTER THE WEDDING

ARCHIE

By late April, we were all ready for the bump to arrive. Frankie's appointments were now weekly, and she still went out for daily walks. Through mutual consent, we scheduled for one of us to be with her or at least close by at all times.

Frankie appreciated the company, but she also got irked if we hovered. So, we split the difference. Today was my day, and I'd come with her to the appointment, sat in the chair while the doctor did her exam and then told her we were still on target for a few more weeks.

That was it.

For some reason, that irritated the shit out of me. I wanted more definitive answers. I wanted actual dates. The doctor, as she had said numerous times before—we really should compensate her for how many times I'd asked—said that the bump would be here when the bump was ready.

Some of my frustration must have shown because Frankie

gripped my hand as we were stepping out of the doctor's office. It was a beautiful day, sunny, breezy, and not too cold. Though Frankie barely noticed the chill at the moment.

"Let's go for a walk," she suggested and I frowned. "Before you tell me it's too far or you don't want me to overdo it or any of the dozen other reasons I can see you listing in your mind—it's a beautiful day, I'm with my husband, Bump is actually quiet, and I want to just take a walk together."

Well, when she put it that way. I frowned. "If you get tired…"

She raised her right hand. "I solemnly swear I will tell you the moment I get too tired."

That was craftily worded. Still, I understood what she wanted to do. "All right, Babe," I said, tucking her arm through mine. "Where do you want to walk to?"

She glanced at the street before looking at me and making a face. "I really don't know what's on this side of town."

Laughing, I pulled out my phone and pressed a couple of buttons to bring up the app and called a car.

"What are you doing?"

"Taking you somewhere you can go for a walk."

Once we were in the car, I said, "Battery Park, please."

"Oh!" Frankie lit up and sent me a bright smile. "I've been wanting to go down there."

I was aware. One of the amusing things about moving to Manhattan and then living here for the past several years, at some point, we'd just stopped playing tourist. Battery Park had been on the list for a long time.

"There's plenty of places to walk, to sit, we can get lunch…"

"A real date." The fact that she lit up at the idea had me kicking myself. We really had been hovering the last several weeks.

"We've been neglecting you, haven't we, Babe?" I turned her hand over in mine. The rings were absent, but when her fingers started swelling, she took them off rather than risked having to cut them off.

"No," she promised. "You really haven't. We've all been trying to get everything ready for the bump. Then there's work—I had so much to do before taking leave. Though Eddie giving me six months seems a bit extreme."

Okay, at that, I laughed. "Dad found out that at six months, it would probably be okay for you to bring Bump to work with you, and don't think he isn't angling for that."

She groaned, but her smile kept winning out. "Does he really think Jeremy is going to let me take the bump anywhere?"

"Probably a battle he's looking forward to waging." The grandparents were all just having way too much fun and we'd let them have it. Our priority was Frankie.

Once at Battery Park, she needed a bathroom, and then after that, we walked through the gardens before we made our way to the waterfront. It was just nice to just be, no rush, no meetings, no press of waiting to get back to testing the engine.

Jake and I were so damn close. So close. We'd found about fifteen hundred ways it didn't work, but I rather hoped we finally had a line on a way that it did.

Leaning against me, Frankie sighed.

"Tired?"

"A little," she admitted. "But it's so pretty out here. Can we just stay for a little longer?"

We could do whatever she needed. But I did move us to one of the benches, even if it involved paying off the folks using it. There were many tourists out actually being tourists. Once we had the bench, I bunched up my jacket for a back cushion, and then we sat there until her yawns took over.

As dates went, it was actually going to be one of my favorites.

JAKE

Three weeks to her due date, and I found myself hating every single time I had to leave the house. Between her libido, which hadn't cooled once in the last few months, her cravings, and how fucking beautiful she was so swollen with our child—yeah, there was nowhere else I wanted to be.

Right now, though, we were in the shower and I was washing her hair. I'd pulled a shower chair inside it because her feet had been starting to swell and I didn't want her overdoing it.

"I miss taking baths," she confessed as I massaged the shampoo into her scalp. "I miss being able to just soak and indulge."

"Soon, Baby Girl," I promised. "After the baby, you just need to heal up—what six weeks? Then we'll make sure you get a long hot soak every single night. We're gonna work out a schedule too so that you have one of us backing you up at night, so we can all look after him or her."

She laughed. "Well, if we go forward with breastfeeding then I'm going to need to pump so you can use bottles too."

"I like this plan, though I freely admit, I love these breasts more." They'd seriously swollen over the last few months. When I'd pushed them together to fuck them, she'd laughed so hard, but she'd let me do it.

A little bit of white foamed over one peek as I massaged her breast. That was going to take some getting used to. But I didn't mind.

"Hair, Jake," she said with just a hint of laughter to underscore the command. "My breasts are a little too sore to come out and play."

"What about your pussy?"

"Actually…"

The minute she said that, my stomach bottomed out. "Actually, what?"

"Actually, it is a little sore. Kind of hard to describe. You know—achy, but you guys were very enthusiastic this weekend, so I am not complaining."

I studied her as I knelt there in the shower. "You sure?"

"I promise." Her green eyes softened as she touched my cheek. I moved my hand to her swollen tummy and the distended belly button. The piercing was gone. Had been since not long after the lines turned pink. Her belly had gotten harder and harder as of late.

All normal, but still… "Maybe we should call the doctor and just be on the safe side?"

"Or we can call your mother, who has had four kids, and we can run it by her?" The suggestion immediately made me nod.

"I like it." When I reached to turn off the water, she stopped me with a hand on my arm. "Baby Girl?"

"My hair?"

I stared at her blankly for a moment then at her hair. "Shit, sorry, Baby Girl."

Her laughter filled the shower. I helped her rinse it, then condition it and after all that, actually helped her finish washing up before I did my own sketchy shower.

We put off calling Mom until after breakfast. Then I got to have a front-row seat to Frankie discussing our sex life with Mom. Not one of my favorite moments ever, but the amusement on Frankie's face and the full-on belly laughs were worth it.

She had an appointment in a couple of days anyway.

IAN

I went through the next set of chords, pencil gripped in my teeth. Frankie dozed in the chair in the garden with Miss Abigail sprawled out on the stone in the sun a few feet away. Tiddles and Tory were sitting in the doorway, well laying in it. They didn't venture out so much as just doze right there.

Since she'd become pregnant, the animals always wanted to be around her. I kind of got that. We wanted to be around her too. Not totally happy with that chord, I switched it to another, and Frankie sighed, shifting in her chair.

"Not that one. Bump doesn't approve."

I chuckled, replaying the earlier one. "Better?"

"Yes," she said with a yawn. "Much. Apparently, Bump has definite opinions."

"Well, Bump's mama has fantastic taste when it comes to helping me with my music," I told her. "And if the bump prefers the first set of chords, then that's what we'll do."

I wrote the notes down on the lyric sheet, then started over again. Frankie rubbed her hand against her belly, humming along, but soon her hand slowed and her eyes drooped.

It was hard for her to sleep at night at all lately. More often than not, she was up every couple of hours to use the bathroom, and then she couldn't sleep after. Mom said it was the body's way of preparing her for broken sleep after Bump arrived.

I was not a fan. As long as she could sleep, I kept playing. It seemed the bump really did like the new song. Which was good, I'd been writing about the bump this whole time, but until the last few weeks, the final bits of the song hadn't come together.

Letting the music drift away, I finished adding notes to the sheets. It was a little under two and a half minutes. Not the longest song, I didn't think, but it was the right length.

"Mr. Bubba," Jeremy said from the doorway. "Mr. Cooper is on the phone. He said you weren't answering yours and he wanted to talk to you about the thing."

The thing.

I chuckled, then glanced at Frankie, where she slept soundly. With care, I pulled a light blanket over her bare legs, then rose. "Can you…?"

"Absolutely," Jeremy said as he stepped out into the garden. "I've also made the Shepherd's Pie she enjoys for dinner tonight and fixed the lemonade."

"You're going to be her favorite until the end of time," I told the man.

Inside, I slid into the kitchen and picked up the house phone. The kitchen smelled fantastic. With her being this pregnant and her due date right around the corner, Frankie had forgotten all about her own birthday.

But we'd all refused to forget it. Instead, we'd enjoyed dinner and a movie here. Still, we wanted to make every night special with her favorite meals and different ways to indulge her.

"Sorry," I said by way of greeting. "I turned the phone to silent cause I finally got her to sleep."

"That's what Jeremy said," Coop answered. There was a lot of noise in the background. "I'm at the jewelry store. Have we decided on what we want to put on the different charms yet?"

We'd debated everything from names to dates, but we couldn't do any of those until after the bump was born. "I think we leave them blank—we want the bracelet so we can give it to her at the hospital with the different pieces on it. If she wants to get them inscribed, we can do it later."

"That was Archie's suggestion, too," Coop said with a laugh. "Jake said he'd go with the majority, so I'm getting the pieces soldered on, and then I'll be home in a few hours."

"Sounds like a plan."

Off the phone, I headed back out to the garden. Jeremy straightened from where he'd been petting one of the cats. "All good?"

"Yep. Thanks."

"Of course, let me know when she's awake, and I'll bring out lunch."

"You're the best."

He slipped away and I settled my guitar back in my lap. Pencil between my teeth, I glanced at the notes on the page and then began to play again. I'd play all day if it let her sleep.

I couldn't wait for Bump's arrival. Not only so Mama could get her sleep but so that we could help more. Not to mention, Bump apparently had a solid ear for music.

Good to know.

COOP

The guys with the more flexible schedules had been handling the majority of the day-to-day over the last month as we got closer and closer to her due date. Not that anything was set in stone, according to Dr. Felucca. Which, fine, but I'd had to be out most mornings early and not get back home until close to six in the evening.

But I'd taken the next week off. We were wrapping up my clinical hours, and I wanted the time with Frankie. Especially once Bump got here.

Chuckling, I shook my head, and Frankie glanced up from her book to stare at me. "What are you laughing about?"

"Wondering how long it's going to take us to learn the baby's name and not call them Bump."

Laughter escaped her and she shook her head. "I don't think it will take that long at all, though…I have almost called the doctor a few times to ask her if we're having a girl or a boy."

"Really?" I mean, it shouldn't have surprised me. It didn't surprise me. Still…

"I know we agreed, which is why I didn't call, but every day I get more curious. I want to know them. I want to meet them and see if they are curious about everything and taking it all apart or if they're protective or musical or…"

"Or absolutely wonderful because we're going to love them no matter what personality quirks they have?" Not that there was an ounce of doubt within me.

"I know—but I want to meet them now, and it just seems like it's taking forever. Well, that and I'm tired of being pregnant." She made a face.

"It's not that bad, is it, Beautiful?"

"Um, no, but…"

"What's wrong?" I was out of the chair and heading to the sofa.

"I think my water just broke."

We both glanced down at the rapidly spreading stain. "Oh."

For a moment, we both just sat there. Well, Frankie sat there. I stood. We both stared.

Then I snapped my head up. "Water breaks. We call the car, get the bag, and take you to the hospital."

We'd been drilling the routine for weeks.

"Stay right there," I told her as I hurried upstairs to get the overnight bag.

"Coop, I can't go soaking wet."

"Stay there anyway," I called down the stairs. "I'll grab you some clothes."

Five minutes later, I was back, shoes on and with a change of clothes in hand. I helped her out of the wet things and into something dryer after I got her to the bathroom. While she peed—yes, definitely pee—I sent the text message to the guys.

Jake and Archie were in Brooklyn, and Bubba was downstairs in the recording studio. A second after it went through, the door flung open downstairs. "We sure?"

"Yep," I assured him. "Car is on the way."

"Why are we out here?"

"Because I looked like I peed myself," Frankie said from the bathroom. "I needed to clean up."

I bit back a smile as Bubba frowned. Jeremy swept through. "I've called the doctor to inform her you would be going directly to the hospital. The private suite will be ready as soon as you arrive. Shall we wait to notify the grandparents?"

I split a look with Bubba, and we both nodded. "We'll call them after. I want to keep it calm for her."

Seven hours later, I debated what calm for her meant because she was leaning all the way forward in the stirrups and glaring at Jake, who was near her feet. He'd already caught her foot when she would have kicked the nurse.

I had her hand, so when she squeezed during a push, it was my hand she was trying to break. Archie was on the bed behind her, bracing her, and Bubba alternated between whispered praises and cool washcloths to her face.

"You're doing great, Frankie," the doctor told her. "Baby is coming right on down, a couple of more pushes and they're going to be out, but I need you to do this—okay?"

"Remind me to never have sex again," Frankie declared and the doctor chuckled. "It's their fault we're here, their dicks—I'm starting to see the benefit of girls—"

I did not laugh. I would not laugh. I swore I wouldn't laugh.

Archie cracked up as he braced her, and Jake's lips were twitching.

"I. Hate. You." She gritted out every word as she pushed.

"Use it. Let it flow through you," Jake encouraged her, dropping his voice. "Let me feel your anger…"

Then she was laughing and I swore the doctor rolled her eyes at her, but then Frankie screamed as she pushed and there was a second scream echoing hers.

Frankie panted, but we were all leaning forward to see the screaming, messy little thing, and all the videos in the world don't prepare you for how like an alien a newborn looks.

I'd keep that choice bit of info to myself too.

"It's a girl," Jake said, laughing as he lifted his head to look up at us. "A baby girl." Tears escaped from his eyes, and he wasn't alone as he clipped the umbilical cord.

He'd won the damn coin toss. Just meant he was out for the next time round.

"She's looking good, mama," the doctor said. "But we have a little more work to do here."

"Wait, what?" I said. Twins? Didn't that shit only happen in the movies?

"We need to pass the placenta," the doctor informed me.

Oh. Ick.

Right.

"Go with Bump," Frankie said to me, and I squeezed her hand gently. I was going to have finger imprints for life and I was okay with it. After kissing her hand and another to her damp forehead, I followed Jake to where they were cleaning up the very angry little thing.

"She already has Frankie's temper," Jake murmured.

"I heard that," Frankie called, and I had to lean on Jake cause I was laughing so hard.

She was so tiny, red-faced, and with a head full of hair. I couldn't tell if it was dark or light since it was so wet. But they cleaned her up, checking her reflexes, her weight, and her measurements.

Nineteen point two inches. A little under eight pounds. Healthy baby. Nine on the Apgar. Then they were wrapping her up and lifting her. "Does one of the daddies want to hold her?"

Hell yes, I wanted to hold her. Jake and I immediately put out fists. Paper beat rock, and they put the perfect little angel right into my arms. She was so tiny, but her grip on me was nearly as fierce as her mama's.

I didn't think there'd been a happier day in my life than when Frankie said she'd marry me, but I was wrong.

This—this definitely topped that. Putting the little girl into Frankie's arms was a brilliant moment. She looked down at the sweet girl's face, and we were all enraptured.

"She's perfect," Frankie whispered.

"Just like you, Babe," Archie said, but that went without saying. Even after they moved Frankie into a room and we got the baby to latch the first time, none of us were going anywhere.

"Is it bad that I kind of want to wait to call the grandparents still?" Bubba asked.

Jake shook his head. "They can wait. We'll send them photos later."

We did.

Much later.

Three days after she was born, we brought baby Isobel home, ready to begin the next chapter in our lives.

Seriously, I couldn't wait.

Epilogue
A FEW YEARS LATER...

FRANKIE

"You're going to be late," I called, almost laughing as the words fell off my lips. I had the lunches stacked together, and Jeremy stood at the door with jackets and backpacks lined up. He still made the best French toast and coffee, and we'd struck a deal regarding cooking. On busy mornings, he took care of it, but when I had a day off or took it off, I was in charge.

Today was Isobel's first day of third grade and Joshua's first day of kindergarten. Big days. The first day of any school year was important. We weren't going to be late, but I still glanced at the clock. No, we had time.

The sound of the backdoor opening had me turning, though, and I grinned as a familiar dark-haired man ducked inside. "Am I late? Did I miss it?" Archie asked, worry in his dark brown eyes.

"Nope," I promised. "You're just in time."

"Excellent, look who I found at the airport." He pushed the door wider and Ian followed him inside. My heart did a little fist bump with my ribs. Archie had been gone for just the weekend. The annual meeting for Standish Enterprises required his presence and he'd stayed over to tour the new R&D facility. Jake had planned on going with him, but Charlie got a cold and Ian had still been in California.

Before I could let out a squeal of delight, the sound of feet racing down the stairs reached us.

"I'm coming," Izzy huffed as she preceded Jake into the kitchen. "Daddy was doing my braid. What do you think?" Skeptical didn't begin to cover Izzy's expression. Her green eyes studied me for even an ounce of doubt, but the wild mass of long blond curls had indeed been tamed into a double French braid with one twist coming from each side of her head to meet in the middle.

"I think it looks perfect," I promised and set my coffee aside. Isobel shot across the kitchen as soon as I opened my arms. She hugged with her whole body and squeezed me for all of three seconds before...

"Dad!" she screamed. "Papa!"

Then she launched toward Archie and Ian. Archie intercepted her first hug, and she squealed in delight as she squeezed him and Ian half-hugged her over Archie's shoulder. But as soon as she squirmed, she was in Ian's arms.

"I missed you!" she scolded him, all serious. "Next time, they can't have you for three whole weeks unless I get to go too."

"Duly-noted, Peanut," he murmured, and despite flying what must have been the redeye to get back in time, he looked amazing.

"Daddy did my hair," Izzy informed them as though they hadn't been standing there when she told me. Jake slid his arm around me and then snagged my coffee cup. At his raised brows, I grinned and he took a grateful drink.

He still had the magic touch when it came to getting Izzy to wear anything she didn't want to. Who knew my daughter could be so stubborn? Not that I was stupid enough to ask that aloud.

"Papa!" Joshua yelled as he streaked through the kitchen ahead of Coop, who arrived with Charlie snuffling against his shirt. Archie caught Joshua as he flung himself at him and oofed dramatically. Ian snorted.

"He's going to master that tackle one of these days."

"Don't I know it," Archie groaned. From the corner of my eye, I caught Jeremy's broad grin as he dusted off Izzy's blouse. I was still on the fence about sending them all to private school, but as long as the kids enjoyed it, I would be okay with it.

Izzy looked adorable in her uniform, and Joshua high-fived Ian before squirming to rush over to me, just as Charlie let out a little wail of sound and tried to pitch himself out of Coop's arms. I caught the red-faced toddler and hugged him close. Most of his cold was gone, but he was such a grumpy little puss when he didn't feel good.

Joshua scowled for a minute as though he disapproved of Charlie's sudden demand for attention, but then he relented when I squatted down, still holding him, and Joshua gave me a careful hug. "Feel better, buddy," Joshua told his little brother. "Don't be a pain in the ass to Mommy."

At my glare, Jake, Archie, and Ian all found somewhere else to look, but Coop just laughed. He was so not helpful.

"Don't say ass, you ass," Izzy informed Joshua. "Now come on, we're going to be late, and I want to meet your teacher and mine before classes start." She held out her hand to him, and Joshua kissed my cheek almost shyly.

"Sorry, Mommy."

"It's all right, big boy," I murmured, then hugged him close. Kindergarten was such a big step. "You sure you don't want us to go with you?"

He made a face, and then he squinted at me before looking at Charlie. "Think it'd be okay if Papa and Dad went? You guys were up a lot with Charlie this weekend."

"That'd be fine, kiddo," Jake told him, and Joshua gave me another kiss before giving Jake a hug. "You be good. Listen to your sister and your teacher. No fighting."

It was my turn to snort. Coop was already putting a hand under my elbow to help me up while Charlie just wiped his damp face against my shirt.

"I don't fight, Daddy," Joshua told him bluntly. "That's Izzy's job."

Laughter rippled through the room, and Izzy gave me a bland look as I shook my head. She was so much like me. "Have a fantastic day, little miss. I want to hear everything when you get home."

"I'll take good notes, Mom," Izzy said, hand over her heart. "And I'll look after Joshua. Max and Brayden are both gonna to be there, and they made me promise they could have some of the fights this year, too."

Oh God, save us all.

Jake had his face buried in my hair as his shoulders shook. Archie's eyes were dancing, and Ian just grinned.

"And on that note," Jeremy said. "Miss Isobel, Mr. Joshua, let's go. Coats on like a little lady and gentleman."

"Bye, Daddy. Bye, Pop," Izzy called. Joshua waved to both of them.

I managed to steal a pair of quick kisses from Ian and Archie before they had to go, and they both nuzzled kisses to Charlie's head.

"He still feels warm," Archie worried. "Do we need to call the doc?"

"No fever, at least not this morning," I assured him, rubbing a hand against Charlie's back. "Pretty sure he's teething again." He'd gotten a bit of a late start to it. "But we'll watch him."

"Okay," Archie said, stroking a hand through his hair. "We'll be back soon and can take over so you three can get some sleep."

Did we really look that bad?

"I have to get to work," Coop said with a stretch. "But it's just the morning, so I'll be back after lunch."

His practice had begun to take off except...

"Be home by lunch," I told him. "It's the five of us today as soon as little Mister Boo here takes a nap, and I want some me time."

"Yes, ma'am," Ian told me and he grinned at Coop. "You have your marching orders."

"Yes, I do."

It was noisy and messy and chaotic, and I loved every single minute of it. Jeremy got the boys and the kids out the door. Coop gave me a long, firm kiss before he headed upstairs to change for work. Charlie had all but gone to sleep while I cradled him. Another sign he wasn't feeling too good.

"You planning on telling us you're pregnant again?" Jake asked quietly, and I shot a look over at him. How had he...?

My coffee cup was in his hand.

"Decaf, it's the only time you drink this swill."

Jeremy had figured it out, but I'd sworn him to secrecy and he'd been damn good about making sure that I got the decaf while not alerting the guys. Honestly, I was ready to let this baby out of the bag.

My heart squeezed, and then I laughed. "Yes," I admitted. "Been sitting on this news for the last week, but I wanted Ian and Archie here..."

"No worries, Baby Girl," Jake promised me, his eyes brightening as he pulled me and Charlie to him. "I'm thrilled," he whispered. "Though the little man here might get pouty."

I chuckled. "We have a few months to get him ready…" That gave us time to do a lot of things, including the tour Ian wanted to do this fall. A month-long circuit of one-night-only performances. He didn't tour as often as he should, but he wouldn't go without me, and I'd been pregnant the last time we did it too.

Coop paused in the doorway, hands on his tie and he studied us. "Huh," he grunted then grinned. "I'll be home for lunch. Promise."

He already knew. It was all over his face.

"I don't know why I try to keep secrets from you guys."

"Cause you're good at it when you *want* to keep it a secret," Coop teased, and then he and Jake boxed Charlie and me up together and I sighed.

Getting here had been a bit of a trial and a whole lot of tears, but every damn day had been worth it.

Very worth it.

* * *

271

Thank you for going on this journey with us. This is the final book for Frankie and the boys. While they will appear in guest roles in future series, this is the happily ever after I promised all the way back in the beginning.

What's next?

KC's story begins this autumn at Blue Ivy Prep,

with Book One: Problem Child.

Blue Ivy Prep
BOOK ONE

PROBLEM CHILD

Enrollment begins this autumn.

Born into Hollywood royalty, I've been making the hot sheet and generating internet buzz since before I could even walk. Doesn't matter that my parents divorced prior to my second birthday, I can't escape the shadows—or scandals—of my movie star mother and my rock star father.

At least, I couldn't until Aubrey, Yvette and I formed Torched and went double platinum as we made a name for ourselves. Four years after taking the world by storm, I'm exhausted. We all are. I'm also ready to try and be a regular kid. Only problem is I've never been normal. I don't actually know what that feels like. Accepted into the prestigious Blue Ivy Prep, I have a lot to prove to the students, the faculty, our fans, but most of all to myself.

Despite my tabloid reputation or maybe because of it, I don't intend for anything to get in my way. Especially not anyone who decided I'm an empty-headed pampered partying princess before I even showed up.

If they want a fight, I'll bring them a war.

Afterword

And they lived happily, crazily, madly, ever after.

Course, with three kids and a fourth on the way, they are probably living it sleep deprived and loving every stolen moment they get with each other.

The epilogue to this story was actually written in August of 2020. This was before I added two more books to the already ten planned books and before a slowdown thanks to a herniated disc in my spine had me putting the books out a little slower.

In all honesty, I hadn't really read that scene for more than a year when I went and opened it for this. I only had to make two small modifications.

Thank you very much for being on this journey with me. Thank you for loving them and cheering them on. Thank you for asking about KC and Rachel and will they get their books.

As you can see by the previous page, yes, they will. First up is KC, Problem Child will release later this year. When Blue Ivy Prep wraps up, we'll dive into Rachel's books.

You may have guessed it, but we will see cameos from Frankie and the guys in those stories. *winks*

I can't wait to see what's next.

xoxo

Heather

Flashback
FISTS AND FRIENDS

FRANKIE

"Cooper Brennen," the teacher called.

"Here."

"Francesca—" I grimaced. "—Curtis."

"Here."

The kid sitting next to me crossed his gray-green eyes and I wrinkled my nose and then focused on the teacher again. He lived in my apartments and I'd seen him outside a couple of times, but I hadn't met him before class today.

I was nervous enough about being here. My tummy kept doing these weird flippy flop things. Mom had told me I wasn't allowed to cry so I hadn't. I also had to be good, so I was doing my best. I'd been to pre-school before, but I had friends there. It was in the same building where Mom worked.

This was not.

And it was so much bigger.

I didn't know anyone.

Tears pricked my eyes but I blinked them back because a girl at another table just started crying. When all the attention swung to her I let out a breath. The kid next to me crossed his eyes again when I glanced at him and I frowned.

"Fran-Chest-Ca?" he sounded out my name and I scowled.

"Frankie."

I liked Frankie *way* better. Francesca was a terrible name.

Mom only called me that when she was mad.

The kid grinned. "That's a boy's name."

Ugh. I made a face. Then stared at the board when the teacher started talking again. She had the crying girl all cuddled up when she called us to sit in a circle. We got to tell each other something about ourselves. I didn't have much to say, but I did get to tell them I was Frankie and the teacher promised to remember my name.

By lunchtime I was exhausted, we got to go out on the playground right after food. We didn't get our first break because we got to go to the library instead.

I *loved* the library.

The lady in charge of it was Mrs. Fredkins. She was the nicest lady ever and promised that by Christmas, we would be able to take books from the library home to read then bring them back.

Best.

Place.

Ever.

I could already read. That was something not every kid in the class did yet. I could even write most of the alphabet neatly. I ate as fast as I could because as soon as I finished I could go outside. The kid who sat next to me in the class also sat next to me at lunch. But like me, he was hungry, so he ate as fast as he could, too.

I won and shot my hand up in the air. My teacher laughed and told me I was excused. I remembered to throw away my trash along with the brown paper bag and then raced outside. It was hot and sunny and there was playground equipment. I knew I had to be careful of the dress, even if I hated it, but I *never* got to go to the park.

Mom never had time. She had to do a lot of work and it was important that I entertain myself. This was the best part of preschool and I needed to know if it would be the best part of school school too.

The playground was *huge*.

I wanted to do everything.

I was up the slide in a heartbeat and flying down.

Stupid skirt got in the way, but I bunched it and made it work. I had on shorts underneath.

The boy from class was at the top of the slide when I got to the bottom and he wooted as he raced down. Then I was back up again.

Next was the jungle gym and I watched him scamper across the monkey bars and I was right behind him.

He laughed when I jumped off and landed next to him. "Swings?"

"Yes!"

We turned and he ran into another kid. "Hey," the kid groused and shoved Cooper. Cooper stumbled into me and then shoved the kid back.

He was a bit bigger than Cooper. But I was taller than Cooper too. Then the kid hit Cooper. I scowled. "You want a knuckle sandwich?" I demanded.

The other kid smirked at me. "Give it to me," he demanded and pushed right at me. I balled up my fist and socked him. The big bully landed on his butt in the dirt. My hand hurt and the kid on the ground stared at me for a beat and then burst into wailing tears.

What a baby.

I was so disgusted.

Cooper stared at me, wide-eyed with his mouth open as one of the teachers charged over to us.

An hour later, I had to explain for the third time why I punched the boy—John—in the face. "I asked permission," I argued tartly. I didn't understand the problem. We weren't supposed to touch other kids without their permission. I learned that *last* year. So I asked.

My teacher seemed to be struggling, mightily. The principal who had come in to talk to me was a big guy and I was a little scared when he'd first come in, but he listened to me tell the whole story and then he and the teacher both seemed like they were going to cry.

"Am I in trouble?"

"Francesca," my teacher began.

"Frankie," I said. "Please."

"Frankie," she continued, this time with a smile. "I am going to have to call your mother."

My stomach dropped. I was in trouble. Mom was gonna be so mad. "But I asked first."

"Yes, you did," the principal said with a sigh. "We have to talk to your mom because those are the rules, and I need you to not ask other kids if they want a 'knuckle sandwich' again."

I frowned. "He said yes."

"John claims he didn't know what it was," my teacher said gently and I scowled. "That said, you shouldn't hit."

"He was being mean to Cooper and shoved him."

"Then you get a teacher," the principal told me. "I know this is new for you, but you have to follow the rules, too."

I folded my arms and leaned back in my seat. "I did follow the rules. I didn't touch him without asking."

The principal cleared his throat. "I'll leave Frankie with you, Ms. Diaz." Then he left the room. It sounded like he was choking or coughing as he left.

Then it was just me and Ms. Diaz. The other kids weren't here, they were in another classroom. I'd had to come sit with Ms. Diaz and talk after the fight. Not that it was a fight. John was just a big ol' baby.

"Frankie," she said, pulling my attention. "Do you understand why it was wrong?"

"No, because I asked first. I didn't touch him without asking."

"That was good. But even if you ask for someone's permission to hit them, you shouldn't hit."

That didn't make any sense. "Do you have to call my mom?"

"I'm afraid so, sweetheart. That's the rules. You're also going to need to sit out from the playground for the next couple of days."

"Fine."

That wasn't so bad. Mom was going to be so angry.

"But Mom is at work and if you interrupt her at work, she'll get mad."

"I'll take care of it. You don't worry. Okay?"

Yeah. I worried.

By the time the other kids came back and Cooper and I were sitting at our table, my stomach was in knots. Not because I was scared of school, but because I was scared of going home.

Cooper leaned over when the teacher told us to color our sheets and whispered, "Hey Frankie...will you be my friend?"

Really? I blinked and stared at him. "Okay."

"Yeah?" he said, grinning.

"Yeah."

He bumped my shoulder and then shared his crayons.

I didn't get to play for the next couple of days and Cooper sat out with me. He wanted to be called Coop. I called him Coop.

Mom picked me up that first day and she wasn't mad at all. She did ask me about it, but she wasn't angry. If anything she laughed then asked me if I really hit the kid hard and I told her I had. She nodded and that was that.

Whew.

Mom picked me up every day after school that week and she met Coop's mom and then...the next week, Mom took us both to school and Coop's mom picked us up after.

It was awesome.

Three weeks later, I was in the principal's office again. I'd torn my last dress and I had a bloody nose. Felicia MacNamara had a black eye. I made sure she hit me first. But she'd been really mean to Coop and called him names.

So I made her mad.

They called my mom.

I got in trouble for this one.

Totally worth it.

Coop wanted to be my best friend after that.

Flashback

BOYS AND BOOKS

FRANKIE

2nd Grade

"Let it go," I ordered Alan Graves. He had his grubby fingers locked around my book and I wasn't giving it up. I'd worked for two weeks straight to earn enough quarters from Mom to buy this book myself. Alan did not get to take it. We were supposed to be having free time on the playground right now and I'd brought my book out to read.

Alan made a face and yanked the book free. "Mine now. Whatcha gonna do?"

Balled up my fist and punched him in the nose was what I did.

He whacked me right back. Even though I had tears from the smack of my book hitting my face, I didn't get to retaliate. A blur of dark hair slammed into him and they both went flying. So did my book. I barely scrambled to grab it and turned when I found Alan on the ground while a boy a little bit bigger than him wailed on him.

We were just out of sight of the monitors but one of the other kids yelled "fight!" and I whistled between my teeth. It sounded pathetic since I was actually missing a tooth but it was enough to get the second kid's attention. Oh, it was the new kid. "C'mon," I told him and curled my fingers. "You're gonna get in trouble."

He scowled. At first I thought he was glaring at me, but he jumped to his feet and then kicked Alan. I winced cause Alan made the mistake of rolling and the new kid got him right in the no-no square. The little squeal Alan made told me, hurt as much as it looked. Then the new kid stomped over to me and looked down at my book.

"You're bleeding," he said.

I swiped a hand at my face and winced at my nose. Yep. There was some blood. "He hits like a little girl."

The new kid snorted.

"What?"

"You hit him pretty hard," he said. Alan had dragged himself up and limped away. One of the playground monitors glanced over at us and I grabbed the new kid's arm and hauled him over behind the jungle gym and the slide. We weren't totally out of sight, but didn't want them to see the new kid with the dust all over him.

He looked like he'd been fighting.

"I said *little* girl," I told him sternly and dusted him off before I straightened and stuck out my hand to him. "I'm Frankie."

"Jacob," he said with a grimace. "I like Jake better."

"Okay, Jake." I said as he shook my hand. "Thanks for helping."

"No problem." He squinted at me. "You sure you're a girl?"

I yanked my hand out of his and glared at him. "Why do you think I'm not a girl?"

"Cause you don't hit like one."

"You've never had me hit you, you don't know." Course, I kind of liked the compliment. Just glad I didn't get caught. I belted Sue Marie last week cause she called Coop stupid. Mrs. Diaz was pretty disappointed in me and Mrs. Hoffman told me I'd lose playground privileges for a week if I got caught fighting again.

Worth it.

"Heh," Jake said, then scratched his ear. "Well, if you wanna hit me so I can find out for sure, you can. I won't hit you back or nothing."

I stared at him. "Why would I hit you?"

"So I can see if you hit like a girl."

I rolled my eyes. Boys were so dumb.

"What?" Jake said. "I could take it."

Yeah. Really dumb. "I don't want to hit you. I wanna read my book."

He shrugged. "Okay."

"Anyway...thanks." I carried my book away from the playground equipment and the other kids and found a place to sit. My nose was tender and there was only a little bit of blood. I rubbed it clean and then wiped my hand on my jeans. So far Alan hadn't told on us. But he was also sitting at one of the picnic tables near the door crying.

I kind of felt bad until I looked at my book and the part where he ripped the cover and I scowled.

He better be crying.

A shadow fell over me where I sat and I glanced up to find the new kid—Jake—standing there. He dropped to sit next to me and I frowned. "What are you doing?"

"Sitting here," he told me. "What are you doing?"

"Reading my book." I mean, obviously, right?

Still, I hated that Alan tore a piece of the cover. I smoothed it down and opened it to the first page.

"What's it about?"

"It's about a girl detective."

"Is it any good?"

I looked at him. "I like all her books. But I haven't read this one before."

"But you read the others?"

"I just said I like the other ones."

"Oh," he said slowly. "Right."

Going back to my book, I turned to the first chapter and Jake scooted closer. Glancing up, I stared at him. "What now?"

"Just wanted to see if it's good or not." He stared at me for a minute. "Is it okay if I read it too?"

I squinted at him and pushed my tongue at the gap in my teeth. I was losing valuable reading time to this conversation. "I read fast."

"I can keep up." He lifted his chin and gave me a grin.

"I won't slow down." Fair warning. Cause Coop always complained about how fast I could read.

"Okay." He nudged my shoulder and nodded to the book.

Fine.

I leaned a little so he could see and then started reading. Like I promised, I didn't slow down. We were on chapter three when a shadow blocked out the sunlight and I glared up to find Coop staring at us. Well, staring at Jake. "Hey," I said with a grin. "I thought you were gonna miss recess."

"Nah," he said, flopping down in the dirt on my other side. "Just had to get my teeth cleaned." Then he looked at Jake. "Who are you?"

"Jake." He scowled right back at Coop.

See, I told you boys were dumb.

I elbowed Coop then said, "Jake's the new kid. He beat up Alan for me."

Coop glanced from me to where Alan was playing now and then

back to me and Jake. "Yeah?"

"Yeah."

"Cool," Coop said and stuck his hand out. "I'm Coop."

"You her boyfriend?" Jake asked and I rolled my eyes.

"No," I said.

"Yes," Coop answered.

"I don't have a boyfriend, Cooper Brennen." I pinched him.

"Yes you do! I'm a boy and your friend. So you have a boyfriend."

We glared at each other. "Fine. I'm reading."

Then I stuck my nose back in my book.

"Can I be your boyfriend too?" Jake asked and I stared at the sky. "I mean I'm a boy..."

"If I say yes, can I go back to reading my book?"

He grinned. "Sure."

"Great, then fine. I have two boyfriends. Now lemme read before the--" Too late the bell rang and I sighed. I closed my book as they scrambled to their feet. Both of them offered me a hand and I snorted, I could stand up on my own.

We were almost to the door when Jake said, "When you're done with the book can I borrow it?"

I glanced at him. So did Coop. Cause I didn't lend books. I didn't have that many.

"I have some books you can borrow," he offered. Coop and I looked at each other and then back at Jake. "I can ask my mom if you guys can come over after school and see."

"How many books?"

He grinned again. "I got a lot of books. Mom likes that I read." Lots of books?

"Yes," I told him. "Coop and I would love to come."

"We would?" Coop grumbled but I stomped on his foot.

"We would."

"Cool," Jake said, grinning wider. "I got video games too."

"Now you're talking," Coop suddenly didn't seem to mind. Games were fine.

I wanted the books.

I finished before school was over and I offered the book to Jake to see if he still wanted it. He grinned. We didn't get to go over after school that day, but Coop's mom promised to talk to Jake's mom and it took us almost a week--Jake brought me my book back the next day and brought one of his with it. Then he asked if I had another of the Trixie books.

We traded books all week.

Coop made fun of us.

But it was still fun and finally, a week later, I got to see all the books he had.

He wasn't wrong.

He had a *lot*.

Boys were dumb but boys with books were cool.

A few months later, I punched Jake. He deserved it.

And you know what, he said I didn't hit like a girl.

Flashback
RHYME AND REASON

IAN

When Dad retired to private practice and a civilian life, I'd actually been looking forward to getting away from living on bases while also soaking up stability of maintaining the same address as well as school for more than two years at a shot.

With his degree and specialities, Dad had often pulled overseas duty assignments. I'd enjoyed seeing the world, but I missed the normalcy of America. Hamburgers. Coke that tasted like coke. The right ratio of onions to burger and the vital ingredient to all of life's pleasures—ketchup

Right, I was a simple guy and I liked simple things. We'd only finished our move the week before once we'd gotten back to the States, done the house-hunting, then pulled everything out of storage in San Antonio. The new place was located in a much smaller town, but I kind of liked it. The open roads. The huge fields. The lakes.

And tons of places to go hiking or fishing when the air wasn't so hot it could cook you in place. Add to that they'd gotten a pool with the house and I was in heaven. Still, enrolling at the junior high so late meant I'd missed out on the pick of the classes and had to stick with whatever was left. I didn't care, honestly, I was kind of looking forward to that "all-American" experience even if it meant homework.

First period was language arts and I found the classroom right before the bell. There was only one desk open. Second row right behind a gorgeous blonde. I'd only gotten a quick look at her as I passed by. She had a book open on her desk and her whole attention seemed focused on it.

I ignored the glances tossed in my direction. Being an unknown wasn't a new experience for me. I'd learned to shrug those glances off a long time ago. Still, I kind of wished she'd glanced up or at least around at me so I could get a better look at her.

The guy on her left reached over to grip it and she smacked his hand without looking up. It was hard not to laugh. The class flew by. Actual textbooks were assigned along with our first visit to the library to get authorized to check out books from there. Independent reading lists and the syllabus for the first six weeks of assignments were also handed out.

Before I realized it, she'd vanished in the library and there just wasn't time to track her down before the bell rang and I had to hurry. My next class was a PE training class. Weights, since all the tryouts for the various teams had happened over the summer, was clear on the other side of the school. I had gym clothes in my bag, but the teacher waved us in without having us get changed. There was a note on the door for the same thing.

"Let's go, I want to go over all the safety rules and expectations before you guys even touch the weights..."

Right, I knew how to use all the visible equipment and had been training with Dad pretty regularly for the last three years. Still, I focused on what he was saying right up until I caught sight of a familiar face. Locking gazes with Jake Benton had me grinning stupidly.

Of all the people to be in one of my classes was someone I actually knew from going to school with him before. Only then, we'd been in Germany and not the U.S. Our parents had also been friends, our dads at least, which meant Jake and I had hung out quite a bit before he'd returned stateside with his mom.

We didn't get much of a chance to talk before the end of class when the teacher—coach—finished going over everything from safety protocols to dress code to expectations. This would be a weight lifting class, we would have reading and tests on major muscle groups as well as understanding how to train them. We would be working out on different muscle groups daily and we had to partner or triple up

Jake and I were in lockstep almost immediately. When we were told to get to know each other and work out our goal sheets, I headed straight for him and dumped my bag to the side. "Man, it's good to see you."

"Same," Jake said, shaking my hand. "Mom told me she'd heard from your dad and that you guys were planning to move here, but I didn't know you'd already made it."

"Barely. We got in like five days ago, and it's been all running to get everything set up. Mom already has shifts at the hospital and Dad will be starting at his job this week or next."

"This is so cool that you're here," Jake said with a grin. "You gotta try out for football."

"Didn't I already miss the tryouts? And the summer practices?"

"Kinda but, I know a guy." He shoulder checked me. "C'mon."

Our weights teacher, the coach, turned out to be the coach for the junior high's football squad. He gave me a once over and then told me to show up after school to run some drills. No guarantees, but maybe I could get some time to fill in until he saw whether I was a good fit or not.

"Catch me at lunch," Jake said when we separated for classes. The gorgeous blonde was in my third period math class but she was up front and the only seat left for me was in the back. Damn, she vanished as soon as the bell rang. I swore she could move.

But this time I had a name.

I'd ask Jake about her. When the lunch bell rang, my brain already ached from the sheer number of "introduction" and "first of the year" speeches I'd received. It was nice that Jake was waiting for me right outside the lunchroom.

"Hold up," he told me when I would have gone on inside. "Waiting on some friends."

"Sure." I'd just leaned back against the wall next to him when I spotted the blonde again. She was strolling in our direction, talking animatedly to a tall, lanky guy next to her. His response made her laugh and I swore it was like being dropped inside of a bell as a gong sounded.

The vibration went straight through me. She was still smiling, laughter in her eyes, when our gazes locked. The lyrics to Savage Garden's "I Knew I Loved You," made absolute sense to me.

"Bubba, this is Frankie and Coop," Jake said and it was like all the sound rushed back in at once. "Guys, this is Bubba. Friend of mine from Germany. He's new."

"Wait," Coop said with smirk. "You have friends outside of us?" He wrapped his arm around Frankie's shoulder and I had the sudden desire to break it. "Well, what do you know?"

"Fuck you," Jake said, laughing as he dragged the door open. Frankie elbowed Coop, then stuck her hand out to me.

"Welcome," she greeted me as she shook my hand, but the eye

contact didn't last anywhere near as long as I would have liked. Instead, she glanced past me to Jake. "You're really growing in your old age. Developing new people skills. Welcoming friends to our circle. I'm so proud."

She mimed wiping away a tear and I cracked up as Jake made a face at her and then shook his head. "Bubba doesn't count as new. So he's in. Deal with it."

I was? Fine by me. I hadn't realized how hard I was staring or how obvious it was as she and Jake led the way toward the line picking on each other or how Jake pretty much body blocked anyone from running into her.

"She has that effect on people," Coop said as he bumped my shoulder with his. At my glance, he touched the corner of his mouth. "You have a little drool right here.."

The flash of teasing in his eyes helped and I shook my head before giving him a little shove away. "Shut up."

He was still laughing when we caught up and she glanced back at us, a question in her eyes.

"Bubba just had something on his face," Coop said without an ounce of apology. "Don't worry, I fixed it."

At her raised brow inquiry in my direction, I found myself thanking Coop mentally. "I don't see anything," she murmured. "All good now."

Yeah. Yeah it was.

Seeing her had captured my attention. Hearing her laugh had snared my heart. But the fact she smiled at me and then talked to me.

All I could think of was soulmate. What a stupid fucking word it was, but at the same time it fit. Clearly, I kept those thoughts to myself. But I ate lunch with them every single day and it wasn't long before I had her number and we were hanging out.

Maybe all the last minute rushing and not being able to pick classes was worth it. Sure, I sat on the bench for half the year in football, but I got my times to shine. I found an old friend and new friends all on the same day.

Even better, I met Frankie.

I had no idea why all of that went through my head as we sat on the bus heading for graduation, but it did. Six, almost seven years ago, I couldn't have imagined how this worked out. Hell, at the beginning of the school year I'd thought we'd doomed it before it could really start.

Yet here we were, beyond rhyme and reason.

All because I met Frankie and she was the best damn thing to ever happen to me.

Flashback
MATH AND MEETINGS

ARCHIE

The car rolled up to the high school and I leaned back in the passenger seat. Jeremy cast a sideways look at me. "There's still time to change your mind, Mr. Archie." It was the first day of ninth grade and not only had we moved over the summer to a new place in Texas of all places, but I'd decided to go to school locally rather than remain at boarding school.

"Nope," I said with a lot more confidence than I possessed. The last couple of years at Andover had been less than stellar. With Nana gone now, there was no reason to stay. She'd been the driving force behind my attendance. Particularly since she and Grandpa lived a few miles away. I could spend weekends with them. Grandpa didn't want the house anymore and I couldn't blame him.

The last weekend I spent there it had just been the two of us rattling around in that big empty house. Now that Grandpa and Edward were no longer on speaking terms, I didn't even have that escape available. Grandpa's last missive—passed through Jeremy since Edward, the asshole, had forbidden me direct contact with him—included the fact he was selling the house but would put the money into my trust for me.

I didn't give a damn about the money. Honestly, I didn't even care about the house. It was just a building without Nana.

This school though was a far cry from the boarding schools and preparatory academies I'd spent the last few years at. No uniforms in sight. The temperatures outside were sizzling. A hell of a lot more kids trailed up the walkways, got off of buses, and made their way in from the parking lot than had been at his boarding school.

A lot more.

Public school. Time to make my own way.

"I'm good," I continued, glancing at Jeremy. The guy, who was pretty much the family manager from butler to chauffer to cook to confidant, regarded me steadily. "Seriously, I'm good. I want to do this. I need air to breathe that isn't loaded down with expectations and plans made three generations ago."

Also, I didn't want any more damn arguments about what my next steps would be. Edward and Muriel both wanted different things for me. From prep school to Ivy League to diving into the family business.

Yeah, none of those were on my list.

There had to be a life outside of the moneyed halls with their polite stabs in the back and poisonous arguments.

"You have your phone, I'll be along directly at four to retrieve you. If that changes for any reason just let me know."

"Thanks Jeremy."

"Of course, Mr. Archie."

At least riding up front it wasn't as conspicuous that I had a driver for school. We'd finished all my enrollment the week before. Jeremy had come with me to do the paperwork and signed everything. He'd pretty much done that since I was five. I doubt Edward or Muriel had ever set foot inside one of my schools.

Ever.

Somehow, I didn't think it would change here.

"See you later," I told Jeremy as I stepped out into the muggy heat and slung my backpack over my shoulder. One look at what the other kids were wearing and I was glad I swapped out the polo shirt Jeremy had put out for a band t-shirt I'd picked up at a concert over the summer.

As it was the khaki shorts were gonna stand out but fuck it. I tapped the top of the Lexus before walking away. I had my schedule in my back pocket and I may or may not have memorized the layout of the school because it was three times the size of the academy. They like everything bigger in Texas apparently.

The first three classes of the day were boring as fuck. I might need to revisit my academic schedule. I was ahead of a lot of these classes, but Jeremy had been right in his advice to test the waters first. Fourth period had potential. I liked math. My engineering classes were in the afternoon, so those were something to look forward to as well as foreign language. Two years of French to meet the requirements.

Another perk for public schools, so far there was no assigned seating. I could skate in and grab a desk in the back row. It put me in the perfect position to watch kids as they hustled in. The other freshmen seemed to be a mixed bag of totally not giving a damn and seriously anxious. The anxious ones earned my sympathy cause if I hadn't practiced hiding my feelings for years, I'd probably look just like them.

The last four to skate in the door laughed their way in the door. Two jocks, though the third guy could be one, too, I supposed, but they weren't what snagged my interest. No, the blonde in their midst with a faint smirk on her lips as she punched one of the jocks in the arm captured all of my attention.

"Shut up," she muttered then hip-checked the second jock.

"Asses."

"Awww," the third guy complained. "It was my idea."

She flipped him off so fast, I had to snort a laugh then she slid into a chair in front of me which worked for me, I didn't mind the view *at all*.

Her friends, however, scowled and the dark-haired guy gave me such a narrow-eyed look I planted my gaze anywhere but her.

For. The. Moment.

As soon as the teacher walked in though, I kept studying her. She barely looked up from her books except to answer questions. That kind of laser focus was scary. Still, math just got a hell of a lot more interesting even if the subject material was easy.

"Psst," the blond jock leaned over and tapped her arm. I'd ended up sitting right in the middle of all of them but I didn't mind.

"Yes, Bubba," she said over her shoulder with a grin. "I'll help with homework after school."

"Awesome," he said, grinning.

With him distracted, I could see his answer sheet. Why did he need help? He had all the problems answered already, but he tucked the page into the back of his book and then put a blank sheet on the problem set.

Huh.

Still, the glimpse of her profile had been like a donkey kick. She really was gorgeous. All too soon the bell rang and she and her escorts were gone before I could introduce myself.

That had to change the next day. Hell, I hadn't even caught her name. I'd do better. I had first lunch so I headed for the cafeteria along with the rest of the herd. A couple of girls smiled at me and a guy from my first period class lifted his chin. I nodded back, but I couldn't remember their names if they'd been said at all. Probably better to just play it cool.

I stood in line with everyone else and grabbed a tray of the most frighteningly greasy pizza I'd ever seen, some French fries (who served fries with pizza?) and grabbed bottled water. I'd kill for a soda but apparently they didn't sell those in the lunchrooms here.

Healthier options or so it had said in the orientation packet. Looking at the greasy pizza, I had to seriously question that particular logic. Whatever. Food paid for, I scanned the cafeteria seating. The tables were packed. I didn't know enough of these people to just swing over and ask for a spot so I navigated the room looking for an open table when the blond from math intercepted me.

Damn if I didn't nearly swallow my tongue.

"Hey," she said and my brain went on hiatus for a solid five seconds. "I'm Frankie. You can sit with me if you want." She indicated the nearly empty table behind her. Well, nearly empty except for her tray and backpack. "My friends will be here in a minute."

The communication lines between my brain cells zapped to life and I grinned. What was I going to say when a beautiful girl—seriously freaking hot—asks me to sit with her? I was not stupid.

"That'd be great, Frankie. I'm Archie."

"Awesome those of us with 'e' at the end of our name need to stick together."

I snorted a laugh as I slid my tray onto the spot next to hers and pulled out the chair. She said her friends were coming. I assumed that meant the guys from math, but maybe she meant girlfriends.

"You're in my math class," I managed as I unscrewed the top from my water bottle. Pithy one there, Arch. Really pithy.

"I know," she said with a grin. Unlike me, she wore jeans, but they were ripped around the knees and her t-shirt was tie-dyed. She kind of reminded me of a cool hippie. The green of her eyes held all of my attention. "Saw you when we came in. Did you go to Freeman?"

I had no idea what that was. "No, just moved here this summer."

"Oh, cool…"

"We can't leave you alone for five minutes," said the guy she'd flipped off during class. "Don't you remember you're not supposed to talk to strangers?"

"Bite me," she said, pointing a plastic spoon at him. Like me, she had a slice of pizza and some fries, but she also had a chocolate pudding cup and was eating it first. "Coop. Archie. Archie, Coop."

"Hey man," Coop said with a grin as he set his stuff down on the other side of Frankie.

"Hey."

"Why are you all the way over here?" Ah, here came the other two guys. The dark-haired one pinned me with a look that was far from friendly. "Who are you?"

"Jake, don't be an ass."

"Hard for him to do that when it's his default mode," Coop said with a laugh. The other blond with "Jake" snorted.

"He's sitting in Jake's spot, Jake never takes that well."

Shit, she was already taken. That figured.

"Jake can sit there," Frankie said, pointing opposite her. "It won't kill him. Also, Archie, that's Jake, he growls a lot but he's much nicer than he sounds and that's Bubba."

"Hey," Bubba said, sliding his tray onto the table. "I don't growl and I'm apparently not very nice." But his laughter decried that as Frankie rolled her eyes.

I found myself grinning as Jake scowled but took the chair she pointed out. I could have offered to move, but I didn't want to. Besides being pretty, she was adorable.

"Guys, this is Archie, he's new, just moved in this summer and he's gonna hang out with us for lunch, so don't be dicks."

"When was the last time we were dicks?" Coop asked with a laugh then bumped his shoulder to hers.

"This morning," Frankie and Bubba said almost in concert, but Jake just snorted. He didn't say much while we ate, but he did slide his pudding cup over to Frankie when she finished hers. The weight of his glare wasn't lost on me, but I played it cool. Frankie chatted with all of us and her enthusiasm for school just seemed to bubble over.

"Wait," I said when something she just mentioned penetrated past my just soaking in her voice. "You have French this afternoon?"

"Yep," Coop said, popping the 'p.' "Both of us do. Sixth period. Excellent. "Me too."

"Hey, that's two classes together. What else do you have?"

"Engineering next then History for seventh."

"You're with Jake next period then," Frankie said, grinning. "Who do you have for History?"

I had another class with Jake. He met my gaze with the same amount of enthusiasm I experienced. That was going to be fun.

"Um… Rogers, I think." I had to pull out my phone and look at the schedule.

"Sweet, you're with me and Bubba."

Three classes with Frankie, but one of the other guys was in it? I could live.

"Well, at least now I have a reason to survive my first three classes of the day."

She laughed and Bubba snorted. He and Coop shared a look. Yeah, I was definitely treading on unwelcome territory, but she invited me so I wasn't going anywhere. The next couple of minutes, she quizzed me about my last school and I didn't mind answering the questions but I kept it vague.

She'd finished her pizza and was down to half her fries when she said, "I see Tiff and Sharon. I gotta go talk to them about the spirit squad." As she wiggled out of the chair, her hip bumped my arm before I could move out of her way. "Sorry." Then she pointed a fry at Jake and Bubba. "You two owe me for this."

Jake grinned at her, it was his first real smile since sitting down. "You're the best."

"You really are," Bubba told her. "Also if I could put in a cookie order for my spirit box..."

"Yeah yeah," she said with a flick of her fingers before walking away. "Don't touch my fries, Coop," she called back without looking behind her as she hustled across the cafeteria. Coop yanked his hand back with a laugh, but I tracked her progress until Jake leaned into my line of sight.

Snapping my gaze to him I raised my eyebrows. "Problem?"

"Keep looking at her that way and there might be."

"Dating?" I asked because sure, if she was *taken* taken, I could bide my time.

"Nope," Coop answered before Jake could say anything. "Frankie isn't dating anyone."

The other guy glared daggers at him but I grinned. "No one, huh?"

Jake scowled, then drained his water bottle. Bubba shrugged. "Frankie doesn't date."

Maybe she just hadn't met the right guy. "So, I'm not stepping on anyone's toes if I ask her out?"

Across the room, she was talking to a table full of girls. Girls who alternated between chatting with her and glancing over here at us. But I wasn't interested in them. Frankie's grin was so damn open.

Finally, Jake sighed as I realized the dead silence meeting my question also involved the three guys exchanging looks. "No," he said after a beat. "But let's be clear, if she says no you take her no and if you hurt her, I'll beat your ass."

"And I'll help," Coop said. "You know, like bring the first aid and stuff."

Bubba just shrugged. "What he said but Jake usually does the hitting first and warning later. So take the warning for what it is."

"Duly noted," I said with a nod. She was on her way back and when she grinned at me, I didn't bother to hide my own smile. "Definitely need to do lunch again."

"We do lunch everyday, genius," Coop said.

"Great, you're just going to open the door?" Jake grumbled.

"I didn't have to," Coop retorted.

"Y'all behaving?" Frankie asked as she dropped back into the chair, a little flushed and breathless. "Also, apparently I have to do this spirit thing every day after school for the next couple of weeks. I officially hate you both."

"Aww," Bubba said. "We'll meet you after football practice."

"Pfft," she said but Jake offered her the pudding cup from Coop's tray and she laughed.

"Hey," Coop complained. "I was going to give it to her."

"You snooze, you lose," Jake said with a grin and I shook my head.

They were nuts.

But they were my kind of nuts.

Frankie popped open the pudding cup and looked at me. "We're probably going to walk down to the diner after practice and spirit meeting stuff. You're welcome to come with."

Oh yeah. "Sure, just let me know when. I'll have to text my ride."

Yeah. School was definitely looking up.

.

About Heather Long

USA Today bestselling author, Heather Long, likes long walks in the park, science fiction, superheroes, Marines, and men who aren't douche bags. Her books are filled with heroes and heroines tangled in romance as hot as Texas summertime. From paranormal historical westerns to contemporary military romance, Heather might switch genres, but one thing is true in all of her stories—her characters drive the books. When she's not wrangling her menagerie of animals, she devotes her time to family and friends she considers family. She believes if you like your heroes so real you could lick the grit off their chest, and your heroines so likable, you're sure you've been friends with women just like them, you'll enjoy her worlds as much as she does.

Follow Heather & Sign up for her newsletter:
www.heatherlong.net
TikTok

Also by Heather Long

82nd Street Vandals

Savage Vandal
Vicious Rebel
Ruthless Traitor
Dirty Devil
Brutal Fighter
Dangerous Renegade

Always a Marine Series

Once Her Man, Always Her Man
Retreat Hell! She Just Got Here
Tell It to the Marine
Proud to Serve Her
Her Marine
No Regrets, No Surrender

The Marine Cowboy
The Two and the Proud
A Marine and a Gentleman
Combat Barbie
Whiskey Tango Foxtrot
What Part of Marine Don't You Understand?
A Marine Affair
Marine Ever After
Marine in the Wind
Marine with Benefits
A Marine of Plenty
A Candle for a Marine
Marine under the Mistletoe
Have Yourself a Marine Christmas
Lest Old Marines Be Forgot
Her Marine Bodyguard
Smoke & Marines

Bravo Team Wolf
When Danger Bites
Bitten Under Fire

Cardinal Sins
Kill Song
First Chorus
High Note

Chance Monroe

Earth Witches Aren't Easy
Plan Witch from Out of Town
Bad Witch Rising

Her Elite Assets

Featuring:
Pure Copper
Target: Tungsten
Asset: Arsenic

Fevered Hearts

Marshal of Hel Dorado
Brave are the Lonely
Micah & Mrs. Miller
A Fistful of Dreams
Raising Kane
Wanted: Fevered or Alive
Wild and Fevered
The Quick & The Fevered
A Man Called Wyatt

Going Royal

Some Like It Royal
Some Like It Scandalous
Some Like It Deadly

Some Like it Secret
Some Like it Easy
Her Marine Prince
Blocked

Heart of the Nebula

Queenmaker
Deal Breaker
Throne Taker

Lone Star Leathernecks

Semper Fi Cowboy
As You Were, Cowboy

Magic & Mayhem

The Witch Singer
Bridget's Witch's Diary
The Witched Away Bride

Mongrels

Mongrels, Mischief & Mayhem

Shackled Souls

Succubus Chained
Succubus Unchained
Succubus Blessed
Shackled Souls (Omnibus)

Single Wicked Wolf
Desert Wolf
Snow Wolf
Wolf on Board
Holly Jolly Wolf
Shadow Wolf
His Moonstruck Wolf
Thunder Wolf
Ghost Wolf
Outlaw Wolves
Wolf Unleashed